MODERN FAIRY TALE

STEVE HIGGS

Vinci Books

vinci-books.com

Published by Vinci Books Ltd in 2025

1

Copyright © Steve Higgs 2024

The author has asserted their moral right to be identified as the author of this work in accordance with the Copyright, Designs and Patents Act 1988. This work is a work of fiction. Names, characters, places and incidents are the product of the author's imagination or are used fictitiously. Any resemblance to actual persons, living or dead, places and incidents is entirely coincidental.

All rights reserved. No part of this publication may be copied, reproduced, distributed, stored in any retrieval system, or transmitted in any form or by any means, including photocopying, recording, or other electronic or mechanical methods, nor used as a source for any form of machine learning including AI datasets, without the prior written permission of the publisher.

The publisher and the author have made every effort to obtain permissions for any third party material used in this book and to comply with copyright law. Any queries in this respect should be brought to the attention of the publisher and any omissions will be corrected in future editions.

A CIP catalogue record for this book is available from the British Library.

Paperback ISBN: 9781036708726

The EU GPSR authorised representative is Logos Europe, 9 rue Nicolas Poussion, 17000 La Rochelle, France contact@logoseurope.eu

By Steve Higgs

Blue Moon Investigations

Paranormal Nonsense
The Phantom of Barker Mill
Amanda Harper Paranormal Detective
The Klowns of Kent
Dead Pirates of Cawsand
In the Doodoo with Voodoo
The Witches of East Malling
Crop Circles, Cows and Crazy Aliens
Whispers in the Rigging
Paws of the Yeti
Under a Blue Moon
Night Work
Lord Hale's Monster
Herne Bay Howlers
Undead Incorporated
The Ghoul of Christmas Past
The Sandman
Jailhouse Golem
Sparks in the Darkness
Shadow in the Mine
Ghost Writer
Monsters Everywhere

Modern Fairy Tale
No Such Thing as Magic

Albert Smith Culinary Capers

Pork Pie Pandemonium
Bakewell Tart Bludgeoning
Stilton Slaughter
Bedfordshire Clanger Calamity
Death of a Yorkshire Pudding
Cumberland Sausage Shocker
Arbroath Smokie Slaying
Dundee Cake Deception
Lancashire Hotpot Peril
Blackpool Rock Bloodshed
Kent Coast Oyster Obliteration
Eton Mess Massacre
Cornish Pasty Conspiracy
The Gastrothief
Lyme Regis Layover
Majestic Mystery

New Partner

WEDNESDAY, 13TH DECEMBER 1116HRS

Tempest arrived at the house, but had to park more than a hundred yards down the road and walk the remaining distance. The parking spaces that might have been available were filled with police cars.

Thankfully, his red Porsche was small enough to slip into the one gap remaining in the street. Had he come with Big Ben, his friend's oversized truck would never have fit.

The constable minding the entrance to the property lifted his hand to stop Tempest when he reached the gate, but saw who it was and gave him a nod instead. Tempest was getting used to it – people recognised him.

At almost exactly six feet tall and broad across the shoulders, his athletic physique drew looks from men and women alike. Unless he was with Big Ben, that is. His six-foot-seven-inch, ex-military colleague looked as though he'd fallen from the cover of a magazine. Chiselled looks and defined muscles ensured he was the focus of everyone's attention everywhere he went.

"You're gonna like this one," the cop muttered, as

Tempest passed him, the cryptic comment only deepening the mystery behind the call that brought him to a peaceful suburb in Offham, a small village a few miles from the larger market town of West Malling.

On any other day, passers by might consider it a delightful place to live: thatched cottages, quiet streets, and a delightful pub with an inviting garden. Today, however, things were different.

There were two more cops inside the door, both men he recognised though Tempest did not know their names.

"Upstairs," one said, nodding the direction with his head.

Tempest mumbled his thanks and took the offered blue plastic overshoes. He slipped them on before trotting up the single flight to the landing above.

The house was a nice place set over two stories. It was a newish build, probably no older than the 1980's Tempest judged, but designed to look much older with fake oak beams set into the front façade and leaded windows to give it a Tudor appearance. Tempest filed his observations away, refusing to draw too many conclusions though it was obvious someone living in the house had money.

Pausing at the top of the stairs, there were voices coming from both directions and no one visible to suggest which way he needed to go.

Anything but timid, he raised his voice and called, "Chief Inspector?"

Almost immediately, a uniformed sergeant stepped out of a bedroom. He clocked Tempest, lifting his chin to indicate he needed to come his way.

"Over here, Mr Michaels," came the voice of Chief Inspector Quinn.

Finding himself at the scene of a bizarre crime was

anything but new; Tempest Michaels' chosen profession as a paranormal investigator almost guaranteed it on a daily basis. However, occasions when the police invited his attendance could be counted on one hand. That it was Chief Inspector Quinn waiting for him was completely alien.

Because they hated each other with mutual dedication.

Quinn saw himself as the lawman which made Tempest Michaels a vigilante at best. In truth, he thought of the P.I. as a conman or charlatan looking to rob the pockets of gullible people, so Tempest felt quite certain in his conviction that it was not Quinn's idea to bring him on board.

They had clashed many times in the past, one occasion occurring on national TV during a press conference where Tempest chose to punch the chief inspector in the face. He spent three months in jail for that infraction and continued to claim it was totally worth it.

Tempest rounded the corner, entering the master bedroom. The bed was dishevelled, the covers pulled back and wrinkled as though the people sleeping in it had just risen for the day. The clock next to the bed claimed the time to be 1116hrs.

There were four officers in the room including Chief Inspector Quinn and his boss, Chief Constable Harrelson. The presence of Maidstone nick's senior man explained a lot. Quinn would never have called Tempest in to consult, but Harrelson held a different opinion.

"Ah, Tempest," the chief constable came his way, extending a hand.

A tall man with a barrel chest and dark hair set above bushy eyebrows, he looked more like a bear than a man and had the grip to match.

"Chief Constable." Tempest let the burly man crush his digits as he always sought to do. Notably, Quinn busied himself with his subordinates, making sure he wasn't available to shake hands.

"Thank you for coming at such short notice," the Chief Constable ignored Quinn as ably as Tempest. "I hope you will be able to lend some expertise to this investigation."

"Am I to be taken on as a paid consultant?"

"Yes," the chief constable nodded. "There is budget to allow for such disbursements in justifiable circumstances."

Tempest flicked his eyes to check Quinn. He possessed a desire to antagonise the man. The chief inspector was known for being petty and vengeful, and it was mostly for those reasons that Tempest forced himself to rise above his childish desires.

Quinn was working hard to not take part in the conversation when it was quite clear the chief constable was going to leave him to run the investigation. Working alongside Tempest Michaels thus became an unavoidable eventuality.

"We can discuss your rate later, Mr Michaels, if that is acceptable. Right now, provided you agree to the work, I would like to get you started."

Tempest let his eyes move to the bed. "Of course. I will have my assistant send a copy of the contract to be signed. To whom should it be addressed?"

"Have them send it to me, please."

Tempest made a mental note to call Marjory when he left the crime scene. She would make sure the contract was signed, correctly filed, and his hours billed.

Curious about the chief inspector's personal involvement, Tempest asked, "Can I ask why you are here, Sir?"

The chief constable's eyebrows twitched; he had not expected to be answering questions, but said, "The victim is a golfing friend and a person I know through a certain society."

So, a mason. Tempest filed the point away for later consideration.

"You said *victim*. I see no signs of a struggle. No blood." The request to come to the address had not come with much of an explanation other than to suggest it was 'just his sort of case'.

"Chief Inspector," the chief constable all but barked to get his subordinate's attention.

Quinn finished what he was saying, passing an instruction to a sergeant who then left the room. About facing to look at his boss, Quinn said, "Yes, Sir."

Lean like an endurance athlete, Ian Quinn had a pinched face and permanently irritated expression. Or perhaps that was the only expression Tempest ever saw him wear because he was largely the cause of it. To Quinn's mind, private investigators ought not to be allowed. They poked their noses in, and they meddled where they were not wanted.

Not once did his eyes stray to take in the man standing next to his superior. It amused Tempest no end.

"Please explain the details of the case. I must be getting back to the station." He lifted his hat, looking ready to don it before deeming it necessary to issue a warning to the men in his presence. "Now I want the two of you to work together amicably. Leave the past in the past. The victims are your priority and must be your focus. I won't tolerate any nonsense." He narrowed his eyes to meet Quinn's gaze, then turned the same expression on Tempest, imparting how serious he expected each man to take his warning.

"Of course, Sir," replied Quinn.

Tempest smiled at his new partner. "Couldn't be more thrilled to be working with Ian again, Chief Constable."

The chief constable eyed them both for a few more

seconds, trying to decide whether he needed to say anything else. Words failed him, and he strode from the room, donning his hat with a final, "Good luck, gentlemen. I expect a swift solution," echoing back from the hallway outside.

Silence fell, neither Tempest nor Quinn saying anything for several seconds while they contemplated one another.

Bored of waiting, Tempest encouraged, "So tell me about the case."

The Frog King

WEDNESDAY, 13TH DECEMBER 1123HRS

Quinn backed away before turning around to stand at the foot of the bed.

"This is the home of Dr Mortimer King, fifty-eight, and his wife Verity, fifty-five. They have no children. Mortimer is a psychiatrist with a practice in Kings Hill.

"A psychiatrist?" He wasn't going to use the term 'crazy people', certainly not out loud, but work as a psychiatrist had the potential to put Dr King in very close proximity to people with mental health issues. Possibly serious ones. He filed the thought away for later consideration.

"That is what I said," Quinn replied, doing nothing to hide his impatience.

Tempest mimed zipping his mouth closed.

"Dr King's wife claims he came home from work last night as usual, had dinner, went to bed, and fell asleep before she could finish brushing her teeth. This morning, when she awoke, he was missing and in his place was a frog."

Tempest blinked.

"A frog?"

"Indeed. Tucked up in bed next to Mrs King. Naturally, she screamed upon discovering the beast, and thinking her husband was playing a practical joke on her, went looking for him."

"But of him there was no sign," Tempest guessed.

"Correct."

Tempest faced the chief inspector. "Am I to believe I was called here to investigate a wizard who turned Mr King into a frog?"

Quinn's expression hardened. "You would not be here at all were it not for the chief constable's insistence. I see no need whatsoever for your involvement."

Unable to stop himself, Tempest made a point of seeking clarity, "Soooo, not a wizard?"

Quinn turned away and started for the door.

"Come with me, please, Mr Michaels."

Tempest complied, following the chief inspector to the stairs and down them.

"The chief constable expects me to work with you and that is what I am going to do. I expect you to conduct yourself in a professional manner and to not get in my way or the way of my men ..."

"Officers," Tempest corrected him, winking at a female in uniform as he went past, then blushing slightly when he sensed it might be taken as flirting.

"Please do not interrupt me, Mr Michaels, it is so tiresome."

"Please try to remember what century it is, Ian," Tempest shot back. "Firefighters, not firemen and all that. The percentage of cops of the female persuasion grows every year. They are officers, not men."

Continuing as though no one had spoken, Quinn said,

"The presence of the frog is baffling, but there is reason to believe this is more than an errant husband wandering off or playing a trick."

He stopped walking in the kitchen, about facing yet again to look at Tempest who met his eyes and waited for the chief inspector to make his point.

Rather than speak, Quinn raised one hand, pointing to the refrigerator.

Playing along, Tempest opened it. He hadn't felt there was a need to brace himself and was used to seeing grisly and unexpected sights. However, the bloodied finger lying on the middle shelf came as a surprise.

"It's King's?" he asked, bending to get his face closer to the severed digit.

"That is being checked, but we believe so. It would have been packed in ice in an attempt to save it, but I am assured it has been removed from the body for too long for that to be viable."

Tempest moved around to look at the severed end.

"Any guessing how it was removed?"

"Garden secateurs is the current theory. I wanted to send it back to the lab, but the chief constable insisted it be left for you to see as Mrs King found it." Quinn took a breath before delivering the next piece of news. "The frog was also missing a finger."

Tempest stepped back from the fridge. "Anything else?"

"Just one more thing. The bloodied end of the finger was used to leave a message."

"That's ticking the macabre meter."

"Indeed." Quinn led the way to the living room where a large mirror set above an inglenook fireplace proclaimed, '*I want my golden goose!*' in large bloody letters.

Tempest studied the mirror for more than a minute, his

brain churning and his mouth closed. When he finally moved, it was to take out his phone.

Another minute passed, silence ruling and only when Tempest put the phone away did he choose to speak.

"Grimm."

"Grim? I don't need you to tell me the situation and the scene we find here is grim, Mr Michaels."

"Not grim. Grimm. The Grimm Brothers. I'm sure you must have heard of them. Famous for collating European bedtime stories and recording them in a book. Walt Disney converted a few of them into movies."

Not following, the chief inspector tilted his head.

Mildly exasperated, Tempest said, "*Snow White and the Seven Dwarfs*? *Sleeping Beauty*? Those are both famous *Disney* films. Red Riding Hood, Rumpelstiltskin. Ringing any bells?"

Annoyed, Quinn snapped, "What of them?"

Fixing the chief inspector with a level stare, Tempest said, "Another of their stories is the Frog King. And so is the Golden Goose."

An Old Friend Comes to Town

WEDNESDAY 13TH DECEMBER 1242HRS

From the Kings' house, Tempest drove to Rochester train station where he parked and waited. The clock on his dash assured him he was right on time, and text messages received over the course of the last few hours confirmed the train he wanted was about to arrive.

Not that he was getting on it.

The quiet of his car provided a good place to start exploring the Grimm case. It wasn't his only ongoing investigation, but it was nice to have something new lined up because his current case felt like it was drawing to a close.

In fact, he had a stakeout and a little light breaking and entering planned for the evening and hoped it might provide an opportunity to find the answers he needed. The B&E wasn't strictly legal, but he didn't plan on any actual breaking, and if he was right about the location, it was unlikely the police, not even Chief Inspector Quinn, would make a fuss about how he entered the premises.

A few minutes passed and the train from London pulled to a stop at platform one. From his position in the carpark,

Tempest could see the passengers disembarking, but failed to spot the person he expected.

The platform was crowded and the station building obscured a good portion of the train, but he left the warmth of his car to make himself more visible and watched the crowd for a familiar face.

"Tempest!" the friendly call echoed in the tunnel that led under the station from the platforms on the other side. The unmistakable Australian twang would have told him it was the right person even if he hadn't recognised the voice.

Emerging from the press of people heading out of the station, Darius Kane, all six feet and two inches of him, waved a greeting.

A smile found its way onto Tempest's face. He first met the Australian in 2002, right before things kicked off in Iraq for the second time. A member of the Australian SAS, Darius took an exchange posting to spend two years with the British elite unit. Tempest and Big Ben were there at the time, all three deploying into the sand along with the rest of the British Army.

They hadn't seen each other in more than a decade, but they shook hands like the old friends they were. They didn't need to express the words; they both understood the depth of the bonds that form in such extreme circumstances.

"Easy flight?" Tempest turned back toward the carpark.

"It got here. That's good enough for me and much better than the alternative."

Reaching his car, Tempest said, "We could walk to the office from here. It's just across the road, but I was coming from a case. Think you can manage with the bag on your lap?"

Darius travelled light, his belongings in a large backpack rather than a giant suitcase most would employ for long haul travel. However, his luggage wasn't the issue, it was the width of his shoulders and overall height that presented a challenge in the low-slung German sports car.

He squeezed in, but they were both glad the office really was just around the corner.

Between deployments, training, and other trips, during the two years he was posted to England, Darius got to spend about six months actually in the country. In that time, he did a little exploring but not much, so faced with the ancient majesty that is Rochester High Street, the castle, cathedral, and city wall, he was unsurprisingly distracted.

"I guess you don't have this in Australia," Tempest remarked.

Darius laughed. "Nothing much there more than a hundred years old. I'll get out and have a look around later, but architecture and history are not what I came here for."

Tempest led his companion through the back door of his office building. It opened into a corridor which accessed storerooms and connected to the office itself at the far end.

Marjory, the office receptionist, looked up when the door from the back rooms opened.

"The contract came back signed already. Was it what you thought?" she asked, turning her attention back to whatever she was doing at her desk.

Tempest shucked his jacket, smiling while he placed it on the stand against the wall. Pleased to hear the chief constable had signed the contract, for it gave him leverage, Tempest said, "Not even close. Chief Inspector Quinn was there."

A quiet expletive escaped through the open door to Amanda's office, accompanied almost immediately by the sound of her chair moving.

Emerging a moment later, she was about to ask him how the meeting went when she spotted Darius.

"Hello. You must be Darius."

"I must be," Darius agreed, shaking her hand. A yawn split his face. "Sorry, jetlag," he managed when he was finally able to force his mouth shut.

Tempest said, "I'm going to drop Darius off at mine to get some sleep in a bit. He's going to come along tonight."

Amanda's eyebrows rose, her focus on Darius. "You're serious about opening a Blue Moon franchise then?"

"I didn't fly all this way for the weather."

His response drew a laugh. It was summer in Australia and significantly warmer than it would ever be in England, let alone as the country settled into winter.

Amanda touched Tempest's arm. "Quinn," she prompted him. "I take it things remained cordial? I mean, you are not in cuffs this time."

"His boss was there."

Amanda hoped that wasn't the only reason the two men hadn't come to blows.

"Is it a real case?" she pressed, following Tempest to the client waiting area.

"Coffee?" Tempest enquired, grabbing a delicate white cup for himself, and holding one up as a question for Darius – did he want caffeine if he was hoping to get some shut eye soon? At his nod, Tempest began to fill the machine and said, "It is a real case. An interesting one too. Quinn's boss is rather keen for it to be solved so I guess I have a contract with the police now."

Amanda sucked some air between her teeth, not entirely happy at the prospect.

"Is that really a good idea?"

"Assuming I don't have to fight them to get the money, it

should be. A woman awoke this morning to find her husband missing. In his place she found a …?" Tempest teased it out, encouraging Amanda to guess.

She jinked a single eyebrow. "A bar of gold?" she tried.

Tempest nodded, showing he was impressed. "Close."

"Really?"

"No, not really. The correct answer is a frog."

Amanda slapped his arm.

"A frog?" Darius questioned.

"Some women might consider that an improvement," Marjory commented, eavesdropping from her desk.

Grinning, Tempest poured the coffee, handed a cup to Amanda and another to Darius, who was looking weary and had settled into one of the chairs already. Making one last cup for himself, Tempest picked the seat opposite Darius and continued to explain the latest case.

"I think we have someone with a Brothers Grimm obsession. The missing man is Dr Mortimer King – the Frog King."

"Is that a Grimm's fairy tale?" Amanda's forehead creased in thought.

Tempest nodded. "So is the Golden Goose and whoever is behind the kidnap made reference to it in a note he left on the living room mirror using the blood from Mortimer's severed right index finger."

Marjory crossed herself and Amanda grimaced. "How do you know his finger was used? Or do I not want to know the answer to that one?"

"It was in their fridge."

They lapsed into silence and drank their coffees.

"Soooo, working with Quinn again," Amanda swung back to a topic she felt required some exploration. "Do I need to run a book on how long it is until you get arrested for throttling him?"

Tempest had to swallow his coffee fast to avoid spitting it out and still ended up with a drip hanging from his nose.

Fighting to rescue his handkerchief from a pocket, he sputtered, "I think I can control my urges for long enough to get through one case."

Amanda's face made it quite clear she wasn't so sure.

"Have I missed something?" Darius asked.

It turned out he wasn't aware Tempest had enjoyed a term in prison after punching a cop during a televised press conference. Amanda felt he ought to condemn her boyfriend's actions and rolled her eyes when he laughed and offered Tempest a high five.

"And you are working with him again?" Darius wanted to check he understood the situation.

Tempest finished his coffee. "Yup. I don't think it will be a problem though. He is under orders to cooperate with me. I think it will be fun."

Amanda didn't look so sure.

Their coffees finished, they retreated to the private offices at the back of the building. Amanda had cases of her own to work on and Tempest planned to show Darius as much of the business as possible. The success of Blue Moon Investigations was such that he now had three franchises operating in America. He wasn't looking to take over the world, but clients with extraordinary cases cropped up more places than he could be.

Darius's interest provided another opportunity to spread the success of the firm he started though he still shook his head at the irony of it all. He never intended to investigate the paranormal, the whole thing came about by accident. A different person might question divine intervention or fate, but Tempest was content to put it down to blind luck.

They were deep in discussion about past cases and how Tempest approached them when Marjory bellowed for Amanda. Tempest might have paid no attention, but upon leaving the office next to his, he heard Amanda say, "Patricia?"

That was enough to make him lean over his desk to check. Of course he knew Patricia Fisher was in the country – he'd raced to Hampshire just a few days ago to lend a hand in case she needed it, but her visit to his place of work was unexpected.

Naturally, Patricia wasn't alone. She is rarely to be found without her butler, Jermaine, by her side, and her stunningly attractive blonde friend, Barbie, was with them too.

Amanda was already crossing the floor, on her way to greet their mutual friend. Rounding his desk, Tempest said, "There's someone you need to meet."

Darius had no clue what was going on until he got to see the visitor for himself. He recognised her face instantly. Patricia Fisher had been in the news plenty in the last few months, most notably less than a week ago when a story about a Spanish treasure ship broke. Patricia Fisher found it ... well, sort of. An order of monks had found it three hundred years ago, but Patricia Fisher's involvement brought the discovery into the spotlight.

Hands were shaken and introductions completed. With visitors on the premises, more coffee was called for. Darius excused himself and left the office via the front door, his confused body clock demanding he go in search of food.

Patricia's visit wasn't social; she was investigating a murder in her village and hoped Amanda could put her in contact with Patience Woods, a cop Amanda used to work with.

Amanda made the call, and the group chatted about the San José treasure since Tempest and Big Ben found themselves drawn into the case and they hadn't seen each other since they found the fortune in gold and jewels just a few days ago.

"Hey, where is the big fella, anyway?" asked Barbie.

"Injured," smirked Amanda, her grin demanding she expand. "Got a little too amorous with some ladies and needed a few stitches somewhere he would rather not have them."

Jermaine tried hard not to wince at the suggested nature of Big Ben's injury.

From the reception desk, Marjory tutted. "*Some ladies*. Serves him right. The way that boy carries on with women. It shouldn't be allowed."

Tempest didn't exactly leap to his friend's defence, but he did say, "I can assure you all parties are consenting."

"What are you guys working on at the moment?" asked Patricia. "Anything interesting to keep you all busy?"

"And where is Jane?" asked Barbie, enquiring after the third member of the detective team.

Tempest fielded. "Jane is currently investigating a private case, by which I mean something without a client."

"She's working with a police detective at Buckingham Palace," explained Amanda. "It started months ago with a case involving a dragon."

Patricia and her companions all looked equally mystified.

"I didn't read anything about that in the papers," Patricia challenged.

Around a nod of acknowledgement, Tempest said

quietly, "It's not the kind of news the palace would ever want to admit. Anyway, with all the recent royal deaths, there are persons who believe there is someone behind it all."

"And that is what Jane is investigating?"

"As well as other cases. Cassie, the detective she is working with at the palace, asked for her help. It would appear she is getting all too little of it from her bosses."

"Goodness." The conversation stalled for a second, restarting when Patricia circled back to her original question about Tempest's current workload. "There must be something weird and fantastic on your books."

Tempest downed his coffee, setting his delicate, white porcelain cup on the table as he considered how to respond.

"Tempest has a case with a demon," Amanda revealed.

Jermaine crossed himself.

"Don't worry, it's not real," Tempest assured everyone. "A few miles from here, out in the middle of pretty much nowhere, a couple came across a seven-foot-tall figure with antlers and cloven hoofs. It was standing in the middle of the road and their attempts to avoid it crashed their car and put them both in the hospital. They are my clients."

"Any leads?" Patricia enquired.

Tempest leaned back into his chair, drawing one leg up to cross it over the other knee.

"I think we have it all figured out, actually. We caught a lucky break with their son. They told us he had a tattoo of the same demon thing on his arm, and it turns out he was coerced into getting it. That led to the poor guy being drawn into a criminal ring. The demon will be nothing of the sort, and we are hoping to find out more tonight."

Amanda gave a small shake of her head and rolled her eyes. "Tempest is planning to break into the tattoo parlour.

By himself," she added, clearly disapproving, "because Big Ben isn't currently up to helping."

Tempest huffed out a breath. "We have been over this, darling. The risk is low, and I am taking Darius with me."

"And what if the tattoo parlour is the base for the gang of drug dealers and thugs? What then? You need to wait for Big Ben to be back to fighting strength."

Unexpectedly, Patricia volunteered, "Can we assist?"

Tempest and Amanda shot her questioning looks.

We," Patricia made sure to include Barbie and Jermaine, "Owe you many times over. I, for one, would feel much better if you would allow us to accompany you tonight."

Barbie echoed her friend's thoughts, saying, "If there are people to thump, Jermaine is very good at it, and I bet Hideki will want to come too. He's like a modern-day Bruce Lee."

Tempest's natural inclination to argue was shot down before he could speak. Patricia's opinion that she owed him was accurate enough, not that he would ever express such a belief, but the truth was that he could do with a hand.

Patience barrelled through the door a few moments later, bringing with her the noise and chaos she always generates. However, by then the deal was done and Tempest had all the back up he was going to need for the evening's planned excursion.

Home Comforts

WEDNESDAY 13TH DECEMBER 1401HRS

With Darius flagging and a plan for the Australian to be out late that evening, Tempest took him home where he could rest.

"So this is where you came to rest?" Darius admired the delightful village of Finchampstead as Tempest drove through it. "Nice place."

"It's quiet too," Tempest shared. "There are lots of places to walk the dogs, the pub is friendly, and the crime rate is about as close to zero as you can get." He chose to leave out that most of the crime in recent times had occurred when witches, Klowns, or other such enterprising criminals had chosen to target him.

Barking from the other side of his front door began the moment he pulled onto the driveway and continued until he used a key to open it. His pair of black and tan miniature dachshunds spilled out through the gap almost before it was wide enough to allow them and achieved the feat by climbing over each other.

Inside the house, the dogs buzzed around the newcomer's feet, dancing on their back legs for attention.

"This is Bull," Tempest pointed to the idiot rolling on his back. "And that one is Dozer. You're okay with dogs, right?" Tempest checked. Needlessly, it turned out for Darius dropped his bag, then sank to his knees so he could pet the excited hounds.

"I've got a dog of my own." Darius laughed, playing with the dogs. "I wondered if I should have something more manly than a beagle, but I guess having these two hasn't hurt your chances with the ladies."

Tempest wondered when Darius would comment about Amanda. Not that he expected his friend to make lewd remarks, but he had managed to land an exceptionally attractive girlfriend and figured some banter was to be expected.

To respond, he said, "If anything, these guys improved my chances. Ladies gravitate toward them."

Darius pushed off the floor with one hand to get up. "I've no doubt they do." Stifling another yawn, he said, "Look, I'm just going to hit the hay. If I don't get a few hours now, I'll be no use later."

Tempest showed him the kettle, the fridge, the bathroom so Darius could freshen up, and the spare room, which was made up and ready to go.

It was his intention to head back to the office, but a phone call changed that plan in an instant.

"Tempest Michaels," he confirmed the caller had reached the person they wanted and listened to hear what Chief Inspector Quinn had to say. That Ian Quinn's name was stored in his phone was a development in itself.

"Mr Michaels ..."

"Call me Tempest, Ian. We are going to be working together."

"No, I think formal terms will suffice. Otherwise, you might think it acceptable to address me by my first name in front of my officers."

Tempest noted that Quinn used the term 'officers' instead of 'men' for what might be the first time ever and had to resist the desire to congratulate him on joining the twenty first century.

"I need you to come to the station."

"What for?"

Tempest got to hear the aggravation in Quinn's voice when he sighed. "Because we *are* working together, Mr Michaels. I have a team of officers assigned to investigate this case and to do my job properly dictates I involve you. I have no intention of giving my briefing twice."

So Quinn intended to talk to his team and wanted Tempest there. Was that a powerplay? Did Quinn intend to make it look as though he was in charge and Tempest worked for him? Suspecting the answer to that was almost certainly a solid 'yes', Tempest chose not to play along.

"Sorry, Ian, I have other cases. Don't worry though, I'm already researching the Frog King and the Golden Goose. I'll get back to you the moment I have something."

"No, Mr Michaels. You will drop what you are doing and report to the station. If you wish to be paid as a consultant, you will obey my instructions."

Precisely as Tempest expected, Quinn was willing to work with him, but only from a position of established power.

Trying to keep the smile from his face, not that Quinn could see it, he said, "No problem."

"Good. I will expect you in fifteen minutes."

"Oh, you misunderstand me, Ian. I'm not dropping anything, and I am certainly not on my way to the nick. I can drop this case though if the police don't wish to pay me. I'll let you tell your boss."

Tempest took the phone away from his ear and waited just long enough to hear Quinn begin to argue before taking great pleasure in thumbing the red button to terminate the call.

He wasn't about to drop the case; it was far too interesting, and he had no faith whatsoever that Quinn would manage to solve it for himself. The man saw things in straight lines. Put him up against a vanilla criminal: a burglar, a stalker, a drug dealer, and he was a capable law enforcer. This case, like most of those that landed on the Blue Moon desk, was anything but straight.

Content his position was now clear, yet certain he was going to argue with the chief inspector about it again before the day was done, Tempest slipped into his car.

Bull and Dozer were with him, the dogs balanced on the passenger seat and happy to be heading out after getting left at home earlier. Tempest took them to work most days, but when he had a crime scene to visit, there really was no place for them and he had made the mistake of leaving them in his car before.

You might think a ten-pound dog wouldn't be able to do much damage, but the bill for his new gear stick suggested otherwise.

Reversing back into the street, Tempest patted each dog and ruffled their ears.

"Come on then, chaps. Let's go see Frank."

Mystery Men Comic Book Store

WEDNESDAY, 13TH DECEMBER 1438HRS

Frank Decaux heaved a thick tome onto the glass counter next to the cash register in his first-floor bookshop. He and Tempest met eighteen months earlier when Tempest's ill-fated newspaper ad claimed him to be a paranormal investigator.

At the time, nothing could have been further from the truth, but Frank didn't know that and was almost foaming at the mouth with excitement when he barged into Tempest's office that morning.

He was a fervent believer in all things supernatural and a great source of knowledge whenever Tempest had a question.

Frank's assistant, Poison, was on her knees behind the counter making a fuss of the dogs.

"You should bring them in more often," she coached.

Tempest was inclined to disagree, far too concerned one of them might elect to lift a leg on one of Frank's expensive displays, but said, "We will be happy to see more of you. Visit whenever you like."

Poison flicked her head around to meet Tempest's eyes. She had a thing for him and rarely bothered to hide it. Now there was a hunger in her expression that made him rerun his previous sentence to see where he might have given her the wrong impression.

"Um, I mean the dogs are at my office most days. You can pop in to see them there."

Poison rose to her feet. "So you don't want to see *more* of me?"

There was no doubt Poison was asking a completely different question to the one she voiced.

Tempest cursed himself. He had no trouble facing down hardened criminals or walking into situations where he knew he would be outnumbered. He was generally unphased by women who flirted with him too, for that matter, provided he wasn't interested in them. That changed dramatically, if he liked them though, and were it not for his relationship with Amanda, which he would never risk, he would almost certainly have explored the charms of Frank's assistant.

"Can I get your attention for a moment, please?" Frank complained, sighing and tutting.

Thankful to have an escape route, Tempest took it.

"Sorry, Frank. You were saying?"

Shaking his head, Frank said, "I was telling you that most of the Grimm tales were based on real events."

Suddenly on much safer ground, Tempest said, "No, they were not."

"Yes, they were," Frank insisted. "Admittedly, Little Red Riding Hood's real name was Birgit. However, the magic inside the folklore, the witchcraft, and demonry was always real. The tales are sold now as stories for kids, for which I blame Disney, but the original manuscripts were written to be a guide, kind of like a combat soldier's bible for what to expect and how to win."

Frank stopped talking, waiting for Tempest to argue some more, but the paranormal P.I. chose not to waste his breath. Countering Frank's barmy beliefs with sound logic and reason never bore fruit.

Instead, he introduced the reason behind his enquiry into the Grimm brothers.

"Brothers Grimm."

"I'm sorry?"

"Brothers Grimm," Frank repeated. "You said Grimm brothers, but to be correct you must say Brothers Grimm."

Tempest closed his eyes and counted to three. "Whichever it is, Frank," Tempest didn't care one way or the other, "I have a missing man replaced by a frog and reference to a golden goose written in the missing man's blood."

"His blood?" Frank questioned.

"Yeah, they cut off his right index finger and used that as a pen."

The face Poison pulled mirrored Tempest's own thoughts on the matter. He explained about the victim's name and how that led him to question a connection to the Grimm brothers' tales.

"It's not a lot to go on yet," he concluded, "so I'm here to ask about the stories as much as anything. I don't recall the Frog King and the Golden Goose having anything to do with one another."

"They didn't," Frank confirmed. "The Golden Goose was one small element in a story about a simpleton who won the hand of a princess and took over a kingdom for displaying kindness to a stranger. It gets confused a lot with

Aesop's fables in which the goose that lays the golden eggs appears. The term Golden Goose in modern parlance has come to mean a source of continual wealth. You say the frog was also missing a digit?"

Tempest nodded. "The right index finger."

Frank sucked some air between his teeth while he flicked pages of the original Brothers Grimm manuscript. Stopping when he found what he wanted, he rotated the book to show Tempest.

"Rumpelstiltskin?" Tempest questioned.

"I want you to suspend your disbelief for a moment, please."

Tempest sniggered. "Okay. Disbelief suspended."

Frank narrowed his eyes but continued regardless.

"In all likelihood you don't have a missing man. The frog *is* Dr Mortimer King. This is bad dark magic, Tempest. Not the kind of stuff you want to mess with."

"And you think Rumpelstiltskin is behind the transformation?"

Frank made an incredulous face. "Of course not, Tempest. Imps don't have that kind of lifespan. I showed you Rumpelstiltskin because he's the best-known example of an imp using magic on mortals for his own gain. He deals in contracts, notably in the original story, doing so to gain the first-born child of a woman. Here, the suggestion is that the magical practitioner behind Dr King's transmogrification, not transformation – those two things are very different, Tempest - had previously entered into a deal with him and that Dr King refused to pay up. Ergo, the imp still wants his golden goose."

Tempest took a few seconds to absorb Frank's words. The bookshop owner was completely bonkers, but a lot of what he said still made sense if you picked between the lines. Not for one moment did Tempest believe Mortimer King had been transmoggy ... whatever the heck word Frank chose to describe the process of changing him from human into a frog. But the concept of a deal gone sour and a debt to be claimed by any means necessary, had a worrying ring of possibility about it.

Most crimes come down to sex or money. That was a well-established fact and while Tempest couldn't rule out the possibility of extra-marital affairs on either the part of Dr or Mrs King, the financial option, given that Dr King appeared to have a profitable business, sounded more probable.

The possibility raised an immediate concern.

If Dr King had been snatched for failing to pay up, it meant he'd made the mistake of doing business with some bad people, the kind who remove fingers when you fail to hold up your end of the bargain. More concerning was that they might come back for Mrs King.

Had she lied this morning? Or did she really not know who was behind her husband's disappearing act? Had it not been for the finger in the fridge, he might have suggested Dr King chose to abscond voluntarily. A quick check of his bank account might have confirmed it. It wasn't as though he would be the first husband with money to find a younger, firmer version of his wife.

However, unless Tempest was prepared to believe Dr King was committed enough to cut off his own finger, he doubted he would be found holed up with another woman. He hadn't been turned into a frog either, which meant someone had him. In turn that meant the clock was ticking.

Thanking Frank, and making sure to give a non-flirtatious goodbye to Poison, Tempest hustled out of the bookshop, down the narrow wooden stairs to the street and around the back of his office where he loaded first his dogs, and then himself, into his car.

If this was about money and the bad guys snatched Dr King in the night to squeeze from him what they felt they were due, they could come back for Verity.

Mrs King

WEDNESDAY 13TH DECEMBER 1517HRS

It wasn't Verity King who opened the door, but a police officer. She recognised Tempest – there were very few local cops who wouldn't.

"I need to check with Mrs King, see if she is okay with the dogs unless you want to leave them in your car."

"No, thanks. I'll wait."

The constable returned less than thirty seconds later, opening the door wide.

"She loves dachshunds."

Acting as though they understood what was said, Bull and Dozer leapt over the threshold, their stubby legs doing their best to drag Tempest behind them. Once inside, he made his life easier by unclipping their leads and shucking his coat while they shot off.

The voice of Mrs King echoed out from her kitchen where she cooed and praised the dogs. He found the lady of the house on her knees on the kitchen tile, both hands providing tummy tickles, one per dog.

He didn't meet her during his first visit, but saw

photographs around the house and could recognise her though she had aged. Verity King looked to be in her very early sixties though Tempest knew her age to be fifty-five. Her hair was dyed to hide the grey, but not recently, an inch of grey root showing through where her hair parted. If pushed to find a word to describe her clothes and general appearance, it would have to be 'frumpy'.

When she rocked back off her knees and came up to her full height, she stood five feet and nine inches tall in flat shoes. She would hit six feet easily in heels.

"You're Tempest Michaels," she observed, extending her right hand for him to take.

"Mrs King."

"Oh, please, call me Verity." Her eyes and face bore the puffiness that went with sobbing. Finding the frog must have been a shock, but not nearly so bad as her husband's finger in the fridge or the blood on the living room mirror.

"Very well, Verity. Shall we sit? Were you advised I had been brought into the investigation?"

Verity nodded that she had.

"Can I get anyone a tea?" asked the constable.

"That would be lovely. Thank you," Tempest replied. "Sorry, I didn't get your name?"

"It's Linda," said Linda, carrying the kettle to the sink. "Linda Matthis."

"She's just here until my sister arrives," explained Verity. "That nice chief inspector didn't think it was fair to leave me all by myself." Proving it was her brave face Tempest was seeing, a tear slipped out and she turned away.

Her shoulders shook and it was clear this was a continuation of a theme, not the first time it had happened today. Linda abandoned her tea making to give comfort, putting an arm around the distraught woman.

Tempest was left to watch, but it wasn't his first time in the company of someone emotionally unbalanced by the impact of their situation. In fact, it was an almost weekly occurrence, such was the nature of his work.

He waited for Mrs King to gather herself which took no more than a few moments. Inevitably, she apologised for her emotional state.

"I just don't know what I will do without him," she sobbed around noisily blowing her nose.

He knew better than to make promises, but Tempest believed he could give hope without overstating the likelihood Mortimer would be returned unharmed.

"If we are dealing with a kidnapper, he won't want to damage his chances of getting paid by hurting your husband, Verity."

"He already cut off his finger!" she wailed.

"And now he must maintain him in his current condition," Tempest reinforced the concept. "I must ask you some questions about your husband's business dealings."

Mrs King stopped sobbing and looked up. "His ... why?"

"Because the crime appears to be quite personal. If the person behind your husband's disappearance merely wanted money, he could have snatched him outside work when he went to get into his car. By staging such an elaborate scene with the frog and the missing finger, it tells me the perpetrator wants to send a message."

"He did send a message," Verity countered. "Or rather, he left one. It was written on the mirror with my Morty's blood," she choked getting the final words out.

"Precisely." Tempest came to kneel on the carpet next to her, taking her right hand in both of his. "I know this is hard, Verity, but the person behind this could be someone your husband knows. It could even be someone you know. The message about wanting their golden goose has hidden meaning. I think this person believes Mortimer owes them."

Tempest searched Verity's eyes, looking for a spark of recognition. Would she be able to help him piece things together?

"Your husband must have treated a lot of people over the years, Verity. Are there any that stand out as having born a grudge? Did Dr King ever mention a problematic patient or one who was violent?"

"Oh, Morty never talked to me about his patients, Tempest. Not once in all the years we've been together."

Disappointed, Tempest tried again from a different angle. "What about money, Verity? I'm sure your husband charged a fair rate for his treatment, but professional psychiatric help is expensive. There must have been times when patients complained and asked for their money back?"

Verity shook her head. "I'm sorry. There might have been, but Morty never talked to me about that sort of thing either. What I can say is that there was never enough money to go around. You might scoff at that because of this house, but we couldn't afford it when we bought the place and nothing much has changed."

Linda delivered cups of tea and Mrs King excused herself to leave the room. Left in the kitchen with the police constable, Tempest turned his questions on her.

"What did the forensics team turn up? You were here for that, yes?"

"I was," Linda nodded. "The official answer is that they are still going over the data and that they collected a lot of samples that will take them some time to work through."

"What's the unofficial answer?"

Linda leaned against the kitchen countertop and blew across the surface of her drink.

"They found nothing."

"Nothing?"

"No sign of forced entry for a start which likely meant the perp had a key, but no fingerprints and no DNA they could immediately identify which beggars belief since whoever did this went up to the master bedroom and put a frog in it."

"And they had to open the fridge to put Dr King's finger in it." Frowning with thought, Tempest asked, "How sure are we that the finger belongs to Dr King?"

Linda shrugged. "About as certain as we can be. Mrs King identified the ring as his. The forensic team will need to run some tests, but the blood on the mirror is a match for his and the fingerprint matches ones found all over the house. I don't think there is much doubt."

Tempest absorbed the news and sipped his tea. Outside it was already getting dark, the late autumn sun racing for the horizon long before the working day could be considered done.

The frog and the finger, plus the mirror and goodness knows what else, were back at the lab in Maidstone Police Station. What secrets the scientists might glean from them Tempest chose not to speculate.

He'd rushed over to speak with Mrs King in the hope she might be able to identify someone who could be behind the kidnapping. Though she could not, Tempest didn't take it to mean he wasn't onto the right idea. He would need to explore Dr King's business and talk to some of his senior employees. Mrs King might not know about any historic or current problematic patients, but someone would.

It was just one line of enquiry and Tempest expected to

have to explore several before he caught a break. The lack of fingerprints and other evidence was a little disturbing, not least because he could not figure out how someone removed Dr King from his bed without his wife noticing.

The Grimm's Fairy Tale case, as Tempest had come to think of it, was going to have to wait though. He was due to meet Jane in just a couple of hours and needed to eat, prepare, and get to the destination in that time.

Scooping his dogs, Tempest clipped them back onto their leads, promised Mrs King he would keep working until they figured out what happened to her husband, and let himself out.

It was time to catch a demon.

Demon Ink

WEDNESDAY, 13TH DECEMBER 1923HRS

Jane stared at the building across the street. "Looks harmless enough, doesn't it?"

Tempest looked up at the sign above the door, 'Demon Ink', and shook his head. It was right there in plain sight for everyone to see. How had it gone unnoticed for so long?

"You get many cases like this one?" Darius enquired.

Tempest shook his head. "We've never had a case like this."

The clients for the case were a couple in their early sixties, Janine and Ken Whelan. They were still in the hospital, their injuries likely to heal before their emotional scarring. Tempest took their case on the spot and would have tackled it for free had they not been willing to pay his usual fees.

"Do we go in?" Darius asked, ready to kick the door off its hinges and charge in fists blazing if Tempest thought it necessary, but he was in the UK to learn from his old friend and prepared to follow his lead.

Tempest frowned in thought before giving a short shake of his head. "No, I think we watch for a while."

"We're waiting for Patricia, right?" Jane sought to confirm as they wandered back to her car.

"Yes and no," said Tempest, seeing no need to expand. It wasn't Patricia Fisher they were waiting for so much as the friends who would be accompanying her. Big Ben, Tempest's usual muscle for this kind of operation, was out of action in more ways than one.

He had Darius with him instead, but since Patricia all but insisted she take part with her friends to make up for all the times he'd come to her aid, he was going to have an abundance of back up for once.

Darius reclined across the back seat of Jane's vintage Aston Martin, and getting comfortable he said, "Remind me what we are dealing with."

Jane twisted around in the driver's seat to meet her passenger's eyes. "A demon!" she croaked in a macabre voice.

Tempest snorted. "An idiot in a suit. You'll get a lot of those." Taking a more serious tone, he explained, "The clients reported seeing a demon in the road on Saturday night as they were coming into the village."

"This village?" Darius questioned.

"Yes, Allhallows. We're right out on the edge of the Grain Peninsular here. Miles from civilisation really though it's only a half hour drive back to the cities and you can see the lights of Southend on the other side of the estuary if you go to the beach. The point is this community is remote from the rest of the county and that can make people …" Tempest searched for the right word.

"Odd," volunteered Jane.

Tempest chuckled. "I was going for superstitious, but I

guess it amounts to the same thing. Anyway, they saw a creature with a blood red face, glowing eyes, a forked tail, cloven hoofs, and antlers like a goat. Their description not mine. It stood approximately seven feet tall and barred their path, glaring at them as their headlights bore down on it."

"This is still an idiot in a costume, right?" Darius didn't sound entirely convinced.

"Wait, it gets better. Ken was driving and by his own admission he panicked. Scared by what he was seeing because apparently there have been tales of the demon going back centuries, he pumped the brakes, but his tyres blew out the very next moment. He lost control, the car left the road and slammed into a tree."

"Hence the injuries?" Darius guessed.

Tempest nodded. "They were lucky to survive even if they did both break bones. The demon could have done more, but didn't, leaving them to be found a short while later by the next car to come along the street."

Darius frowned. "Okay, so why are we outside a tattoo shop?"

Jane took up the narrative. "Ah, well that's where things get interesting. The Whelans had no idea why they might have been targeted or if it was perhaps poor luck on their part to have come across the demon by accident. However, when we asked their son, Arnold, if he knew anything, he started sobbing."

Darius leaned forward in his seat. It was a fascinating tale that sounded like ridiculous fiction, but was no less true for it.

The door to the tattoo parlour opened, a thin man in his early twenties leaving, the right sleeve of his jacket rolled up to show the plastic wrap over his new ink. He lit a cigarette before wandering away.

"More demon ink," Jane muttered, her words part question but not aimed at anyone to provide an answer.

"Wait, that's the connection?" Darius asked. "But what does one have to do with the other?"

Tempest's tone was grave when he said, "That's what we are here to find out."

Drugs Mugs

WEDNESDAY, 13TH DECEMBER 1926HRS

"When Arnold Whelan broke down and started talking, we couldn't stop him," Jane explained. "He got some ink here three weeks ago, which was a harmless enough thing to do. I have some tattoos of my own."

"And the tattoo he got is linked to the demon thing?" Darius guessed.

"In a way. The tattoo is of the demon and apparently quite a popular design about these parts. The day after he got the tattoo, the demon appeared to him. It was at night, and he was on his way home from the pub."

"Read into that what you will," remarked Tempest, his eyes still fixed firmly on the door of the tattoo parlour.

"Yes, well," Jane continued, "the demon threatened to suck out Arnold's soul, or words to that effect, and made his tattoo glow."

"Glow?" Darius questioned.

Jane shrugged. "Apparently so. "Arnold said it glowed and the demon told him it wasn't ink in the tattoo but the demon's blood. Through it he owned Arnold, and he was to do the demon's bidding or suffer the consequences."

Adding up what he'd already heard, Darius said, "This is where the parents come in, right? Failure to comply resulted in his loved ones being targeted. Do I assume Arnold has no girlfriend?"

"Well, he's gay," Jane replied, matter-of-factly, "but yes, he is single."

Tempest twisted to face the back seat. "We had a look at the tattoo, and it seemed perfectly ordinary. Until we shone a black light at it."

"Fluorescents in the ink?" Darius guessed. "Looks like nothing until you hit it with UVA light. They were all the rage for a while about a decade ago. I remember seeing girls sporting them in nightclubs and they looked pretty cool. They certainly stood out."

"Indeed," agreed Tempest in a rather non-committal way. "The point is, the demon must also be using a UVA light. However, I doubt he is working alone because of the next part."

"The next part?" Darius had one eyebrow hitched.

Tempest settled back into his seat, facing the tattoo parlour once more.

"Tell him, Jane."

"Arnold refused to play along. Refused to obey, so the demon appeared to his parents and almost killed them."

"Play along with what?" Darius wanted to hear.

"Drug smuggling." Jane said the words and let them hang heavy in the air. "It seems Arnold was coerced or possibly tricked into getting the tattoo. It's a picture of the demon which a couple of his so-called friends already had. It's an in-joke for the local population. The demon legend goes back to the eighteenth century."

"Well," Tempest interrupted, "that's as far as we traced it. Frank – that's our local font of all supernatural knowledge – would be able to produce a small Bible's worth of detail and records if we asked him."

"Which is why we didn't," finished Jane. "Arnold got tricked into joining a gang and now he is living in fear and needs our help. He believes his friends were also suckered into getting them and into doing the demon's bidding and were forced to recruit him, if that's the right word for it."

"Either way," Tempest took over again, "the demon is elusive, but the entire enterprise leads back to here."

Darius frowned deeply. "But surely Arnold told you where he had to go for the drug smuggling thing. He could operate as an inside man and the police could raid it."

Tempest smiled broadly. "Ah, yes, the police. You will find they are generally reluctant to listen to stories about demons or anything else that suggests the supernatural world might exist. Anyway, poor Arnold was transported to wherever they took him in the back of a van. He says he has no clue where they were other than close to the coast, and we have a lot of that around here."

"What drugs are we talking about?"

"Marijuana so far as we know. Arnold said there was tons of it and more than a dozen of them handling the load. The demon wasn't present, but Arnold reported a slew of armed guards who kept them working until the task was complete. According to Arnold, the armed thugs appeared to be under the demon's control too."

Darius fell quiet, his face thoughtful until he said, "I wanted to question why they would pressgang guys like Arnold using fear and terror tactics when they could just bring in paid thugs to do the work, but it's a money game, isn't it? If they can make these mugs do it for free, so much the better. Have there been many other instances like the Whelans?"

Tempest nodded. "Yes. Not recently, but going back over newspaper clippings for the last hundred years we found lots of sightings and reported attacks. There was even a big hunt back in the 1920s when a chap from the Natural History Museum believed the people here were seeing a new species of ape that he was going to discover."

Falling silent again, Tempest checked his watch. "I'm going for a look around." He looked at Jane. "Ready to do our bit?"

Jane sucked in a deep breath, clearly not ready though she said, "Always."

Acting the Part

WEDNESDAY 13TH DECEMBER 1930HRS

The tattoo shop's windows were screened off to give privacy to those inside, and festooned with hundreds of images to show examples of the available artwork. It sat on the corner of two streets, the door mounted at the apex so the two floor-to-ceiling window displays shone out on either side.

Inside, there was a faint smell of alcohol. Not the kind you drink, but that which you use to clean skin before making lots and lots of holes in it.

Hearing someone enter, a voice echoed out from a back room.

"Won't be a minute." It was a man's voice, but they already knew the shop was operated by Ross Dickerson, a short man with an abundance of ink, a six-month stint inside for fraud, and a terrible mullet hairstyle that deserved to be forcibly removed.

The constant buzz/whine of the tattoo gun filled the air, stopping now and then as the artist changed position or perhaps ink colour.

"Place looks harmless enough," murmured Darius, his

voice low. "What's the plan? Grab him, hang him by his feet, and make him tell us everything?"

Jane gave a small shake of her head.

"Tempest thinks this place is linked to the building next door somehow." To explain, she added, "Two nights ago he saw more people going in than a tiny space like this should be able to comfortably hold. They didn't come out for ages. So, his hope is that the tattoo shop is actually the headquarters or base of operations; whatever you want to call it." Explaining a pertinent point, she added, "You'll spend a lot of time on stakeouts. That's just how it is. Make sure you have a box of snacks in your car so you don't starve."

Catching on, Darius surmised, "We are in here to keep the owner distracted so Tempest can poke around. That's why he didn't come in with us."

"Yes, there is a side door. He's hoping to pick the lock and needs me to make sure the owner is out here and not back there where he might hear him sneak in."

"Then what?" Darius kept his voice quiet, unsure how far his deep tones would carry in the quiet space.

"If we get lucky, Tempest finds the demon costume and we can build a solid case. Or, if he finds evidence of the drugs, he can get the police involved and have the place raided."

"Wait? The police? How does he get paid if the police deal with it?"

They heard a squeak of leather and fell quiet, waiting to see if the tattoo artist was about to appear. When he didn't, Jane said, "We can't arrest anyone. I mean, obviously we can restrain criminals, and the guys do all the time, but gathering evidence to make a case that will hold up in court – it's just better having the police do it."

"But Tempest said not five minutes ago that they don't respond to claims of supernatural activity."

"That's why we have to figure out the truth before we call them."

The sound of feet on the lino drew their eyes toward the door in time to see Ross Dickerson coming through it. He wore a baggy black t-shirt with a metal band motif, skinny black jeans, and mostly-dead, black Converse hi-top trainers. Tattoos poked out from every hole in his shirt, running from just beneath his chin all the way down to his hands and onto his fingers.

"Evening," he greeted his customers with a professional smile. "Looking for something in particular?" He had a nasal voice which Jane surmised to be caused by a deviated septum – someone had done a good job of breaking it and Ross had never bothered to get it fixed.

This part had been rehearsed a little, Jane stepping in to take up the discussion, but only after shooting the tattoo artist an apologetic smile while she finished sending a text message – to Tempest to tell him it was go time.

"I was hoping you might be able to do something I've seen on a friend of mine." She made a show of looking around the displays inside the shop. "I don't see it though."

Keen to help the blonde woman and make a sale, Ross kept his smile in place and asked, "Can you describe it?"

"Oh, um, it was kind of like a demon face. It had antlers and it was coloured a deep, vibrant red." Jane held a hand, palm down above her right breast. "I would like it here if that's possible. I have quite a bit of ink already," she admitted, sounding somewhere between ashamed and excited.

Darius let a smile tease his lips – Jane was good.

Ross had tried not to react when he heard the description, but he wasn't fast enough to hide the concern in his face when it surfaced.

"Oh, well, we certainly have a lot of great designs to pick from," he was trying to deter her. "I'm sure we can come up with something that will suit the lady. Can I ask where you saw the demon tattoo?"

"In the pub, actually. It was last weekend. I don't recall the guy's name, but he was very cute with dark brown hair and stubble. He said he got the tattoo here, but his was on his right deltoid. Would it help if I got a photograph of it?"

The worried look crossed Ross's face again. "Oh, um, well, I mostly stick to what I know. Sorry. There really are a lot of designs here to pick from."

Asking about the demon tattoo was nothing more than an exercise to see how he would react. He had to be complicit in the crime, but at what level? Was he a pawn? Was he involved at the upper end of the organisation? He certainly wasn't the idiot in the costume since the Whelans described it as seven feet tall and Ross had to be eighteen inches shorter than that.

Moving on to keep him talking and distracted, Jane walked to a stand of designs.

"Can you talk to me about this one?" She pointed to a giant dragon, its wings spread magnificently. "That would look amazing across my back."

Clearly seeing a score, the tattoo was the kind that took multiple sessions and cost hundreds, Ross followed Jane.

"This is one of my favourite pieces," he bragged. "It's my design, in fact."

"Hello?" called a voice from the back room. It belonged to a man, and he sounded impatient. "Are you coming back anytime soon? If I wanted to hang around waiting for someone to hurt me, I would go home to my wife."

"Won't be a moment," Ross apologised, turning imploring eyes back to Jane – he wanted to make the sale and get her lined up for the work, but had to return to his current customer very soon.

Jane exchanged a glance with Darius; they needed to give Tempest more time. Assuming he'd managed to pick the lock, he still needed time to get in and explore and then get out again.

"Shall I leave you to look around some more?" Ross suggested, his feet slowly edging back to his impatient customer.

Jane grabbed his arm, smiling coyly, "No, tell me more about your genius. If I'm going to spend so much time with your hands on my bare skin, I'm going to want to know I can trust you."

Darius watched with interest. Jane stood at least six inches taller than the tattoo artist and her heels added another couple. Towering over him, she was acting sultry and manipulating the poor man as only a woman can.

Ross swallowed visibly and it wasn't hard to guess what might be going on in his head.

"Hey!" called the voice from the back room. "Do I get a discount for being messed around?"

They all heard the squeak of leather as he left the recliner and his feet on the floorboards when he began to stomp their way.

Darius, large and capable, moved to intercept. A certain look from a tall, muscular man usually proves enough to deter lesser mortals from any foolish course of action they might have in mind.

However, before Darius could get to the doorway from the shop to the backrooms, the man appeared. He was naked from the waist up and had the build and physique of a professional wrestler.

Darius wasn't against mixing it up and fighting when the situation called for it, but so far as he knew, the man, giant or not, was an innocent.

"Ten seconds," the man growled at Ross, "or I'm not paying for the work you've done so far and I'll get someone else to finish it."

Ross's feet moved instantly. "Sorry. Sorry. I'm coming right now."

"What about me?" asked Jane, trying to keep Ross in the front of the shop for a few moments longer.

Ross twisted his body as he went through to the back room, but kept walking when he said, "Sorry. I really won't be long if you can hang around."

That was all they got.

Left alone in the tattoo parlour, Ross and his customer would be able to hear them if they spoke aloud and a camera mounted above the door suggested he had a screen from which he could monitor his shop from the ink room.

Jane inclined her head toward the door – it was time to go.

All the Gang Is Here

WEDNESDAY, 13TH DECEMBER 1937HRS

Leaving the shop, Jane spotted a car parked behind hers. Her heartbeat increased, but only for as long as it took for her to realise the car belong to Patricia.

The passenger's window opened, gliding down far enough for the middle-aged blonde woman to lean out and wave hello. Also inside were Jermaine, Barbie, and Hideki, all of whom Jane knew from past encounters.

"Hello again, Darius," Patricia looked around. "Standing in for Tempest?"

Darius chuckled, "Not exactly."

Jane huffed out a worried breath. "He's inside. At least I think he is. He got me to create a diversion so he could sneak in through a side door."

"You look concerned," Patricia observed. "Is he in danger?"

"Probably," Jane conceded. "He usually is."

Jermaine picked up his bowler hat, a steely determination in his eyes. "We can effect a rescue if one is needed."

"Let's give him some time," Jane suggested. "He went in

to see what he could find. He'll holler if he gets into more trouble than he can handle."

Returning to her car, this time with Darius in the passenger seat instead of in the back, Jane watched the door of the tattoo parlour.

Half an hour passed. She sent text messages to Tempest without getting a response. Fighting against rising nervousness, Jane told herself the issue was probably one of poor signal quality out here in the sticks. Her messages were not getting through. Or his, perhaps. He could be deep inside the building or even in a cellar where reception might be non-existent.

Of course, inside her head, Tempest got caught the moment she left the shop and was currently being tortured for information.

Her discomfort rose significantly when the wrestler wannabe left the shop, his clothes now covering his body, and the lights inside went off.

Expecting to see Ross Dickerson leave the premises and lock up, she waited ten minutes before the lump in her gut demanded she do something.

Darius agreed. He wasn't used to taking the figurative backseat. A man of action, he was more than ready to storm the tattoo parlour to get his friend back. However, just when Jane was sending an update to Patricia, a man walked down the street and went inside the darkened building.

Darius leaned forward in his seat, peering through the windscreen. "There's another one coming this way."

Jane was just about to reply when a shadow went by her door as yet another man headed in the direction of the tattoo parlour.

He crossed the road right in front of Jane's car, his

attention on where he was going, thankfully, or he might have noticed the two cars filled with people.

Sucking air between her teeth, Jane said, "I don't like the look of this."

Tempest was inside the building and still men came. They counted more than twenty in the space of ten minutes. That they might be there to deal with Tempest went without saying.

A knuckle rapped against the driver's side window making Jane almost leap out of her skin.

"Good thing I don't need to pee," she moaned, lowering her window to see what Jermaine wanted.

Patricia appeared beside him. "Do you think we should go in?" she asked, cutting her eyes toward the shop. "What if Tempest is in trouble?"

Darius grabbed his door handle. "I don't think we have a choice at this point." Clambering out to stand up and look over the top of the car, he said, "I'm going in either way. Tempest would do the same for me."

Patricia was swift to point out, "Tempest *has* done the same for me."

There being no further need to argue, Barbie and Hideki left the Range Rover to join their friends and the six checked the street before stealing through the night.

Stairway to Hell

WEDNESDAY, 13TH DECEMBER 1947HRS

Darius got to the door first, but only because Jermaine was too polite to shove him out of the way. They were expecting resistance from the moment they opened it, but there wasn't even a guard inside to deter them from entering.

The interior of the shop was dark, but there was enough light coming from the streetlamps outside for them to be able to see.

"Please stay behind me, madam," Jermaine requested, advancing across the room with silent steps.

"Maybe you want to hang at the back with me, Patricia?" Jane suggested. Not long after starting her job at Blue Moon, she took up self-defence classes. But learning a few moves was a long way from feeling confident walking into an environment where they would be outnumbered many to one.

Taking the lead, Darius indicated, "It's through here. After that, I have no clue where we need to go."

Patricia said, "Didn't you say Tempest went in through a side door?"

Jane nodded, "That's right. It's outside and round to the right."

"Maybe we should check that out," suggested Barbie. "Us three girls can tackle it."

The guys were already progressing through the back rooms of the tattoo parlour. It was eerily quiet, no noise at all save for a low humming sound coming from somewhere.

"Does anyone else hear that?" asked Hideki. His question enough to stall the ladies' feet before they made it back to the exit.

"The humming?" questioned Jermaine. "Any idea what it is?"

Everyone stopped to listen, holding their breath to focus only on the strange noise.

"Hold on," hissed Darius. "I think I've found something."

Yet again, everyone stopped moving and turned to face him. It meant they were looking in the right direction when he opened a door and a thin shaft of dim light shone out. What was more notable was how the humming noise increased in volume. Not only that, without the door muffling the sound they could now tell they were hearing voices.

"Stairs," Darius whispered. Four steps down they took a ninety-degree right turn and kept going, descending into the darkness.

Barbie retraced her steps across the shop. "Where do they go?"

Darius double pumped his eyebrows and grinned evilly in the darkness. "They go down."

Dark Cellar

WEDNESDAY 13TH DECEMBER 1932HRS

The dark basement wasn't the first Tempest had ever wandered willingly into and he doubted it would be the last. Slipping inside the building via the side door, he managed to avoid the owner returning to the back rooms by being still.

He considered it a little-known skill and one he discovered playing outdoor games as a boy scout in his youth. Movement is one of the easiest things for the eye to track. Straight lines don't occur in nature so they stand out, and sound will always attract attention, so staying still and quiet while shrouded in the darkness of a shadow, well that was almost the same as turning invisible.

Ross walked right by his feet, as did his customer on his way out to the shop and again when he'd finished complaining about being made to wait and headed back to the chair. Once they were out of sight and the buzz of the tattoo gun returned to mask the sounds of his movement, Tempest slipped deeper into the back rooms, checking those before finding the cellar door.

He knew there would be a cellar, the tattoo parlour had once been a public house and the evidence of its former life was obvious from the outside.

What he had not expected was how extensive the cellar would be. It clearly covered a greater area than the building above it, extending into the derelict building behind it. Exploring, it took no time at all to find where the walls had been removed. To open the space up, someone had simply knocked out the walls and employed builders' acrow props to keep the ceiling from falling in.

The shoddy building work was, however, of little interest compared with the enormous, raised pentagram. Built up from the dusty floor and reflected in paint on the ceiling above, it measured twenty feet across.

Tempest entered the building hoping to find evidence he could take to the cops, but so far there was no trace of drugs that he could find, and no demon costume that would have at least confirmed he was in the right place.

Until he found something to provide a concrete link between the Whelans' injuries and the tattoo parlour, it was nothing more than a contentious connection. Arnold could provide nothing, not even anecdotal, to suggest Ross Dickerson was involved. Sure, he provided the tattoo, but there was nothing illegal about that.

However, just as his frustrated feet were getting ready to give up and leave the cellar, the sound of feet on the stairs drove Tempest into cover. Mercifully, there was plenty of that to be had.

Making himself comfortable in a darkened corner behind the raised pentagram, he watched Ross Dickerson enter the room. He was tearing off his shirt to show the full range of his tattoos.

Curious to see what might happen next, Tempest took

out his phone. It had no signal underground, but that didn't mean it was useless. Tracking the suspicious tattoo artist, he began to film.

He was still filming when people started to arrive a short while later.

Welcome to the Party

WEDNESDAY, 13TH DECEMBER 1959HRS

Darius placed his right foot on the first step. It was concrete rather than wood, he noted with relief, since it was less likely to creak and announce their approach.

The humming sound was clearer now and it wasn't voices at all. Someone was talking, a deep bass resonating through the walls and floor as though it was coming from the depths of hell itself. But the humming was something else, something machine based as he first believed.

Indicating his plan to descend, Darius took another step, but movement ahead made his feet freeze.

Stepping out from behind where the stairs turned a corner, a rough-looking man with a shaved head covered in tattoos aimed a gun squarely at Darius' midriff.

A second man joined him, though he did not appear to be armed. Both were dressed in dirty jeans, t-shirts, and sports jackets unzipped at the front.

The shorter man grinned, showing his poor dentistry.

"Welcome to the party."

Darius weighed up his odds. In the narrow confines of

the stairwell, the man with the gun could hardly miss, but it was a small handgun, a .38 from what he could see.

"Madam, we appear to have encountered a problem," Jermaine reported.

Patricia squeezed in tight to his side to look for herself, uttering a quiet expletive when she saw the two men.

Barbie grabbed Patricia's arm, "Let's go, Patty! Time for some of us to be somewhere else!"

Patricia wholeheartedly agreed. However, there was no opportunity to beat a hasty retreat, for the moment they turned to face the shop door, the trap was sprung.

Four men with handguns rushed in through the shop's entrance, flicking on the lights to sting eyeballs and add to the shock of their capture.

Facing Darius, the short man with the bad teeth continued to grin when he said, "We clocked you lot ages ago. Sitting outside in your cars and watching the place. Did you not wonder why there was no one guarding the door?"

Darius narrowed his eyes and kept his body loose. If the shaved-head ugly bloke with the gun took his eyes away for a second, he was going to attack. There were no more than two yards between them. He could get to the gun before Shaved Head realised what was happening.

It would even the odds.

Unfortunately, the kerfuffle behind him reached his ears to give him pause and the opportunity, however slight it might have been, was lost.

Sandwiched between the two groups and facing automatic weapons, Darius, Patricia, and the rest were escorted downstairs.

They exited the stairs into a musty-smelling basement. The walls were bare brick, the floor bare concrete if one discounted the layer of grimy dust. It was lit only by a couple of bare lightbulbs hanging from the ceiling, but brighter light with an eerie red edge shone out from a gap in the wall to their front.

The space was bigger than expected, they all noted, and certainly bigger than the footprint of the building above it. The deep voice which, now they were hearing it without walls or floors to muffle it, had an alien, evil darkness to it. It was also the deepest bass any of them had ever heard.

"This way," sneered Shaved Head, beckoning they follow as he led them across the basement floor in the direction of the voice.

The man with the bad teeth walked backwards so he faced his captives and continued to grin and talk, identifying himself as some kind of low-level boss or spokesperson for the group.

"Some of you lot look tough." He eyed Darius and Jermaine. "That will change when Bakasura marks you. That's if you are lucky. He might decide he doesn't need any more slaves and just kill you all instead."

"Bakasura?" Patricia repeated. "That's your little demon, is it?"

Bad Teeth quirked an eyebrow. "Well, how about that? You're even dumber than I thought. You willingly walked into a demon's lair. Now you get to pay the price."

"Yeah, I've got a price the blonde one can pay," muttered Shaved Head lewdly, his tone sinister.

Patricia narrowed her eyes at the man. "Excuse me?"

His face crinkled into a disgusted grimace. "Not you. Her," he jerked his gun in Barbie's direction.

The men surrounding Patricia and her friends chuckled darkly, one showing his bravado by smacking Jane on her rump.

"I quite fancy the skinny one, myself," he growled.

"Is that so?" asked Jane, dropping her girl voice for a beat. The sound of the man's voice coming from the petite blonde's mouth startled the armed men, but they had crossed the basement and could be seen by the people in the next room.

"What is this?" asked the deep bass voice. "We have unexpected guests," it announced, sounding pleased.

Coming through the space where a wall had once been, Darius, Patricia, and the rest found themselves in another room. Roughly the same size as the one they were leaving, the walls were decorated and it was better lit.

A group of about twenty men, all bare from the waist up, their ink on display, knelt on the floor. They were facing the other way but twisted around now to see who was coming in behind them. The men were tattooed to varying degrees, but each had a distinctive red devil on their right deltoid, easy to see because it glowed faintly.

Around the periphery of the room, another half dozen men watched over them. In contrast to the men on their knees, they were fully dressed and hefting clubs or bats threateningly.

Patricia took all that in as she came into the space, but her eyes were drawn to the far side of the room where a giant demon stood. It had to be close to seven feet tall though the antlers sprouting from its skull made it over eight. The prongs almost scraped the ceiling where a large white pentagram was crudely daubed in white paint.

Like the men kneeling, the demon was naked from the waist up. It wore black leather trousers that ended with cloven feet. Its skin was a dull red like the colour of dried blood and its eyes were pure black like a shark's.

Spearing the newcomers with a hate-filled gaze, it raised one hand, fingers extended, palm down.

"Come forward and kneel before me," it commanded, lowering the arm. "You have chosen to invade the sanctity of my sanctuary here on this mortal plain and you must pay the price."

The armed men behind Patricia's group moved forward, expecting them to also move.

Clearly used to fear-induced compliance, they seemed confused when no one moved.

"I don't think so," snarled Darius, narrowing his eyes at Shaved Head, the nearest of the goons and the one he planned to take out first.

Beside him, Jermaine tensed, ready to act and only waiting because their situation was problematic and the likelihood someone might shoot or hurt Patricia was too great. Outnumbered wasn't too much of a problem, he'd fought multiple opponents before and believed he could rely on both Darius and Hideki. The guns, however, gave his opponents an unfair advantage.

"Kneel!" Bakasura barked, the half-naked men to his front flinching at the stark increase in volume.

"Or we could do something else," said a new voice. It seemed to come from nowhere, yet also most definitely from inside the room. "Ooh, what does this button do?" it asked, the dull red light around Bakasura changing to a sky blue.

Comically, it made him look a bit like a Smurf. A muscular Smurf with antlers, for sure, but kinda the same, nevertheless.

Patricia, despite the armed men around her, couldn't stop the smile sneaking across her lips.

"Tempest," she murmured, catching Barbie's eye to wink at her.

The demon's expression changed from one of total confidence and control, to one of mild panic.

"Oh, great Bakasura!" Tempest's headless voice echoed loudly around the chamber. "Reveal your true self I beseech you!"

Two of the men with clubs closest to the raised pentagram started running down the side of the room.

The half-naked men on their knees were looking around and at each other. Whatever they had experienced before, this wasn't it. Their questioning faces were reflected by their master who watched the two men with their clubs held high disappear behind a wall neither Patricia nor any of her friends had noticed yet in the dimly lit space.

The sound of fighting broke out, a few expletives let loose to the accompanying whack of a club hitting something with a great deal of force.

A triumphant grin crossed the demon's face, and he raised both his arms.

"Now ..." the deep bass was gone. In its place a nasal whine. Bakasura said but one word in a voice that wasn't his before slamming his mouth shut again.

Jane jolted the moment she heard the new voice and in the stunned silence that followed, shouted, "That's Ross Dickerson!"

The men on their knees were becoming agitated and one or two started to rise.

Bakasura tried to speak again. "Stay where you are! I command you!" However, the small nasal voice didn't carry the same ability to terrify obedience.

Darius seized his chance. The armed men surrounding their group looked just as confused as the demon-inked victims in the centre of the chamber. So far as he was concerned it was now or never, and with that in mind and Shaved Head's attention distracted, he lunged.

Jermaine was already moving, giving Hideki a nudge to

Modern Fairy Tale

spur him into action. Where the Jamaican was tall, muscular, and powerful, the much smaller man from Japan was faster.

All three men struck out at the armed men surrounding them, aiming their first blows at the weapons or the arms holding them. Barbie and Jane attacked too. While neither was a trained fighter, it felt like enough of a life-or-death situation for them to throw themselves bodily at their captors.

Darius grabbed Shaved Head's gun, stripping it from his hand even as he continued to power forward. Using his body mass and inertia, he slammed through Shaved Head, propelling him backward into Bad Teeth.

They were both going down, but Darius didn't hang around to watch it happen. He spun around, adjusting his grip on the gun as he brought it to bear on a man struggling with Barbie.

Easing back the trigger, he calmly expected the buck of recoil, and was surprised when none came.

Looking startled by the sudden turn of events, Bakasura shouted, "Kill them! Kill them all!"

Patricia swung her handbag – a terrible cliché – she thought to herself, but having learned a lesson from a mad old woman she met along the way, she'd taken the time to load it with a house brick before leaving home.

Yelling, "Barbie! Heads up!" the handbag swiped through the space her young blonde friend's head occupied a moment earlier, striking her assailant across the top of his skull with a terrible crack.

One handle of the handbag snapped, the contents flying free to scatter in the air.

Darius looked up. The magazine of the weapon he'd taken was empty and a closer inspection showed it to be a harmless replica. A good replica, but a toy just the same. Since none of the armed men had discharged their guns yet, he chose to assume they were all replicas and used the one he had as a missile, launching it at the head of Bad Teeth as he wriggled out from under Shaved Head and started to get up.

The gun hit him square in the forehead, leaving a dent. Bad Teeth wavered for a moment before his eyes went blank and he collapsed back to the floor.

At the far end of the chamber behind the raised pentagram, Tempest emerged holding a club. There was blood coming from a cut above his right eye, but other than the look of determined rage on his face, he looked fine.

"Do you want to see your demon?" he bellowed loud enough to be heard above the cacophony of battle.

The men in the middle of the room were on their feet now with one or two exceptions. Terror had kept them compliant, but the changes in the demon they feared and the melee breaking out around them gave question to the balance of power.

Tempest threw the club, sending it sailing on a horizontal trajectory through the air toward Bakasura. The demon didn't flinch. In fact, he didn't even seem to notice when it went straight through him.

The sight was enough to make everyone in the room pause, just for a second.

It was all Tempest needed to take three paces to his right and vanish behind a wall.

On the raised pentagram, Bakasura spun around to look behind him. There was no one there, or didn't appear to be, but the giant demon started flapping his hands at an unseen assailant, trying hard to make them leave him alone until an even bigger hand grabbed him by his throat and gave him a yank.

To everyone looking, Bakasura simply ceased to be. Pulled off his feet, he vanished into thin air, but his nasal voice could still be heard protesting.

Tempest appeared from behind the wall again, his body emerging first followed by his right arm which he held out at shoulder height. Dangling from it and fighting was Ross Dickerson, the tattoo artist's toes barely touching the floor.

"Here he is!" Tempest announced.

Ross fought and bucked, tearing at the arm that held him with no visible gain.

Tempest threw the smaller man down and stood over him, facing the crowded chamber.

"An image projector!" he shouted into the quiet of the room. "That and some clever theatrics are what created the demon. Bakasura is nothing but your own subconscious fears convincing you that what you saw could be real. You have been duped by a petty criminal."

Shaved Head said, "What? Ross said he was the demon's conduit. Cursed at birth, he's been forced to suffer the company of Bakasura whenever the sun fell."

Darius kicked his foot and when Shaved Head looked his way, said, "You're as dumb as you look."

The men in the centre of the room were yet to move, but when the first of them moved toward the little man now cowering at Tempest's feet, the rest followed. They surged forward, reaching the raised pentagram in a heartbeat.

Behind them, Bakasura's thugs chose a different strategy: they ran for the door. Admittedly, several of them, Bad Teeth included, were down for the count and with Darius crowding him threateningly, Shaved Head chose to stay put on the floor.

To stop his friend from giving pursuit, Tempest shouted, "Let them go!" There was no reason to fight them or try to stop them leaving. The safe play was to let them leave.

That left Bakasura's minions though and they were looking for blood.

"I've handled drugs for you!" accused one man.

"Ha! He made me bury a body!" raged another.

They all had grievances and were likely to tear Ross Dickson to pieces if they got their hands on him. To avoid that end, Tempest held up a hand like a cop stopping traffic.

"Hold," he commanded, his voice carrying an air of authority and expected compliance.

Impressing Patricia, Darius, and the rest of his friends, the advancing menace of Bakasura's minions stopped.

Speaking calmly, Tempest offered sympathetic eyes.

"He needs to answer for his crimes, gentlemen. To the police though, not to you. It would seem you all have enough blood on your hands."

"Wait. Are we going to be in trouble for what he made us do?" asked a voice in the crowd.

Tempest didn't want to give them false hope, so he said, "That is not for me to decide. However, I expect your case will be considered groundbreaking. Unless any of you are guilty of murder, I believe the courts will hear your pleas favourably. Now, gentlemen, it is time we all vacated this gloomy place."

"But what about the rest of them?" asked someone. "They've been threatening us and making sure we did Bakasura's bidding for years."

"Yeah," said another. "And you just let them all escape."

Tempest smiled. "Did I?"

No Escape

WEDNESDAY 13TH DECEMBER 2009HRS

Tempest remained tight-lipped about what his cryptic comment might mean – a trait Patricia found most entertaining since she did it to Barbie all the time. However, when they reached the top of the stairs, Jermaine leading with Tempest and Darius manhandling Ross Dickerson, and Patricia, her friends and all the demon-tattooed following, it was instantly apparent what he was choosing not to tell them.

The flashing lights of almost a dozen police cars strobed into the night air. The flickering shadows they created danced against the walls of the tattoo parlour, getting brighter and brighter as they came from the back rooms, through the shop, and out the door to reach the street.

Bakasura's thugs fled the building via the front door and side door, but the cops were waiting for them regardless.

"I made the call when I was stuck in the basement," Tempest revealed on his way out of the door.

Jane frowned. "But we couldn't get you to reply to a text. I figured you had no signal."

"I didn't," he admitted, adding confusion. "I had to find a spot right next to the outer wall where I managed to get one bar. Thankfully, that turned out to be a great spot to leave my phone, so I sent the signal to YouTube, sent the link to a certain Chief Inspector …"

"Quinn?" gasped Patricia.

"Fraid so," Tempest smiled. "Remember that Grimm's fairy tale case I told you about?"

"Yes."

"He's my client." When Patricia's forehead crinkled with her lack of understanding, Tempest explained, "I was asked to investigate by Quinn's boss, the chief constable. I get to work side by side with the chief inspector and they pay me for it."

The face Patricia pulled reminded Tempest of his sister's kids when they filled their nappies.

Sniggering, he explained his take on things. "He hates me, and I loathe him. It allows us to do business without wondering if the other has some hidden agenda because we both do. In circumstances such as tonight, I knew his desire to grab the glory would overwhelm his desire to see me fall. And lo." Tempest spread his arms to indicate the scene in the street.

Bakasura's thugs were either on the ground with cops cuffing them or already being hauled away to waiting police vans which would take them to Maidstone nick.

Darius gave the tattoo artist a shake. "What should I do with this one?"

"I'll take him," said Patience Woods, stepping out from between two police vans parked nose to nose.

"*I'll* take him, thank you, Sergeant Woods," argued a voice everyone bar Darius cringed to hear.

Tempest swivelled around to face the senior officer.

"Chief Inspector."

"Mr Michaels."

Their eyes met and it seemed as though they were entering a staring competition so intense were the looks they gave each other.

"You have all you need?" Tempest asked after a few seconds.

"For now," Chief Inspector Quinn nodded. "But statements will be required."

"Really?" Tempest challenged. "The video footage showing everything that transpired won't suffice?" He was joking and the Chief Inspector refused to rise to the bait.

"Tomorrow, Mr Michaels. You and all your ..." Quinn glanced at Patricia Fisher, "friends will need to explain the events leading to tonight's activities."

He moved away, busying himself giving orders to people already doing what was required of them and Tempest let him go.

There was nothing to be gained by exchanging verbal volleys with Ian Quinn and there was another matter of business he was far more keen to tackle.

"Sergeant Woods?" he beamed, twisting around to face Patience again.

Her smile matched his and they embraced, hugging like the friends they were for more seconds than decorum might normally allow.

Patricia and Barbie were next in line, overjoyed to share the moment with their friend.

"When did this happen?" Barbie begged to know. "We only saw you a few hours ago and you were still a constable then."

"This afternoon," Patience admitted, near vibrating with excitement. "The Chief Constable for the whole of

Kent gave it to me himself. Said I was a shining beacon for all officers in the county."

"It's not going to her head at all," remarked Brad Hardacre on his way past, pushing a suspect in cuffs toward the nearest van.

Patricia said, "You have every right to be pleased with yourself. This is a big achievement."

Patience continued to beam. "I am and it is. I never thought I would last long enough to even look at promotion. Now though … well, I think I might go after a certain chief inspector's job."

They talked for a few moments, but it didn't take Quinn long to decide he needed Patience doing something else.

In the quiet that followed, Tempest asked, "You fly tomorrow?"

Patricia nodded. "That's right. We're meeting the ship in Los Angeles. It will be good to get back. I miss my dogs."

"You miss Alistair," Barbie teased, her arm looped through Hideki's and her head resting on his shoulder.

"True," Patricia admitted. "In fact, we really need to go if we are going to get any sleep before our flight. Thank you for letting me even up the score a little. I'm sure I still owe you many times over though."

Tempest waved her comments away. "Friends help friends."

"Before we go," Patricia started, "How did you know about the projected image?"

"I was in the basement before the other guys arrived. By the time they came in to set up I had figured out how he was making himself look like Bakasura. It's a clever bit of software actually. Like the stuff they used in the *Avatar* film to make actors look like giant blue ape people, but this one operates in real time. I guess the technology is twenty years old now though."

"And it's portable?" Darius challenged.

Tempest said, "Yup. Battery pack rigged up to a trolley with the computer and projector loaded on top. I guess that's how he appeared in the road and made the Whelans crash. In fact, I reckon Dickerson has been using that same trick for a few years, building up the legend and inciting fear."

The mystery explained, Tempest suggested everyone get moving. It was cool out less than two weeks before Christmas, and he rather fancied a beverage at the watering hole not far from his house.

Hugs were exchanged and Patricia promised to look Darius up the next time the ship docked on the Gold Coast.

"That's in about seven weeks," Barbie confirmed.

Darius smiled, "See you then."

Second Victim?

THURSDAY, 14TH DECEMBER 0537HRS

The sound of his phone ringing drilled through the fog of Tempest's sleep, spoiling his particularly vivid dream about Amanda, and rousing him to alertness to find Dozer snoring noisily on the other side of the bed.

Bleary eyed, he swiped his phone, squinted at the screen until it came into focus and stabbed the green button to answer it before it switched over to voicemail.

"Quinn."

"No, sir, this is Constable Wragg calling from the Chief Inspector's phone. He is busy dealing with a case and respectfully requests …"

"That is not what I said, Wragg," echoed Quinn's voice in the background. "Do not put words into my mouth."

Tempest chuckled sleepily, wishing someone would shove something into the chief inspector's mouth. A hedgehog perhaps. Or a full-sized cement mixer.

"Um," Constable Wragg attempted cautiously to finish his message. "Um, there has been another attack, by the, um, by the Grimm's Fairy Tale person. You are needed at the station."

Tempest yawned deeply, letting it control his face until it was done. When it subsided, he stretched his neck and rolled his shoulders while saying, "Please let Ian know I will be along just as soon as I can."

Dropping the phone onto the bed, Tempest rolled off it and fell into push ups. His workload recently was such that he wasn't finding time to exercise. That was fine for a while, but he got twitchy when too many days passed, so five minutes of strenuous exercise would do no harm at all.

He debated waking Darius, who would undoubtedly complain later that he was here to shadow Tempest and thus needed to be included, but jetlag is a tough beast to battle, and the Australian had looked done in when they got home the previous evening.

There would be time to do stuff together later today, so having let the dogs out to relieve themselves in the garden before settling them in the living room, Tempest slipped quietly from the house with a travel mug full of hot tea to find a steady downpour falling.

Constable Wragg gave no clue as to the nature of the latest attack, but made it clear they believed it was another Grimm's Fairy Tale incident. Tempest was curious to learn why.

He felt certain there would be an obvious link, but what did that mean? Had Cinderella escaped her evil stepmother? Was he about to meet a woman in a coma playing the role of Sleeping Beauty?

Choosing to leave his car in the staff carpark behind the station, Tempest dodged the rain and puddles on his way into the nick through a door he had only ever used before when under arrest and being escorted inside. Getting 'nicked' was something that happened all too frequently in his early months as a paranormal P.I. The police regarded him with great suspicion for a long time, and it was only when the press began to glamourise his successes that general opinion turned.

The desk sergeant looked up from his magazine, his eyes registering mild surprise and a touch of confusion at the civilian wandering through the station.

"Special consultant to Chief Inspector Quinn," Tempest announced on his way through. "I'm expected." He was already halfway through the room when he stopped and backtracked. "Actually, I could probably do with a pass for my car and some kind of badge for my jacket. Who should I see about that, please?"

Advised to speak with Chloe in the admin office, Tempest pushed the task down the order of priority – he could deal with it on his way out – and went on his way, correctly assuming he would find someone to point him the right direction if he wandered far enough. He'd been aiming for Quinn's office, but Constable Wragg spotted him.

"He's in interview room three. I'll take you there," Wragg offered.

Tempest followed but had questions. "Is he interviewing a victim or a perp?"

"Victim. Young woman. Gorgeous young woman, actually. Russian, I think. Used to have long blonde hair but someone hacked it off. She ended up in the hospital following her attack and it was the staff there who reported it to the police. Following up was a routine thing, but when the detectives started asking her questions, they phoned the chief straight away."

"Why?" Tempest wasn't seeing the connection.

Wragg paused, his hand on the door handle for the interview room when he turned to look Tempest dead in the eyes.

"The guy who did it kept calling her Rapunzel."

Wragg knocked on the door and opened it a crack. Levering his head around the frame, he said, "I've got Mr Michaels, Sir."

Quinn spoke to the woman still out of sight behind the door, his words kind and soothing, and then to the recorder to explain the interruption before saying, "Send him in."

Wragg stepped aside and Tempest put on his professional game face. He and Quinn had major beef with each other most of the time, but the victim didn't need to see it.

His expression suitably sombre, Tempest strode into the room, extending his hand to shake Quinn's. He turned his eyes toward the victim, noting how fragile she seemed, like a porcelain doll. Guessing her age at perhaps twenty-two, she was petite and had to weigh less than ninety pounds.

Her hair was cut away, just as Wragg claimed, but roughly so as if performed by a blind barber using his feet to control the clippers. In places it had been taken down to the skin, and in some spots even deeper than that. There were dressings here and there and random tufts, some of which were an inch long.

Settling into the chair next to Quinn with the chief inspector introducing his new colleague and explaining his presence, Tempest waited for him to finish before saying, "I'm terribly sorry for what this person did to you. I hope you will be able to help us catch him. We are after a man, yes," he sought to confirm with Quinn.

"Indeed. Thankfully, Miss Rudokova has been able to provide a good description. One of our best artists is on his way to produce a likeness."

"When did the attack take place?" Tempest's question was aimed at the woman sitting opposite. She appeared tired, and the puffiness around her eyes showed recent tears, probably the result of trying to relive her experience.

"Last night," she replied. Twitching her eyes across to spear Quinn with a sad expression, she asked, "Am I going to have to go through it all again now?" Her Russian accent was there, but her English was impeccable.

Tempest shook his head. "There should be no need for that, but I need to know what the chief inspector knows before I can ask what has not been asked." The truth was that Quinn should have waited. The poor woman had suffered a terrible attack, and he hoped she had friends or family nearby she could go to for comfort and support. "Perhaps we should adjourn, Ian?"

A muscle by Quinn's right eye twitched; he didn't like being addressed so informally. Nevertheless, he said, "Yes, perhaps that would be wise. Let's give you a break Miss Rudokova. I will have one of my officers escort you to a private room where you can relax."

In Quinn's private office a few minutes later, Tempest listened to the chief inspector's report.

"She reports the man to be in his late twenties and of very slim build. His face was pockmarked from teenage acne, he is approximately five feet six inches tall and referred to himself more than once as the architect of the story."

"Architect of the Story," Tempest repeated, framing the words with different emphasis to the way Quinn said them. "He's acting out scenes. He turned the king into a frog and now he's created a real live Rapunzel."

The grimace of disgust on Quinn's face was epic.

"Acting out stories, Mr Michaels? These are real crimes. Not someone's games."

"Why can't they be both?" Tempest shifted in his chair, angling a hand up his back to deal with an itch. "Whoever this guy is, I think it would be wise to assume he is operating with a different belief system to the one you employ. Hacking off a woman's hair while calling her Rapunzel is not the usual way a man attacks a woman. The hair thing is very personal, like throwing acid into a person's face. It's not the sort of thing you do to a random stranger. However, Miss Rudokova ... what is her first name, please?"

"Olga."

"Good. You have this thing with addressing people formally all the time, Ian. It makes you sound like a master criminal." Pushing on before Quinn could argue, Tempest said, "Olga would have told us if she recognised her attacker, so I believe he picked his victim based purely on her looks. She had long, blonde hair, yes?"

"She is ... was a hair model," Quinn revealed. "Among other work. It fell to her buttocks."

Tempest wondered if she was smart enough to insure it but wasn't going to ask.

"Is there anything to link her to Dr and Mrs King? Does she know them?"

Quinn shook his head. "That requires some more exploration. She might not be aware of the link if one exists, but in questioning her, she has no knowledge of the Kings and no idea why she was attacked."

They moved on to where the attack took place and the specific details about the time, place, and nature of it. "She was grabbed from behind getting into her car in a multistorey carpark at the nearby Blue Water Shopping Centre. He used chloroform to render her unconscious which could mean he had limited resources or just that he liked the classics."

"When she awoke, she was in a dark room that she reported to smell of damp and mud. She heard a train go by and said there were old posters on the walls that made her think the place used to be a gym. She was tied to a chair and believed she was going to be raped or murdered. Instead, he talked to her about her starring role in his latest tale, called her Rapunzel, and hacked off her hair with a large kitchen knife, the kind you can buy in any store. While he did so he remarked on her looks."

"Then he used the chloroform again and when she came to the next time it was late last night and she had no idea where she was. He'd dropped her still dressed and, with the exception of her hair, entirely unmolested, in Mote Park in Maidstone. Her phone was still in her car which was recovered from Blue Water where they do not have CCTV cameras in the carparks."

"She wandered until she found a woman out walking her dogs and was rescued from there. I have officers combing the area to check if anyone saw anything and plan to release an appeal for information on the local morning news. It might yield something."

It might, but Tempest knew such requests for help more often resulted in thousands of wasted police manhours. They would get hundreds of phone calls, many of which would require follow up and all of which would lead nowhere. Only because sometimes one phone call among the hundreds would identify the criminal and solve the case did the tactic still find itself in use.

"There is one more thing," Quinn said.

"And that is?"

"He left a child's picture book in her coat pocket. A

Ladybird book printed in 1978. It is faded and worn, but as if to reinforce the point, the story he left with her is Rapunzel."

"Can I see it?"

Quinn picked up his phone, issued an instruction and waited less than a minute for a constable to arrive with an evidence bag in which the book had been sealed.

Tempest removed it, took some pictures, and inspected it to confirm there was nothing special about it. It was just a kid's book with pictures and some words to tell the story at a child's reading level.

"Was there one at Dr King's house?"

Quinn pursed his lips. "Not that we have found so far, and a thorough search was conducted."

Tempest didn't know what to make of that, but it bothered him. He decided there was no good reason to bother Olga with more questions. He might have questions later, but for now they were best served waiting for the artist's impression.

That could go out on the local news as well. If it was accurate, it could end the case in an instant. However, unless he assumed the Storyteller — it felt like a good enough name for now — was too stupid to hide his face from his victims, it seemed likely he wasn't worried about being seen.

Did that mean no one would know him?

Leaving the station, his stomach rumbling for breakfast, Tempest feared things were just getting started.

Breakfast

THURSDAY 14TH DECEMBER 0922HRS

Darius was walking the dogs when Tempest got home, a hundred yards from the house and heading for it when Tempest angled his car onto the driveway.

"Thanks for taking care of the boys."

Darius shrugged. "They were dancing by the back door, and I know what that means." He made a show of looking around at the hills surrounding Finchampstead. "Nice area for walks. It must be beautiful in the vineyards in the summer."

Tempest led the way into the house. "It sure is. It's beautiful here all year around though I'll admit you have to look for it when the rain is coming in sideways in the middle of winter. Have they eaten?"

"None of us have. I wasn't sure how much to give them and didn't want to overfill their little bellies. Also, no idea where you keep their food or bowls. Took me five minutes to find their leads."

The remarks promoted a quick 'show and tell' inside the various cupboards and drawers in the kitchen.

Bull and Dozer continued to get under foot until Tempest portioned kibble into the bowls, but they repeated their deliberate tactic ten seconds later until he provided their morning portion of cold milk.

"Got good appetites," Darius remarked.

"Find me a dog that doesn't."

The kettle went to work and they settled on omelettes with thick cut sourdough toast from a loaf Tempest made himself the previous day in anticipation of his guest's arrival. While they made food and ate, Tempest brought Darius up to speed on Rapunzel.

"You think it will continue?"

Tempest swallowed the last of his breakfast and wiped his lips with a napkin.

"Yes. There is yet to be an actual ransom demand for Mortimer King – I don't think we can count the message about the golden goose - which means he wasn't kidnapped to make money. Likewise, our hair model was attacked without identifiable purpose. It wasn't a sexual attack, I don't believe he knew the victim, so this wasn't some twisted revenge against a girlfriend for getting dumped. He called himself the Architect of the Story and I think that is the key to this."

"He's acting out scenes from Grimm's Fairy Tales."

Tempest nodded. "For whatever reason, he has a fetish or something, our perp is going to keep going and the only good thing is that he wants people to see. It will mean there will be clues to follow."

"Won't that mean he gets caught? I mean, unless this fool is some kind of genius."

Tempest put his plate in the sink, much to the disappointment of the watching dachshunds by his feet.

"He wants to get caught. I would imagine it is part of

his whole game plan. What good is a story if no one hears it? Stories are to be told, to be repeated. This storyteller wants the world to witness his genius, but he wants to get caught only when the story is told."

The Storyteller

THURSDAY, 14TH DECEMBER 0948HRS

In a small office in an abandoned building on the outskirts of West Malling, Andrew Grimwald worked on a book. Not one he was writing, but one he was physically creating. It took a long time to find an old version of the Grimm's Fairy Tales, and it really was old.

Andrew's aim had been to find a first edition, but there simply were none to be had. However, when first published in 1812, *Children's and Household Tales* contained only some of the stories Andrew wanted to incorporate, so it was perhaps serendipitous that he was forced to settle for a seventh edition.

By 1857 when it was published in Germany, the contents had grown from the original eighty-six stories to more than two hundred. Now he was going to add more.

Removing the spine and painstakingly adding fifty more pages to the back of the book using the exact same quality of paper cut to the exact right size was not a feat the average person could perform. Not that he was a librarian or typesetter; no, his skills were learned from many hours of online tutorials. Plus practice. Lots and lots of practice.

He was directly descended from Jacob Grimm who reputedly died unmarried and childless. Andrew knew it wasn't so, his sponsor had revealed it to him. He had documents showing the line of his parentage going back two hundred years.

His sponsor told him it was his right to continue the tales, his duty, his destiny, but it had to be spectacular. The world had to see it if Andrew wanted his name to join his forebears. He would be famous, and the deeds he needed to commit to perpetuate his family name would echo through time, just like the stories Wilhelm and Jacob collected.

Stitching and sticking the final lip of the spine into place, Andrew carefully set the book aside. Now it was ready for him to add his own words, but he needed to rest first.

Creating the start of his story with Rapunzel was necessary and it had all gone according to plan. He swivelled his chair around to look at the seat where she had been gagged and tied just a few hours earlier.

He held no sense of remorse. In fact, were he to be asked about his victim he would express joy for her. She got to be part of something glorious and though she cried and screamed and fought the whole time she was conscious, Andrew knew in his heart she would be glad he selected her once she better understood what it was for.

Of course, Rapunzel really was just the start of it. He needed to get some sleep, but not for too long because there was vital work to be done.

Returning his chair to face the desk, he leaned forward and from a drawer to his right selected three small books. They were thin, containing few pages, each of which was adorned with a picture. He placed all three face down on the surface of the desk, setting them an inch apart. Then he closed his eyes and began to shuffle them like a man playing three card monte.

Content they were shuffled, he reached out with his right hand and picked one up. He turned it over before opening his eyes, holding it in front of his face so the first thing he would see was the book cover.

It was Red Riding Hood, the children's edition from a boxed set in his house.

Andrew smiled though he resisted the urge to pump the air with his first – the Brothers Grimm would not have approved of such frivolity.

Replacing the selected book on the desk, he pushed back his chair and stood up.

Much of the groundwork for his next story was already done; he knew which school he planned to visit and when. He also knew for certain he would find the students there wearing coats with red hoods as that was part of their winter uniform.

Rapunzel would have created a rumour, but Red Riding Hood was going to get the tongues wagging.

Wrapping Things Up

THURSDAY, 14TH DECEMBER 1100HRS

Tempest took Darius to the home of Ken and Janine Whelan. It was his first visit to their property since they were in the hospital the only other time he saw them. It was from his sick bed that Ken made the initial call, and he hired Tempest on the spot, his less badly injured wife in a wheelchair at his side to confirm they wanted to spend their money.

"There is always a need to wrap things up," Tempest explained. "Clients want to know as much detail as possible and will ask questions you don't have answers to because it has nothing to do with how you solved the case. I try not to lose too much time on giving them the closure they want, but they are paying me to find the truth, so I feel a responsibility to give it to them."

Darius absorbed it all without taking notes.

Wrapping things up, as Tempest put it, seemed like an easy part of the process. When compared to sneaking about beneath tattoo parlours and getting into it with armed criminals. Okay, so their guns turned out to be replicas, but they had bats and knives and were not shy about using them.

Darius knew Tempest had taken some knocks in his job and had more than one stint in the hospital to justify his rates. It wasn't exactly safe work, but the likelihood of getting killed was significantly lower than life in the armed forces.

Visiting the Whelans didn't take long, and Tempest's clients already knew some of what happened from their son. Arnold used his one phone call from Maidstone nick to let his parents know the demon was just a man in a costume, just like Tempest Michaels said it would be.

Arnold Whelan wasn't going to get out in the next few hours, but Tempest expressed how he doubted his clients' son would be locked up for long. He'd handled drugs, but unwillingly and not for money. Provided his lawyer could argue those points successfully, he would be home soon enough.

The stupid tattoo was forever – the primary reason Tempest had none – but whether Arnold chose to keep it as a reminder to be displayed proudly at the pub like some macabre badge of honour, or if he might choose to have it removed or covered, Tempest opted not to speculate.

Back in the car and heading for the office in Rochester, Darius asked what Tempest planned to do about the Grimm case, specifically how he might tackle it.

"I have an email with the artist's impression of Rapunzel's attacker. I haven't looked at it yet, but it clearly hasn't triggered a positive identification yet or the police would have let me know. I need to have a look at it and do some research and I might drop in on Frank too."

"That's the bookshop guy?" Darius questioned his

memory; there had been a lot of information in a short space of time.

Tempest confirmed with a nod. "Often as not his ideas are completely wrong, but equally he has given me the very answer I need too many times for me to ever discount him. He still acts as if it is all real and I've just been lucky not to run into a real demon or vampire, and I have to read between the lines of his 'facts', but I went in yesterday and he produced an original copy of the Grimm Brother's first book. It was more than two hundred years old."

"I guess that must be worth a few pennies."

"So is Frank," Tempest remarked, following up with an explanation because most people would not associate running a bookshop with being a multimillionaire.

At the office things were busy. There were clients in the waiting area when Tempest walked in with Darius on his heels. Amanda was just on her way to meet them and paused for the guys to catch up.

"I've got nothing much on," she admitted. "Their case sounds legitimate; something about a fortune teller predicting their deaths and demanding money to help them avoid their impending doom. I was about to take it."

The clients, a couple in their twenties, had risen to their feet with Amanda heading their way, and chose to settle back into their seats now that the party of investigators had stalled part way across the office.

Tempest said, "Please do. I think this Grimm case is going to keep me busy. There was another attack last night while we were rounding up the demon and his minions." As an afterthought he said, "You should include Darius," and he moved to one side, opening their circle to include his friend. "I'm going to be doing research, which is a necessary but boring part of the job. Looks like Amanda has one of those cases that will prove to be easy to solve. You'll likely get more of them and very few like the Grimm Storyteller. She can take you through the whole thing from start to finish hopefully."

"That's if there isn't something more sinister to it," Amanda pointed out. Turning to Darius though, she said, "Tempest is probably right. I think we will wrap this up in a few hours."

Decision made, Tempest let Amanda and Darius greet the new clients while he went to see Marjory and Jane at the front reception desk.

He'd dropped Jane a line as he left the police station, asking if she had time to research Olga Rudakova and Dr Mortimer King. Her reply sounded hopeful and from the snippets of conversation he could overhear between her and Marjory, it sounded like that was precisely what the pair of them were doing.

Jane was a whizz with social media, often hacking into people's profiles to learn things they intended to keep private. Sure, it was invasion of privacy, but no one was getting arrested for it and the Blue Moon team were not about to use what they found for extortion. Basically, if the people with secrets weren't doing criminal things, they would be safe.

Regardless, Tempest hoped there would be a connection between the two or something would give him a direction for the investigation to go.

"Whatcha got, ladies?" he asked.

Jane looked up. She'd taken one of the spare chairs from the private offices and was sitting on it squeezed in next to Marjory so they could fit her laptop on the reception desk as well.

"Nothing, so far. Olga arrived in England six months

ago having been hired by a modelling firm here. I thought maybe there would be some sugar daddy website that linked her to Dr King and that perhaps he'd stumped up the cost to bring her here, but her entry to the country looks completely legitimate."

Marjory said, "I've been going through what I can find online for Dr King and his wife. He doesn't have a social media profile, which as a shrink is probably not a big surprise, but he is registered with Companies House and he sits on the board of two businesses beyond his own. Both of them psychiatry firms."

"Are they doing well?" Tempest enquired. Money could be such a motivator. "Any staff recently laid off from either business? Board members sacked? Anything like that?"

Marjory picked up a pen and made a few notes on a pad to her left.

"I will expand my search to include those parameters. Do you think I will find that kind of information online?"

Tempest pursed his lips. "Some of it. Companies House will show former board members. Let me know if there is anyone who left either firm in the last year. Obviously, the more recent it was, the more pertinent it might prove to be."

Jane held up her hand to interrupt. "This might be nothing." She rotated her laptop to give Tempest a better view. "I've been cross referencing people against pictures to see if Olga has an ex-boyfriend with a grudge and I think she does. Sort of. She tapped the screen with a manicured fingernail that could be better described as a talon. "This is Sasha Rudakova, her husband."

Tempest had not expected that.

Jane continued, "Her profile says she's not in a relationship and he doesn't appear anywhere on her profile apart from in some old pictures which are just impossible for the average person to remove. In contrast, his profile claims that he is married to Olga and there are pictures of their wedding day. Clearly, there is some disparity in the way they view their marriage. She thinks it is over, and he might not be taking no for an answer."

Tempest looked at the picture of the happy couple. Olga was tiny and her husband towered above her. He had to be six foot four or something close to it and that was a world away from the description she gave the police.

Remembering the picture, Tempest produced his phone. "Sorry, I should have shown you this earlier. This is the man Olga described as her attacker. Seen anyone who looks anything like him?"

Jane shook her head. "Not so far."

Marjory said the same.

"Well, I'll send it to both of you, so you have it for reference. I think the husband is worth looking into, you can leave that with me, but unless we can find some link between him and Dr King, I doubt he will prove to be the guy. If Olga has ended her marriage and moved on ..."

"Which it looks like she has," Jane agreed.

"Then it feels likely she would have named her husband if he was behind her attack."

"Unless he orchestrated it and had someone else carry it out," Marjory suggested.

"I'll look into him," Tempest repeated his intention. "Hey, how's the palace thing going?"

Jane pushed back in her chair and let her shoulders drop in a show of defeat.

"It's just dead end after dead end. Cassie is pulling her hair out and she has no support. No one even believes there is a person behind the deaths and that's the most worrying part. If she is right, then we have a serial killer systematically picking off members of the royal family. Not just any old distant relatives, but ones near the top who could feasibly ascend to the throne if enough people above them were to die."

"Is that likely?" Tempest asked. He knew Jane was giving up a lot of her private time to pursue the investigation alongside Inspector Cassie Munroe and missing out on paid work at the same time. That wasn't a problem from the perspective of the business, but he worried she might be on a wild goose chase.

Jane's face was grim when she met his eyes.

"There is a royal wedding in a couple of months. All the royals will be gathered in one place. Cassie thinks we have some anti-royalist with a plan to remove the entire family. Will the monarchy survive if the only person left to take the throne is a distant cousin with about as much royal blood as a dockworker? Alison Tyler is seventy-fifth in line to the throne, and she's a traffic warden. Kill everyone above her and that will be the end of it forever. We have to take the threat seriously."

Tempest could understand why his colleague was getting so emotionally invested.

"And you have no leads?"

"Not really. We have a couple of clues we are following up, but the case needs an entire unit behind it and Cassie was accused of harbouring delusions last time she tried to get her boss to discuss it."

Further talk on the subject halted when the office door opened, cool air accompanying clients coming in off the street.

Except it wasn't clients.

It was Tempest's parents.

Choose Your Parents Wisely

THURSDAY 14TH DECEMBER 1127HRS

Tempest wasn't expecting his parents to drop by, but unannounced visits were not that uncommon. They lived on the other side of Rochester bridge in the smaller town of Strood. It was easy walking distance from one to the other provided the weather was inclined to behave. On windy days, crossing the bridge over the churning river could be a less than pleasant experience.

He noted they were not soaked to the bone, so the rain must have cleared away.

"Hello, Tempest," his mother greeted him with a pleasant smile that put him immediately on guard.

He air-kissed her cheek and shook his father's hand.

"Coffee?"

"Cor, yeah, kiddo." Tempest's father possessed an exuberant streak that manifested, on occasion, in a need to be mischievous. "I'm parched."

Tempest loved his parents dearly, but they both delivered headaches in different guises, and he had far more pressing matters to which he wanted to attend. He couldn't say that though because his mother would start praying or remind him that being a paranormal investigator was hardly respectable work, and his father ... well his dad would just try to help by getting involved.

Invariably that ended with something getting blown up.

Tempest made coffee, presenting his parents with a cup each and another for himself. While he did, his mother jabbered about church matters, the latest list of old people who had died, and enquired if he had gotten around to 'popping the question' yet.

A muscle in Tempest's jaw tightened.

"When did we last discuss this subject, mother?"

"No idea, love. Must be months ago. I take it that means you still haven't found the courage," she muttered bitterly.

Keeping his cool, Tempest said, "It was five days ago, mother. On Sunday when I came for dinner. I'm quite certain you remember."

His mother focused her attention on her coffee, acting as though she had no clue what her son was talking about.

"Do you recall how we left the conversation?" Tempest prompted her to respond.

"Probably the same way we always leave it," she accused, "With you doing nothing."

"Leave the boy alone, Mary," chided Tempest's father. "He'll live his life the way he wants to and you pushing him only ever results in him pushing back."

"Oh, you've got an opinion now, do you?" She twisted in her seat to glare accusingly at her husband.

"Yes," he argued defiantly, "despite your belief that I should exist only to back up whatever you say."

Tempest knew his parents well enough to read the signs

of an impending fight. Not that it would be a serious one, but they were in his place of work, he had clients in Amanda's office, and his mother was about to start getting loud.

He put his empty coffee cup down with a thunk.

"That's enough." His tone brooked no discussion. "My relationship with Amanda and the future of it is not a topic I have any need to discuss with either of you."

"Never going to get any grandkids," his mother moped, muttering under her breath.

"You already have three," Tempest pointed out, "and me getting married does not guarantee you any more. Now, can we talk about something else? Did you just happen to drop in on your way to somewhere, or was there a specific reason for your visit today?"

"We're meeting friends for afternoon tea," his mother revealed.

"You're meeting friends, dear," dad countered. "I'm meeting a gang of moany old bags who will talk around me and pretend I'm not there the whole time."

"That's because you are not interesting enough to include. It's hardly my fault you don't have the intellect to keep up."

Tempest saw his father's eyes narrow. He was moments away from raising his voice. Only able to guess what might have precipitated their bickering, Tempest found his mouth volunteering to solve the problem before his brain had a chance to figure out what was going on.

"I could do with dad's help today, actually."

"I'm in," his father snapped at the chance.

Mary eyed him sceptically. "You don't even know what he wants help with."

"I'd sooner pick poop out of a goat-headed demon's

hooves than go to tea with your friends, so it doesn't really matter what the job entails." However, displaying that not all tasks were equal, he asked, "It doesn't involve any sewers, does it?"

Tempest remembered only too well the time he took his father to hunt for a fish in a sewer. Between the giant beast they discovered and his dad's homemade grenades, they were lucky to still be alive.

"No, Dad. No sewers. I need to quiz a few people, that's all."

"Oh, good. Actually, there was a thing on the local news this morning about some goat demon out in Allhallows. Mum said it was probably one of your cases."

"That's not what I said, Michael." She aimed an elbow at his ribs which he was too slow to block.

"It's precisely what you said, you mad old bat." Michael rubbed his side. "You heard the reporter say something about the old peninsular demon and went on a tirade about how it had to be your son who was out there at night battling drug dealers and dodging bullets."

"Well, it clearly wasn't him, was it, dear," Tempest's mother argued. "There's not a mark on him."

"That's because I had help, Mum. I was there. It was my case, and the person behind the demon will be spending the next few years in jail."

Mary crossed herself.

Ignoring his wife, Tempest's dad asked, "It went well, then?"

"It did." Tempest forced the tension in his body to release. His mother's need to marry him off was nothing new. In fact, it started not long after he turned twenty. To his mind that was far too young to be tying himself down, but his mother held the opinion that it didn't matter which girl he dated so long as he put a ring on her finger.

His father agreed, sort of. At the time, he said something along the lines of no matter which woman he married, she would be sure to make him miserable in the end. He'd also been sure to say it loud enough that Tempest's mother would hear and was swift enough to duck the table fork that zipped through the space his head previously occupied.

Dad got to his feet. "Right then, love. I guess I will see you at home later. We will be home for dinner?" he fired the question at Tempest.

Tempest cleared away the coffee cups. "Should be. We're just asking a few questions." In truth Tempest was yet to figure out what he was doing with his afternoon, but he could keep his father entertained easily enough and that would stop his parents from fighting.

"There's one other thing," Mary introduced a new subject and when she was sure she had Tempest's attention, said, "Rachel, Chris, and the kids are coming to stay. They expect to arrive by lunchtime tomorrow. Can we expect you and Amanda for dinner tomorrow?"

So that was why his mother had been pushing so hard about the engagement recently. She wanted something to announce at dinner.

"I cannot speak for Amanda, but barring unavoidable work demands, I will be there and will do my best to bring my girlfriend."

His use of the term 'girlfriend' caused a frown to set on his mother's brow, but she let it go without comment.

"Six o'clock for seven. I'm serving a Mexican feast."

Tempest made a mental note to get there as early as he could to help rescue the food. His mother was a thoroughly enthusiastic cook, but equally untalented.

Dad held the door for his wife and was sure to kiss her goodbye before sagging against the doorframe.

"You don't know how much you have saved me today, kiddo."

Tempest snorted a small laugh. "Well don't get too excited. I haven't actually got anything for you to do."

A Suspect

THURSDAY 14TH DECEMBER 1158HRS

To kill time, his father went for a poke around the local shops, but they were going to head to Tempest's house for lunch within the hour.

Tempest wandered to his office and there he spent a few moments cleaning one of the large whiteboards he used for scribbling ideas and linking thoughts.

The demon case was done, so beyond filing his notes and making sure the final bill was paid – both tasks for Marjory, there was nothing left to be done and no need to keep his scribbled ideas.

With the board wiped clean it was time to start filling it again, this time with the Grimm case.

He started with the names of the two victims: Dr Mortimer King and Olga Rudokova. Beneath them he listed the location each was attacked, persons associated with them, and other pertinent information.

This was the first time he'd given real thought to the case and having done so reflected again on the pool of people with a direct link to Dr King – his patients. Asking

Mrs King about it achieved nothing, but Dr King had to have staff.

Obtaining a list of patients and more pertinently, their case notes, would be next to impossible through legal channels.

Plonking into his chair, a flick of the mouse brought his computer to life. The website for Dr King's practice was up and running as usual. To his surprise, there was no page showing staff as one might expect to find for most businesses. However, a few moments spent exploring revealed the name of the practice manager: Mrs Katherine Frobisher.

Opening a new tab, Tempest searched her name and found the woman instantly. The first photograph showed a very attractive woman in her forties and a further search confirmed her age as forty-eight. Her lustrous, dark brunette hair was either permed or naturally curly – Tempest suspected the latter. It framed her face and combined with her makeup and tan led him to believe he was looking at a shot from a professional photoshoot. The kind a model would have.

He called the number for Dr King's practice and though he wasn't sure if the business would be operating today with the good doctor missing, the phone was answered on the first ring.

"Is that Mrs Frobisher?" Tempest sought to confirm. "My name is Tempest Michaels."

"This is she. Do you wish to make an appointment, Mr Michaels?"

Thinking quickly, he said, "I wish to view the premises before I do so. I have paid to speak with other mental health professionals and found myself in depressing surroundings, if you know what I mean. I want to make sure your practice will soothe me, not stress me."

Mrs Frobisher made no comment, but said, "You can visit the premises any time, Mr Michaels. Do you have the address?"

He confirmed that he did, asked about opening times, and suggested he would try to visit before they shut for the day. With the call ended, he took a moment to consider what Dr King's practice manager had said and what she had not said.

He got no sense that she was upset about her employer's disappearance. Did she know? Or was she operating under the belief that he was too sick to come to work?

Would it help if she didn't know and he could deliver the news? It would shock her and that could make her reveal secrets she might otherwise withhold.

Picking up his phone, he called Quinn.

"Mr Michaels."

"Ian, have you been able to get a list of Dr King's clients?"

"That is medical in confidence, Mr Michaels. In order to force Dr King's practice to release it, we would first have to prove it was germane to the case. At this time there is nothing to indicate he might have been targeted by one of his own patients."

And therein, Tempest considered, is the problem with having to operate within the confines of the laws. The practice wouldn't want to give the information to him either, but he wasn't used to bothering to ask for things. It was far easier to take them in secret.

"Okay, Ian. I'm looking at a few different angles, but we want to avoid both doing the same legwork. Have you got anyone on Olga's husband?"

"We are not complete imbeciles, Mr Michaels. Mrs Rodukova assured me her attacker was not known to her and the description she gave is a world away from her husband. However, being thorough, I had his location checked. Sasha Rudokova returned to Russia more than a month ago. According to his wife, he was here only to win her back and when she convinced him their marriage was over, he chose to leave."

"Okay, well he could still be behind the attack, but it doesn't feel likely." Tempest struck Olga's husband from his mental list of people to investigate. "Did the artist's impression turn up anything?"

"Not so far." Quinn was being typically brief in his answers, but whether he was doing it to be annoying, Tempest couldn't tell. They were supposed to be working together, not that Tempest wanted to. In truth, Quinn's standoffish attitude played into his hands. He could conduct his own investigation and if he found something, he could let the chief inspector know after the fact.

Or not.

"Has there been any development with the forensic evidence taken from Dr King's house? Do you have anything to go on?"

"No, Mr Michaels. Do you?" growled Quinn, annoyance bubbling to the surface.

Choosing the patient route, Tempest said, "No, but I am working on it. What I don't want to do is waste my time exploring avenues your team have already exhausted."

"There will be daily meetings at the station and updates given to the team whenever there is a development."

"And since I won't be attending those meetings, how do you intend to include the information I obtain?"

In a bored voice, Quinn shot back, "If you expect to get

paid for your efforts as a consultant, Mr Michaels, you will have to turn up to be consulted. The next meeting is scheduled for five o'clock."

A small snort of amusement escaped Tempest when he said, "You'll need to check my contract, Ian. The one your boss signed. I can do all my consulting over the phone or even by email if I choose. As for getting paid, I doubt you'll be able to hold back my fee when I solve the case ahead of you."

"Why you ... Just you listen ..."

Tempest slid his phone back into his pocket, the call terminated before Quinn had a chance to reach full ranting speed. He almost felt sorry for the man; he was such an idiot. It would have helped to have access to police resources and whatever information they might uncover, but it wasn't like he'd ever had it before.

Tapping his chin with the whiteboard marker, Tempest stared and thought and would have continued to do so had Marjory not hailed him from the other end of the office.

"You have something?"

Marjory's eyes were fixed firmly on her screen, her right hand beckoning Tempest to come closer.

"You asked me to look for Board members who had recently left their positions or people who had been laid off or whatever. Well, that proved to be nothing but dead ends, but I stumbled across this guy." She aimed an index finger at the screen.

Tempest read the name, "Dr Douglas Sloan. Great work. What makes him interesting?"

Marjory rotated her chair a little, so she was looking straight into Tempest's eyes.

"He publicly threatened to kill Dr Mortimer King."

"Do we have an address?"

The Practice

THURSDAY, 14TH DECEMBER 1311HRS

With his dad in the car, Tempest took the scenic, cross-country route to get to his house. On the way, he explained the Grimm's Fairy Tale case and then the new development.

"Dr Sloan accused Dr King of stealing his work. They had worked on a paper together – they are both psychiatrists with their own practices. Anyway, Dr King submitted the paper, which was published and won awards, but failed to give any credit to Dr Sloan who claimed at least half of the work was his."

"This all happened more than a year ago and resulted in a libel case which Dr Sloan lost. If we assume Dr King did steal his work, Dr Sloan not only got stung for his efforts on the paper, but he then lost a court case and was forced to pay Dr King compensation."

Tempest's dad puffed out his cheeks. "I could imagine being jolly upset about all that."

Tempest nodded. "People who cannot get justice have a

habit of taking matters into their own hands when the legal system fails them."

"And we are going to see him now?"

"Yes, but we have another stop on the way to his address, plus we need to eat and deal with my dogs."

The sun was low in the sky as it always is in winter months, the angle it carved through the windscreen making it hard to see at times. It was bright and sunny now, the earlier rain almost forgotten if one ignored all the puddles.

The sunshine highlighted the glorious rolling hills either side of the Medway River Valley. They crested the hill on the new link road on the outskirts of Burham, an almost weightless sensation gripping them for a half second before Tempest's car plunged down the other side.

Barking and snuffling came from inside the front door of his house as always, Bull and Dozer climbing over each other to be the first to greet the humans. Bringing a guest home to make a fuss of them only added to their excitement.

"I'll let them into the garden," dad volunteered, splitting left at the front door to lead them through the dining room/office and out through the sliding patio door.

The dogs shot off across the lawn, chasing garden birds into the sky with great enthusiasm and even more barking.

In the kitchen, Tempest pulled ingredients from the fridge, and they enjoyed sandwiches with cold cuts, pickles, and Swiss cheese. The dogs got some carrot slices which they crunched into oblivion on the kitchen tile.

"Take them with us?" dad suggested.

Tempest shrugged. "They'll be on your lap."

"Suits me. You could think about getting a different car though. You have room on your drive and money, so it's not like you would have to sell the Porsche."

It was a fair point, and one Tempest had considered many times. However, the two-seater sports car met his needs ninety-nine percent of the time and getting a second car meant twice as many trips to the dealer for a service, twice as many annual road tests ... all of which meant an equivalent amount of not getting anything else done.

With the dirty plates in the dishwasher, Tempest led the way back to the car, Bull and Dozer bouncing along excitedly by his heels.

Kings Hill, a new development of houses and businesses just a few miles to the east, started life as a second world war Spitfire base. Indeed, the public house at its centre is called the Spitfire and there is a brass statue of a pilot running to get to his plane.

Knowing the business area from previous visits, Tempest was surprised when his satnav took him straight through it and out the other side.

Seeing his son squinting at the screen, Tempest's dad asked, "Everything okay?"

Tempest nodded but continued to look perplexed. "We are heading for Dr King's practice, but I expected it to be back there."

"Did you input the address wrong?"

"I guess we shall see."

It transpired that the address was right. Turning a corner in the middle of what was obviously the oldest part of Kings Hill, they discovered a parade of businesses.

"I had no idea this was here," Tempest admitted.

They chose to leave the dogs in the car. They were well exercised and looking sleepy, so Tempest chose to risk it rather than taking them into the building where they would almost certainly not be wanted.

A brass plaque outside the main entrance listed all the

businesses to be found inside. Among them 'The King Wellness Clinic' cleverly disguised what the practice did for those who would rather not have their personal business known.

They found it on the first floor where a frosted glass door held them at bay until a voice answered the buzzer.

"Mrs Frobisher?" Tempest was ninety-nine percent sure he recognised her voice. "This is Tempest Michaels. We spoke on the phone just a short while ago."

"Please come in," she replied, a different buzzing noise indicating the door was now unlocked.

Katherine Frobisher met them just inside the door, emerging through another door to the left.

Tempest's dad muttered, "Hubba-hubba," under his breath and had to narrowly avoid a sharp elbow from his son.

However, Mrs Frobisher was indeed worthy of such a comment. Trim, elegantly dressed, well made up, and with the hair, figure, and face that ought to grace magazines, posters, and red-carpet events, she was an absolute knock out.

Tempest shook her hand.

"Pleased to meet you, Mrs Frobisher. This is my father, Michael."

She shook his hand too and tried not to look surprised when the senior Mr Michaels bent at the waist to kiss it.

Tempest resisted the urge to flick his father's ear and got to the point.

Producing a business card, he said, "Are you aware that Dr King was kidnapped last night?"

Mrs Frobisher's eyes were on the business card when he delivered the shocking news and shot up to check his face.

"Is that supposed to be funny?" she asked, very much

not amused. "And what is this nonsense? Paranormal investigations?"

"Mrs Frobisher, I am working as a consultant to the police. Your employer was taken from his house last night and whoever took him saw fit to cut off his right index finger and leave it behind."

The colour drained from her face, and she looked about ready to faint.

"Whoa!" Tempest's dad swooped in to catch her before she could topple. Not that she was going to, but she did want to sit down.

Tempest apologised for the abruptness of his revelation but continued to explain that time was a pressing factor.

"I need to ask you about his patients, Mrs Frobisher."

"Kathy," she murmured, her head hanging down, so it was almost in her lap. "Call me Kathy."

"Can I get you a glass of water, Kathy?" Tempest's dad enquired.

She gave him directions to find the kitchen, but as he went to open the inner door to access the clinic, it swung inward.

"Oh!" said a young female voice, following her exclamation with a laugh. "Goodness, you scared the life out of me!" Spotting Mrs Frobisher sitting with her head between her knees and Tempest crouched at her side, the young woman asked, "Is everything all right?"

The young woman introduced herself as Faith Gasbjerg, an intern working at the practice during her Christmas break from university. Studying to be a psychiatrist, she wanted the experience and was willing to work for nothing. In her very early twenties, she had a slim figure, blonde hair, and a pinched face.

She offered to fetch water for Mrs Frobisher, but Tempest seized the chance to explore the clinic – he had a sneaking suspicion he would be returning after hours at some point.

Mrs Frobisher, though startled by the news of her employer, was sticking with the standard answer that she could not reveal anything about any of Dr King's clients. Not their names, ages, problems, or anything else. In fact, all Tempest got from her was that to her knowledge, Dr King owed no money to anyone and none of his patients had ever proven to be violent.

"I have worked with him for fifteen years," she stated, "and there has never once been a complaint from a patient."

Leaving her with his father, Tempest noted the layout of the clinic as Faith led him through it.

"What will we do if Dr King doesn't come back?" she asked.

"That I cannot say. I think perhaps you should both take the rest of the day off though. Mrs Frobisher appears rather shaken." She really did and Tempest felt responsible. He intended to shock her, but not to the extent that she would become physically ill. Her reaction to her employer's abduction was more severe than he could have anticipated. "Mrs Frobisher will be better off at home. Does her husband work, do you know?" Tempest hoped the chap might take a few hours to tend to his wife.

Faith pulled an 'oops' face. "Um, he left her just a couple of days ago. She's been throwing herself into her work to keep her mind off it I think."

Tempest closed his eyes and berated himself silently for kicking a woman when she was already down.

"He just up and left at the start of the week. I don't

think she had any idea he was even unhappy," Faith babbled to fill the quiet.

Tempest filled a glass with water and went back to the reception area where he handed it to Mrs Frobisher. She was still bent over but sat up to sip the drink.

"Thank you," she murmured, prompting Tempest to apologise again.

"Do you think you can catch the people who did this?" she asked.

He didn't want to make promises, so chose his response carefully. "In my experience, criminals make mistakes. They try to be clever to throw investigators off the scent, but the cleverer they try to be, the more likely they are to slip up. Whoever took Dr King left an elaborate hoax intended to confuse the police. That is why they called me." Worried that he now sounded like a braggart, he added, "I have had some success with bizarre cases like this one. Rest assured, I will not rest until we have answers."

Mrs Frobisher tilted her head to look up at the man standing over her.

"Thank you. I wish you every luck."

Tempest thought it odd, given her general state of despair, that there were no streaks in her makeup where tears sought to ruin it. Kicking himself again, Tempest concluded the poor woman was all cried out after her husband's unexpected and sudden departure.

Having achieved very little, Tempest nodded to his father that it was time to go. They thanked both ladies for their time and candid answers, left them with business cards so they could make contact if they thought of anything they believed might prove useful to the investigation, and beat a hasty retreat.

The dogs were both asleep on the passenger seat,

twisted around each other so each dog had their head resting on the other's rump. They looked up when the doors open, yawned, and attempted to go back to sleep.

Tempest's dad scooped them onto his lap as he slid into his seat.

The clinic was a bust, but perhaps their next destination would deliver a better result.

Trespass

THURSDAY, 14TH DECEMBER 1412HRS

Dr Douglas Sloan's listed address was in Greenhithe, a stone's throw from Bluewater Shopping Mall where Olga was grabbed getting into her car. Quite how her attack connected to Dr King's remained a mystery, and perhaps it didn't, Tempest mused openly in the car.

"You think the two crimes could be unconnected?" his father questioned.

"I don't yet see anything to connect them. That's not the same thing," Tempest tried to clarify. "However, at this time I am operating in an information vacuum – I know almost nothing. There is still no ransom note to suggest Dr King was taken for money despite the cryptic message about the golden goose. I have no idea where he could be, but the longer he is missing, the more likely it is that he will turn up dead. There appears to be no motive for Olga Rudokova's attack unless it was orchestrated by her husband. Either way, it is a completely different crime to Dr King's kidnapping and the only thing that links them is the loose connection both have to the Grimm Brothers' stories."

Modern Fairy Tale

Powering north up the M20 motorway toward London, they turned off long before the giant buildings of the capital rose to dominate their view.

The car's built-in satnav led them away from the bulk of Greenhithe and to a postcode on the periphery where trees lined the road and properties were hidden behind them. Slowing to check the signs outside each gate, they found the one they wanted.

Looking out under the canopy of trees, Tempest's father said, "Being a psychiatrist sure pays well."

Tempest made no comment; he was too busy questioning how best to approach. If Dr Sloan was in any way involved in Dr King's disappearance, ringing the buzzer to be let in would tip him off and give him time to prepare.

Whether that meant arming himself, hiding Dr King's body, or just making himself scarce, Tempest chose to avoid giving the potential suspect any forewarning.

Twisting his head as they drove straight by the place they wanted, Tempest's dad said, "Wait, isn't that the address? Aren't we going in?"

"Yes, and yes," Tempest gave a cryptic response.

He found what he was looking for – a layby – less than a hundred yards down the road. Pulling in, he switched his shoes, doffing his leather oxfords in lieu of army boots he had in the boot alongside his Kevlar vest and other hard-wearing items. He'd learned to keep such things to hand long ago.

"You want to stay here, Dad? I'm going over the fence and will be trespassing. It could be trouble if he's innocent."

"Ha! I'm not staying with the car while you get all the fun, kiddo. Count me in. What do we do with the dogs?"

"Take them with us," Tempest replied as though that were obvious. "They need some exercise anyway."

They backtracked to the edge of the property. All the houses in the street were big, detached places set back from the road by fifty yards or more. Most had six-foot-high fences bordering all sides, though some had gone to the extra expense of brick for longevity.

Fortunately, Dr Sloan's was one of the fenced properties and that made getting in easy.

Approaching the fence, Tempest's dad turned around and placed his back to it. Cupping his hands above a knee, he was offering to provide a bunk up to get over.

"Would I be better going over first?" he asked. "I think you're more likely to be able to vault it than me."

Tempest reached down to grip the bottom edge of the fence panel.

"When I said I was 'going over' I meant that metaphorically." With a grunt of effort, he levered the fence panel upward. The posts on either side were solid concrete items which formed channels into which the wooden panel slotted.

Once he had it six inches off the ground, the dachshunds bounced through the gap, vanishing instantly on the other side. Joining in, Tempest's dad helped to balance the load until the gap reached three feet.

"Now you go through and hold it for me," Tempest instructed, the pair of them dropping it slowly back to the ground once they were both on the other side.

"Neat trick," his dad remarked as they strolled away through the woods.

The house looked peaceful, which is to say there were no dead bodies lying on the lawn, no fire licking at the side of the conservatory ... It was as one might expect on a Thursday afternoon two weeks before Christmas.

They made their way through the trees, staying out of

sight and pausing occasionally to observe the house for signs of life.

A new plate Audi sat idle in front of a double garage door. It was facing outward and looked ready for someone to take a trip though whether that might be to a landfill at night to dispose of a body or just to the local supermarket there was no way to tell. Across from it, a twenty-year-old Renault with a broken number plate, a cracked windscreen and a thick layer of dirt looked very much out of place. Tempest assumed it would be the car of a teenager at the property.

Their route took them to it, a cursory glance through the windows enough to confirm it contained nothing to indicate it had been used to transport victims. Likewise, the Audi contained nothing to indicate it had recently been used in a kidnapping.

Satisfied there was nothing further to be gained by their stealthy approach, Tempest strode boldly along the front of the house to the door.

"I'm going to knock and see if he answers."

"Okay, kid. I'll hold the dogs." Tempest gave his father a few moments to get the dachshunds under control, but the door opened before he could.

Swinging inward, Tempest guessed they had been spotted and the owner was coming to demand to know what they wanted. However, he was wrong and the person coming out squealed in alarm when she found Tempest looming on the doorstep.

Dressed in Crocs, jogging bottoms, and a dirt-streaked sweater, her choice of clothes would have told anyone she was a cleaner if the bucket of sprays and cloths she held failed to get the message across.

A hand flew to her heart, the woman speaking rapid-fire in a language Tempest believed to be Polish.

He apologised in English, hoping she would understand, but in focusing on her, he forgot that his dogs were loose and they never wait for an invite.

Bull whipped past the woman's feet closely followed by his brother.

Tempest swore under his breath and tried to follow, but the cleaner was still trying to get out and her collection of equipment blocked his ingress.

Worse yet his boots were muddy and the carpets were not only pristine following the cleaner's best efforts, but cream in colour. Too late, the dogs streaked across them, their paws leaving behind a wonderful pattern of tiny paw prints.

The cleaner swore – at least that's how Tempest translated her tirade of emotionally-charged words.

All that was problematic enough, but when Dr Sloan swung into sight at the end of the hallway, took one look at Tempest and started running, everything changed.

Chasing a Suspect

THURSDAY 14TH DECEMBER 1421HRS

Barking, "Dad, go around the back!", Tempest took off through the house.

The cleaner still blocked his path and though he was as gentle as he could be in shoving past, it did little to soften the fact that he barged her out of his way. Worse still, as he pelted across the cream carpet knowing full well the mess he must be leaving behind, a burst of foreign-language expletives followed him, accompanied by the sound of the poor woman throwing her bucket of sprays and cloths to the floor in anger.

Staying on the doorstep was never an option though. The look on Dr Sloan's face made him give chase. It was pure panic, the look of a person who knows they have been caught.

From the small amount of research Marjory conducted, Tempest knew Dr Sloan to be fifty-eight years old. He was short, balding, fifty pounds overweight and unlikely to give Tempest much trouble in a foot race.

However, they were inside Dr Sloan's house where he had the home advantage and the first thought going through Tempest's head was to do with how Dr Sloan might arm himself. Now believing he'd managed to track down Dr King's kidnapper at his first attempt, it was reasonable to assume the man had weapons.

He was yet to use a firearm that Tempest knew of but engaged in a deadly game he was bound to have knives if nothing else.

The police were required, but that call needed to wait. For all he knew Dr Sloan had Dr King locked up in his basement and was on his way to kill him before anyone could deny him the chance.

At the end of the hallway, Tempest grabbed the wall to swing himself around it and took a fast glance back the way he'd come. The carpet was wrecked, and it was going to take more than a quick vacuuming to remove the dirt left in his wake.

The cleaner offered a gesture consisting of not very many fingers.

"Dr Sloan!" Tempest bellowed, bursting through a door and into what turned out to be the kitchen. "Dr Sloan I have already called the police!" he lied. "There is nothing to gain by hurting Dr King. Surrender now before this gets more serious!"

A flash of movement caught his eye to the left and he flinched involuntarily. Almost ducking, his brain needed a moment to decipher that it was his father he'd seen through a window. Dad was outside still and looking for a way in.

The kitchen door was there but had to be locked. The question was whether he had time to turn the key and let his father in or whether the extra few seconds that took would mean Dr Sloan was able to barricade himself, open a shotgun cabinet, or otherwise gain an advantage Tempest might struggle to overcome.

The dogs provided an answer with their barking. They were faster and their low centre of gravity meant they could corner like they were on rails. Dr Sloan's verbal rebukes rang through the house to tell Tempest he was still on the move with the dachshunds hot on his heels.

"What's going on, son?" Tempest's father gasped breathlessly as he barged through the now unlocked door to catch up.

Tempest had flicked the key, but didn't wait around for his dad to catch up. Running through a door on the far side of the kitchen, he called back, "Dr Sloan took one look at me and ran. If he has Dr King here, or anyone else he is holding hostage, he might hurt them before we can stop him!"

However, bursting into the next room, Tempest got just a half second of warning to duck and had to throw himself to the carpet before Dr Sloan could pull the trigger on the giant, double-barrelled shotgun he held. Expecting to hear the deafening roar of the weapon discharging, the fact that it didn't provided no comfort. It just meant it was still loaded.

Tempest rolled, crunching his left shoulder painfully, and let his momentum carry him behind a sofa. Not that a spongey, upholstered item of furniture offered much protection, but it was the only thing to hand.

Diving through the air, the room and its contents hard to decipher as his world rotated, Tempest noted that he could hear his dogs' muffled barks, but not see them. Dr Sloan had successfully managed to trap them behind a door.

That meant they were safe for now, but the bigger issue

was his father. Thundering through the house as he tried to keep up, he was about to run into the same room and Tempest couldn't permit the possibility that Dr Sloan might panic and pull the trigger. At such range the shot would shred a body. There would be no surviving it.

So Tempest did the dumbest thing possible. He stood up.

The shotgun twitched every so slightly, the double barrels aimed right at Tempest's core.

Tempest drew a slow breath through his nose, his eyes locked on Dr Sloan's. The look of abject panic was still there, but now that he was getting a proper look for the first time, he could see rage in the man's eyes too. Rage and possibly … righteousness, which made sense if he had targeted Dr King to get his own back when the courts failed him.

Tempest's dad skidded into the room, his feet slipping to a stop. He saw his son, hands aloft, and the man holding the shotgun. Not that anyone could call it unwavering. Whether nerves, the weight of the weapon, or a combination of the pair, the barrels were wobbling all over the place.

"Ha!" Dr Sloan spat. "I've got you. You're not getting a penny out of me, do you hear! Mortimer King can burn in hell if he thinks I'm paying up, and I don't care how many bailiffs he sends. You're trespassing and I don't care tuppence what your court orders might empower you to do."

The frown on Tempest's face was sufficient that Dr Sloan ran out of words. It was helped by Tempest waving a hand to get his attention.

"We are not bailiffs," he announced.

Dr Sloan's forehead creased with confusion.

"What?"

"We are not bailiffs," Tempest repeated, his voice calm. "We are not here to collect anything from you and have nothing to do with the court. My name is Tempest Michaels. I am a private investigator. I am looking into the disappearance of Dr Mortimer King."

"What?"

To help move things forward, scintillating though the conversation was, Tempest began to lower his arms.

"I am going to show you my business card, Dr Sloan."

"Here's mine," said Tempest's father, producing one in his right hand with a practiced flick reminiscent of a street magician. He threw it across the room, the small rectangle of card fluttering and spinning until it landed close to Dr Sloan's feet.

Glancing at it quickly, Dr Sloan read, "Global Superstar Detective, Michael Michaels."

Tempest shot his father a look, one eyebrow hooked. "Really?"

His dad shrugged. "I figured I might need a business card if I keep getting involved in your work. Remember that ghoul case last year? I could have done with some business cards back then let me tell you."

"Hey!" Dr Sloan interrupted. "What is going on?" Aiming his anger at Tempest he demanded, "What did you just say about Morty King? Did you say he's gone missing?"

Bored with holding his arms aloft, Tempest dropped them completely. Dr Sloan wasn't about to shoot, and it was becoming obvious they had the wrong guy. Dr King wasn't locked in the basement or anywhere else.

"You can put the gun down, Dr Sloan. We are not here to hurt you and I'm quite certain you don't want to kill anyone today. It sounds like you have enough legal problems in your life already."

Dr Sloan kept the shotgun pointed at the two intruders for a few more seconds, the muzzle constantly twitching between Tempest and his father. However, when Tempest came around the sofa and dropped backward to rest on it, the homeowner finally allowed the barrels to droop.

When his dad joined Tempest on the sofa, the fight went out of Dr Sloan. He wobbled in place, looking a little faint before backing up a pace and lowering himself into an armchair. The shotgun stayed in his hands but came to rest across his knees, no longer pointing at anyone.

"Is that thing loaded?" Tempest asked.

Dr Sloan shook his head and let out a sad little laugh. "No. I don't have a licence for it either. I bought it years ago, but my wife went nuts and refused to allow me to go through with getting a cabinet and cartridges."

"Is the lady of the house here?" Tempest worried she might be hiding somewhere afraid to come out.

His question drew another sad chuckle. "No, she left me. She wanted me to drop the case against Morty and told me I was going to lose. She never understood. He stole from me and he's still doing it. I can barely keep my own practice going now. My clients have all wandered off, some of them even going over to Mortimer's practice to really rub salt into the wound. I probably should get some bullets for this thing. Then I could ..." he trailed off, choosing not to finish the sentence.

Tempest chose not to correct the doctor on his use of the term 'bullets'.

Instead, he asked, "Where are my dogs, please?"

They had stopped barking, but the sound of their little

claws on hard flooring and the occasional snuffle of a nose made it clear they were not far away.

As if only then recalling there were two sausage dogs chasing him through the house, Dr Sloan twisted in his chair. "Oh, um, I managed to shut them in the library." He pointed. "That door over there."

Tempest retrieved the dogs and chose to remain standing while they sniffed and snuffled around Dr Sloan's living room.

There followed a short discussion to allay any lingering concerns that Dr Sloan might be a world class actor, but it didn't take long to reassure Tempest that the sad defeated man shrivelled into the corner of an armchair was in no way involved in Dr King's disappearance.

Nor could he have been involved in the attack on Olga Rudokova since he had an alibi in the form of his lawyer – someone else who was happily taking Dr Sloan's money – for the time when she was been held.

Dr Sloan wanted justice over Dr King and made it sound like he would merrily throttle the man if he was permitted to do so. Having lost his final appeal months ago, he was out of options and expected to pay Dr King in full for the compensation awarded by the court. He continued to refuse and believed Tempest was part of a team of bailiffs coming to collect by force.

Tempest felt a little sorry for the psychiatrist, but there was nothing he could do to help the man and zero to be gained by loitering any longer.

He apologised for the mess, offered to pay, and when Dr Sloan refused to take anything and he found the cleaner on her hands and knees scrubbing the carpet by the front door, Tempest handed her a wad of notes instead.

Leaving the property, they went through the gate rather

than under the fence, and back to the car with nothing much to show for their time.

Dad asked, "So what now?"

It was a good question, but when an answer presented itself on the way back to Rochester, it came in a most unexpected guise.

Little Red Riding Hood

THURSDAY, 14TH DECEMBER 1518HRS

The M2 was busy, and rather than crawl in the traffic, Tempest took the first exit they came to and wound through the leafy towns and suburbs, wending his way south once more.

The glut of traffic came as no great shock; it was school run time, thousands of parents clogging the roads to get their little ones. It had started to rain again too, adding to the water already sitting on the road from the earlier downpour to make drivers cautious, and the sun was falling out of the sky in the way that it does so close to the winter solstice.

Paused at a pedestrian crossing to let a mum with a pushchair and a little girl cross, Tempest's mind wasn't thinking about the case at all. At the time, he was running through proposal scenario's and wondering whether he ought to take Amanda somewhere exotic before producing the ridiculous diamond he'd purchased almost a year ago.

However, somewhere at the back of his brain, two neurons connected, lighting a pathway that made his eyes focus on the girl walking beside her mother. It wasn't the little girl that got his attention so much as the red coat she wore with the hood up.

"Red Riding Hood," he breathed so quietly his own ears barely heard the words leave his mouth.

In the passenger seat, his father said, "Hmm?"

Tempest pointed. The girl was maybe eleven or twelve years old, but it wasn't just her. Coming down the road toward them were more kids, each wearing a red coat emblazoned with a logo over the left breast.

"What school is this?" Tempest voiced a question he had no reason to believe his dad could answer and ignored the angry beep from behind when he failed to move forward and yet more kids started to cross the road.

He had to wriggle to get to his phone which was trapped underneath his backside – no easy feat in a bucket seat.

The kids made it to the other side of the crossing, and when he still failed to get going, the car behind pulled around him. He got some more horn, and the chap inside – a kid in his early twenties with tattoos on his neck and knuckles – paused to hurl some verbal abuse too.

Normally, Tempest might point out their close proximity to children and possibly punch the fellow on the nose as a stark reminder not to use profanity in public, but he didn't even spare the man a glance.

The internet being a wonderful thing, he now knew the name of the school and was hurriedly thumbing the button to call Ian Quinn.

Putting it on speaker, he handed the phone to his dad. "Here, hold this, please. We need to park."

There were kids in red hooded coats everywhere, the

school clearly a local one that had just opened its gates to send them all home.

Tempest had to cruise past a bunch of them, looking for a spot and only getting lucky when an indicator came on. The road was lined with the cars of parents collecting their children, all of which were in different stages of getting ready to go.

Tempest, however, was not the only one trying to park as yet more mums, dads, or grandparents arrived.

His phone continued to ring, Chief Inspector Quinn either unable to, or very possibly choosing not to, answer it.

Tempest was about to thumb the red button to kill the call when he spotted him.

Him.

He looked just like the drawing the artist made from Olga's description. His head, tucked deep inside a hood, red to match the kids all around, was looking almost directly at Tempest. His hair was a bright orange, though natural, Tempest believed, not dyed. It hung on both sides of his face to form lank curtains, and his complexion was challenged with the remains of teenage acne refusing to give up quite yet.

Tempest killed the engine, his car abandoned at an angle rather than parked. The back end was sticking out into the road and begging to be caught by someone driving past, though he was oblivious.

"Dad, we have to go. Leave the dogs in the car." The grave tone of his voice was all his dad needed to hear. He asked no questions, gripping the door handle and shuffling his legs around to leave space on the floor for the dachshunds.

Plopping them on the carpet, he had to ward them off

with his hands to keep them from leaping out, but shut the door with care to hurry after his son.

Tempest lost sight of the Storyteller – the name had stuck – the moment he took his eyes off him. He was short for a man and that made hiding in the busy street easy.

Dad hustled around the car and into the street where Tempest now stood. "You saw something?" he asked, his eyes trained in the same direction as his son.

Tempest nodded, straining his vision and begging it to pick out the one red hood he needed.

"He's here. I saw him." Tempest started walking, crossing the road much to the consternation of yet more drivers. He was badly parked, in the way, clearly not collecting his kids, and was now holding up traffic.

"Get out of the road!" yelled one woman on her way past.

Heads turned and seeing that Tempest stepped right out into the path of the next car.

The instantly irate driver hit her horn, a loud blast penetrating the air.

More heads turned to see what was occurring, parents and kids alike stopping halfway into their cars or twisting around as they walked home to gawp at the man stopping traffic.

Only one head didn't turn.

"There!" Tempest snapped, convinced he'd caught sight of his quarry. He took off instantly, darting through the gap between cars, his legs already moving him at twice the speed his father could manage.

"Go, kid! Don't wait for me!" Tempest's father wasn't entirely certain who his son had seen and was sketchy on the whole concept of the Grimm case and who might be behind it. Lack of understanding was nothing new though when it came to Tempest's cases, and he'd learned to just go with it.

Arriving on the other side of the street, a mum asked if he was all right and he took the opportunity to ask for her phone.

"I need to call the police," Tempest's dad explained, getting the lady to dial three nines before handing her phone across.

By then, Tempest was no longer in sight, his passage known only by the shouts of alarm as he parkoured his way around the press of schoolkids and parents in the street.

Tempest had to commend the Storyteller for his choice of outfit. The coat was the same model as all the others being worn by the schoolkids and his diminutive size allowed him to blend in where a taller or broader man might have been easier to pick out.

Twice he'd already gripped a shoulder thinking he might have the right person only to find a bewildered child. He'd almost caught a handbag to the face the second time, the swing missing by a hair's breadth when Tempest dodged.

The only element in his favour was that most kids had their hoods down. Only about ten percent wore them up despite the drizzle.

He pressed on, running to catch the next group of kids, scanning the houses and alleyways as he passed them, and the other side of the street in case his quarry had already crossed. The tightly packed cars were making it harder as they provided excellent hiding places for someone to duck behind.

Tempest knew he might have already passed the man he sought, but pressed on, determined not to be stymied by indecision.

The crowd was thinning, the initial press of kids outside the school filtering down as more and more turned into side streets or got into waiting cars.

Heart pounding, Tempest forced himself to keep going. He would double back at the end of the road which was less than a hundred yards ahead of him now. There it met a main road where cars flashed by in both directions.

Ahead, a group of five boys sauntered lazily to wherever they were going in a typical teenager's lack of hurry. Two were wearing hoods, their features obscured and either one could easily be the Storyteller, tagged on to the back of the group and acting as though he belonged there.

At twenty yards, his lungs protesting, Tempest yelled again.

"Hey!"

The kids twisted to see who was shouting, took one look at the man running after them and took off like greyhounds from a trap.

None of them were the Storyteller.

Slowing to a halt, Tempest heaved in a deep lungful of air, followed by another and another, his eyes all the while scanning back down the street. He'd lost his quarry in the crowd, the slippery monkey using his camouflage to blend in and vanish.

But where had he vanished to? That he was here watching the school did not bode well; he planned to target the kids, telling the next chapter of his sick story by attacking a little girl, Tempest guessed.

In the same heartbeat in which Tempest questioned what that could mean, a loud wolf's howl split the suburban air and a woman screamed.

The Wolf

THURSDAY, 14TH DECEMBER 1521HRS

Propelled into action once more, Tempest flew back the way he had come. The pavement, still busy with kids and parents making their way home from school, presented nothing but obstacles. Leaping the bonnet of an ageing and rusty Ford Capri, Tempest landed in the road.

Cars were still passing in both directions, but accelerating into a sprint, Tempest matched their slow pace. Faces gawped from inside the vehicles going past in the opposite direction, music or conversation inside meaning they hadn't heard the scream.

Elsewhere, the street was a frozen plateau.

The wolf's howl came again, eerily out of place among the houses and modern scene, yet somehow in Tempest's head, completely fitting for the unfolding horror.

A small crowd were gathering not far from the school's entrance, a woman's voice at its centre babbling and wailing about her Sophie.

Tempest cursed himself. He'd missed his target, running

by him in the confusion which allowed the Storyteller to double back.

He couldn't get near to the woman, the crowd formed around her was too thick and she was far from his priority. The little girl was obviously not in the same place as her mother, so dismissing it, Tempest leapt onto the boot of a Volvo estate and up onto its roof, his shoes slipping on the almost friction-free surface. There he skidded to a stop.

The driver jumped out, yelling blue murder and making a fuss. Tempest tuned his words out and stayed out of reach when the man tried to hook his ankles.

Squinting into the gloom of the street, the trees lining it making the streetlamps almost pointless for all the light that penetrated to the ground, Tempest searched. Olga was drugged when she was taken, the Storyteller using chloroform to knock her out. Why do anything different here? Grab a kid in such a crowded street and their first scream would bring every eye.

That meant Sophie was unconscious. It would make her more pliable, but hopefully easier to pick out.

The driver of the Volvo decided he'd had enough of being ignored. Slamming his door, he started to climb up the bonnet, meaning to rid himself of the man on his roof by physical means.

Tempest questioned why the fool hadn't simply driven off, but as the driver attempted to negotiate the slippery windscreen to access the roof, a dirt bike angled between two parked cars to appear in the road fifty yards away.

Bathed in a patch of overhead light coming from between two trees, the figure astride it stopped to stare at Tempest.

The sight chilled his blood.

Draped across the seat in front of the rider, the inert

body of a child. It was too far away and too dim to make out any detail, but the light illuminated enough that Tempest could see the girl's bare calves sticking out.

More horrifying was that the rider had a wolf's head.

It revved the engine, the wolf glaring down the street at the one person looking its way. Tempest's feet twitched, but there was no chance he could catch it. The bike would be gone before he could even get back to his car. He would report it to the police, but with alley ways, canal paths and dark parks through which the Storyteller could escape, he would be long gone before the cops could respond and he would take Sophie with him.

Tipping back its head in a final taunt, the wolf howled to the moon high above, revved the engine, and took off.

"Hey," snarled the Volvo's driver, "What's the big idea?"

Had no one else seen it? Angry, his body shaking from adrenaline, and fighting hard to process all he'd just witnessed, Tempest took out a business card.

"My apologies. Please have your car assessed for damage and send a bill directly to me."

Leaving the confused driver on the roof, Tempest dropped back down to the pavement.

"Tempest!" his father forced his way through the crowd, battling with elbows to go in the opposite direction to everyone else. "Did you see it, kid? Some little girl got snatched. Grabbed right out of her seat when the mum was pulling away."

His voice quiet, Tempest said, "Yeah, I saw it."

Modern Fairy Tale

THURSDAY, 14TH DECEMBER 1542HRS

The police came, responding to the garbled and somewhat confused call from Tempest's father and the dozens of panicked parent calls that followed when Sophie Banbridge was abducted from the back of her car.

The Storyteller chloroformed the mother first, but perhaps in his haste to grab the girl and get away, he'd only given her a partial lungful, and she had come around only moments later.

According to Mrs Banbridge, a man knocked on her door just as she was getting ready to pull away. She wound down her window to see what he wanted, assuming it was one of the other students – a boy from her daughter's class perhaps, but he thrust his arm through the window, smothering her face and as she drew a breath to scream, the chloroform did what it does best.

When she came to, the back door of her VW Golf was open, and Sophie was gone. Obscenely, the Storyteller upturned a wicker picnic basket across the backseat, sandwiches, fruits, and cake spilling out onto the pavement outside.

Leading away from the car was a trail of little white cubes.

Tempest retrieved a couple to confirm what he was looking at: breadcrumbs.

Somehow Tempest knew they were on their way to grandma's house. It turned out to be almost the case. Instead, they lived with grandma. Mrs Banbridge, having recently left her husband, was back with her mother.

Quinn arrived thirty minutes after the first cops on the scene. By then the pedestrian traffic had dwindled to nothing, the street cleared so the police could look for evidence. Dozens of statements were recorded but listening in it came as no surprise to Tempest that no one had seen anything worthwhile.

There were some who claimed to have seen a man carrying a small girl – Sophie was in her first year at the school and was only eleven years old. Others reported hearing the wolf or the bike, but only Tempest saw it silhouetted in the street.

Ludicrously, the one thing the witnesses agreed on was the presence of a crazy man blocking traffic and running in the road shouting at people. Tempest identified himself quickly so the police could dismiss the notion that the crazy man was in any way involved in the abduction.

Quinn spoke with the senior officer at the scene, another chief inspector, before approaching Tempest.

"I'm told you saw the person Olga described."

Tempest and his father were sitting on the bonnet of his car. Each held a dachshund, both of which growled when Quinn drew near, proving what great character judges they could be.

"That's right. The artist got him down to a tee. He wore one of the school coats so it could be that he is a former pupil."

"I have officers looking into that already," Quinn reported.

"Or maybe he just picked one up at a shop. There will be a uniform shop selling these somewhere nearby. They might recall him visiting the shop if it was recent. Equally, he might have picked it up at a second-hand sale and there is no chance to trace it if that is the case."

They were after a name for the man Olga described. Now responsible for two of the Grimm attacks if not very probably all three, they had a face, but no idea who he was. Kidnapping a child was an escalation and would grip the attention of the nation.

"That's probably what he wants," Tempest voiced his thoughts. "There has been no ransom demand …"

"Yet," Quinn corrected him.

Tempest inclined his head, conceding the point. "Correct. But unless one comes soon, I think we can assume money is not the motivator here. The picnic basket, the wolf costume, it's overly dramatic. He is telling a story and there will be a reason behind it. The good news is my gut tells me he isn't going to hurt Sophie until the story is told and I don't think he is halfway done."

Quinn scoffed. "Your gut? I'll let Mr and Mrs Banbridge know, shall I? Don't worry, everyone, Tempest Michaels has a feeling this will all be okay."

Tempest bit down his natural inclination to knock the smile off Quinn's face. Doing so would be satisfying but would result in his arrest and in getting kicked off the case.

Instead, he said, "Acting the fool helps no one, Ian, and it makes you look petty. If I am right about this guy's motivation, he needs the characters for something, some new modern fairy tale he wants us all to bear witness to."

"A modern fairy tale?" Quinn repeated the words. "Well, I shall not be using that phrase when I give my press conference later. A little girl was kidnapped, Mr Michaels. Finding out who has Sophie Banbridge and securing her release is now the priority. I expect your full cooperation from now on."

"And you shall have it provided I have yours, Ian. You are not dealing with a regular criminal. Thinking in straight lines and expecting a ransom note won't get the little girl back."

"And what is it that you suggest?" Quinn asked the question, but his body language showed his disinterest in hearing Tempest's response.

"Cut him off. Give him no platform for his story to be told. He wants the spotlight. He wants people to see. Deny him that opportunity and work with me on figuring out who he is." Tempest almost suggested a next move, but he knew the chief inspector would never go for it. Admittedly, what Tempest planned to do was illegal.

"Thank you, Mr Michaels," Quinn began to walk away. "I'll take that under advisement. Don't go anywhere, I still have questions for you."

Tempest watched Quinn merge with the officers still massing outside the school. Mrs Banbridge had been joined by her husband, the estranged couple coming together in their mutual horror. They were no longer at the scene though. In fact, looking around, Tempest judged that he and his father were the only civilians left in the area.

And there was no good reason to stay.

Sliding off the bonnet, Tempest fished out his car keys.

"I'm heading back to the office," he announced,

opening the driver's door. "You want me to drop you off at home?"

Tempest's dad, still holding Dozer who was asleep and being cradled like a baby, cocked an eyebrow.

"You're not going to hang around here?"

"Nah. I want to research the Grimm stories further. The police will dust for prints, take measurements, have their forensic team examine the chloroform on Mrs Banbridge's skin and none of it will tell them who this guy is. Quinn's right that the little girl becomes the priority, but he's wrong about everything else."

As he talked, Tempest heard his own words and they stuck in his head. There were no prints at Dr King's house. It bothered him when he first heard it and while fingerprints themselves are not that hard to hide – a pair of latex gloves will do it – the report was of no physical evidence at all. There was no sign of forced entry either and no sign of a struggle. Mrs King claimed she woke to find the frog in her bed which meant she slept through her husband being taken.

How could all those things be true? It bugged him almost as much as the strangeness of the Storyteller and his motivation for the crimes.

The Phone Call

THURSDAY, 14TH DECEMBER 1652HRS

Tempest drove a little faster on the way back to the office. He dropped his dad off with a hopeful promise to see him tomorrow for the family dinner. Dad understood that solving the case and rescuing a little girl had to come first, but both acknowledged that his mother wouldn't see it that way.

For her, dealing with kidnappers, or any other form of criminal for that matter, was a job for the police. If Tempest wanted to be a detective, he needed to focus on lost cats and missing keys.

Bursting through the back door of the office with the dachshunds dancing along either side of him as they fed off his excited state, he found Marjory at her desk.

It was the end of the day and Marjory was not the sort to work overtime. She kept strictly to the clock, coming and going within a minute or so of her appointed work hours every single day. She looked up when Tempest swept in through the back door, but when all he did was wave and carve a path into his office, she went back to her crossword.

Amanda's office was still empty; her excursion with Darius keeping them busy and Jane was nowhere to be seen either.

Stripping off his jacket, Tempest grabbed his whiteboard marker and started to scribble ideas.

"Anticipate," he explained to Bull and Dozer, both of whom chose to ignore him and burrow into the blankets in their little bed under the radiator. "If I can anticipate where or who he might target next. I might be able to catch him in the act."

Tempest thought it a little hopeful, but while there were many Grimm's Fairy Tales there were only a handful that were well known. He quickly scrawled a list: Red Riding Hood, Tom Thumb, Cinderella, Sleeping Beauty …

Sleeping Beauty could be a woman in a coma or one that he puts into a coma. That was too hard to pin down.

"Rumpelstiltskin," he said aloud, writing the name on the board beneath the others. "Snow White. Hansel and Gretel. Puss in Boots." With each character he identified, Tempest made an entry on the whiteboard and thought about how the Storyteller might choose a target.

With Tom Thumb there was a chance he might grab any man of reduced height. People suffered from dwarfism, so would he simply do something to one of them?

Puss in Boots could be a cat the twisted mind of the Storyteller chose to snatch. Heck, it could be the man's own cat with tiny shoes glued to the end of its paws.

Tempest ran out of characters he could name without the need to look them up, and using his laptop to extend his knowledge decided he had all the main ones. There were more, many more stories, but since he'd never heard of them, Tempest elected to ignore them rather than make his search window impossibly wide.

However, remembering the wolf, he started a new column of names, this time listing subsidiary characters. The evil queen from snow white, the poison apple, the woodcutter. From Red Riding Hood came grandma and the wolf. From Hansel and Gretel he lifted the old witch in the house made of sweets.

There were too many possibilities, too many next chapters the Storyteller might want to tell. Regardless, Tempest kept going, researching the tales, looking for links between them for another hour.

Marjory called out when she left, locking the office front door and turning out the lights. It left him alone in the building with two gently snoring sausage dogs.

In many ways Tempest knew he was stalling. He'd made a decision to do something illegal waiting for Quinn outside the school. Now he needed to get on and do it, but it wasn't the kind of job you did while people were still up and about. Indeed, it was very much a 'dead of the night' kind of operation.

It might not yield the answer he wanted, but it was a whole heap better than doing nothing.

With dogs gamely scurrying after him, he left his office, killing the light to plunge them into darkness. Streetlight filtered through from the High Street outside his building's glass front façade, but the passage to the back door and carpark beyond required the use of the torch on his phone to navigate.

It was that or step on a dog.

Arriving home twenty minutes later, he sent a message to Amanda. He hadn't heard from her or Darius since the pair left the office around lunchtime. Not that he was overly worried about them.

Their case ought to have been an easy one, but that was

based on some unfounded assumptions. The very nature of their business was its unpredictability.

A text from Amanda pinged back while Tempest was feeding the dogs. The fortune teller case was bigger than anticipated, the scope of it going way beyond the couple who came into the office. Reading between the lines, Tempest guessed Amanda meant there were more victims, but she made it clear the fortune teller wasn't working alone.

She finished by saying they were wrapping up for the night, but was tired and heading home once she'd dropped Darius off.

His fingers dithered over the phone, trying to find the words to let her know about the dinner at his parents' house the following evening. Not that such an affair was necessarily contentious. But it involved exposing his girlfriend, the woman he planned to marry, to the entirety of his family and his mother could be hard work.

Rachel was likely to quiz Amanda too having only met her a few times in the past.

In the end he settled for a quick note to say he would miss her company, changed his mind, chickened out, and sent the original message. Only after it was gone did he send an additional note to say they were invited to dinner and that his sister and her family were in town.

With the dogs happily face down in their dinner bowls, Tempest took out the diamond engagement ring. It was becoming a habit.

The ring was exquisite. It came from an exclusive jeweller in London who was appointed to the royal household and had recently been involved in a scandal at the palace. Tempest read the report of the jeweller being arrested for murder with surprise when the story broke a few months ago.

None of that had anything to do with the ring though and the fact that he'd been holding onto it for a year when it was supposed to be on Amanda's finger.

His mother was right in many ways that he needed to be pestered. Of course, pestering on her part would never get the job done. What he really needed was a chat with the guys. Jagjit and Hilary were both married, and Basic was about as attached to his girlfriend as a guy could get.

That only left Big Ben. Tempest liked to think there was a woman out there who would curb his ways and make him want to settle down, but at the same time worried the planet might stop spinning without Big Ben constantly trying to nudge it onward with his groin.

Tempest ate a tuna salad with couscous, drank water, and retired to his office where he continued to wonder about the Storyteller.

When his phone rang, he was staring at the screen of his home computer reading the story of *The Giant and the Tailor*. Too focused on that, he spared only a cursory glance at the screen before answering it.

It displayed a number, not a name, which usually meant it was a client.

"Blue Moon Investigations. Tempest Michaels. How can I help you?"

"Run, run, as fast as you can! You can't catch me I'm the Gingerbread man!"

Every muscle in Tempest's body stilled. His tongue darted out to wet his lips and he chose his response carefully.

"I've been calling you the Storyteller. Is there another name you wish to be known by?"

Silence filled the room and Tempest thought he was going to have to goad the Storyteller into talking.

"No, the Storyteller is good. I like it."

Tempest noted a heavy German accent affecting the Storyteller's words. It was not what he expected and had not been reported by Olga, though she was Russian and perhaps missed the nuance of her attacker's accent the same way he would struggle to pick apart Germans from different regions of the country.

"I note your accent," Tempest said, wishing to God he had some way to trace the call. "Are you German?" Waiting to hear the reply, he carefully fished around in the drawer to the left of his desk. There he found an old Dictaphone, a relic from the days before mobiles.

"You have a good ear, Tempest Michaels," his response came out with an amused singsong cadence. "I am directly descended from Jacob Grimm himself."

"Jacob Grimm had no children," Tempest countered, patting himself on the back for remembering one brother from the other. He put fresh batteries into the Dictaphone, pressed the record button and watched the tiny tape inside begin to turn.

"That is incorrect," the Storyteller snapped, instantly aggravated. "I will admit, however, that my line is illegitimate. Jacob never married the woman who would bear his child."

"Shall I assume that you are hoping to cash in on the fortune the books still generate to this day?" Tempest chose to ask about money because he wanted to eliminate it and get to the real cause.

"Of course not. After all, my predecessors never wrote the tales. They had not one original thought between them. However, one cannot dismiss the brilliance of their decision to take folklore from every region for free and sell it to the masses for enormous profit."

"And you plan to do the same?"

"Yes, Tempest Michaels, but not for personal wealth or gain. I am an artist. The original tales must be brought up to date with some modern retellings, just to capture the public imagination. Then I will deliver the new stories, the ones that will set the literary world alight."

Tempest cracked his knuckles. The crazy child kidnapper was on the line talking to him. He needed to learn something from the exchange.

"I have a question, if you will permit me."

"Go on."

Tempest leaned closer to his phone. "Why did you call me?"

"Run, run, as fast as you can! You can't catch me, I'm the gingerbread man!"

"You think I won't be able to catch you? Is that it?"

"Yes, Tempest Michaels. I saw you today. Racing here, running there. I must commend you for coming so close, but that is as good as you will ever get. Consider this a friendly gesture. I admire you and the work you have done, but you are wasting your time trying to stop me. Do yourself a favour and give up."

A smile lifted the corners of Tempest's mouth. If the Storyteller had encouraged him to try his hardest, it might have worried him. But to be told there was no sense in trying, Tempest knew it could only come from a place of concern. The Storyteller was right; he had come close today. Had he turned around at the right moment, he might have caught the man in the act of taking Sophie.

That it was pure chance that put him in the right location at the right time was not something he chose to share.

Grinning and feeling a whole lot better, Tempest said, "I'll tell you what. You let Sophie and Dr King go and I will take it easy when I do catch you. I will let you keep the use of your limbs." Tempest wasn't one to make threats, especially not idle ones. The fool on the phone had kidnapped an eleven-year-old girl and in his books that meant he had already forfeited any right to decent treatment. If Tempest caught up to him and the police were not around ... well, he wondered at what point his fists might stop swinging.

The memory of Deadface the Klown swam uninvited into his mind, how his eyes registered shock when Tempest chose to drop him. There was a moment when their eyes locked and Tempest made a decision that cost the other man his life.

Sometimes, Tempest wondered if it was bad that he had no regrets.

"Dr King and Sophie?" the Storyteller questioned. "Who are these people?"

"The ones you kidnapped," Tempest accused. "Sophie is the name of the little girl you took from her mother this afternoon."

"Oh, you mean Little Red," the Storyteller sounded happy to be able to talk about her.

"Is that how you think of her?" Tempest asked. "She is not a character in a story. Nor was Rapunzel, and neither is the Frog King. Why did you take the Frog King and Little Red Riding Hood but leave Rapunzel to be found?"

Several beats of silence passed and when the Storyteller spoke again, he sounded confused.

"I do not know what you are saying about this Frog King, Mr Michaels. The Frog King is not part of my story. Do you think perhaps he should be?"

Now it was Tempest's turn to feel confusion.

"Are you telling me that you haven't kidnapped Dr King? Are you one of his patients? Is that how you know him?"

The line clicked, the call terminated at the Storyteller's end, but not before Tempest caught the sound of an announcer in the background.

Destination Unknown

THURSDAY, 14TH DECEMBER 1919HRS

Tempest looked up when he heard the door opening. Voices told him it was Darius getting back and that Amanda was with him.

The dogs reacted a half second before he heard the door, somehow detecting the sound of their shoes outside the house despite the fact that he would swear they were both asleep.

He drained his green tea which had gone almost cold through neglect such was his concentration on other tasks.

"In here," Tempest called out, stretching in place and getting up slowly – his back had begun to set. Coming out of his home office to find his guests kicking off their shoes, he said, "That was a long day. Get anywhere?"

Darius deferred to Amanda, ducking into the downstairs toilet while she explained.

"We got it sewn up. That's why we are so late."

Tempest led her through to the kitchen where he spotted the ring box still sitting on the counter. Amanda continued to explain the case and how her day went while his eyes flared wider than dinner plates and he tried to mask his movements.

"The whole thing was a big scam as we expected, but it had a traveller family behind it and there is evidence they have hurt other people who haven't paid up."

Tempest used his body to block her view of the countertop, quickly opening a drawer and sweeping the ring box into it.

"Something to drink?" he asked as innocently as he could manage.

Amanda eyed him suspiciously, picking up that he was behaving oddly. Choosing to let it go she said, "Sure. A small glass of wine sounds nice."

Tempest joined her but kept his even smaller as he was going out again.

Darius opted for a beer, though he called it a 'tinny' and together with Amanda explained how they had involved the newly promoted Sergeant Woods so she could notch up another bust. It was going to take some work to make the fraud charges stick and that comment led nicely into Tempest and Amanda explaining that side of the investigation business.

Darius was coming into it with open eyes and a sensible head; Tempest believed he would do just fine flying the Blue Moon badge in Australia and was more than happy to stump up money to get him off the ground.

When the conversation dried up, Amanda asked, "How was your day? Anything much happen with that Grimm case? I note you are still free to wander, so I'm guessing you haven't had to spend much time with Quinn."

Tempest laughed. "That was a lot of questions." He was

brief in his outline of the visit to see Dr Sloan and didn't dwell too long on the fun and games outside the school because he wanted to ask them about the announcer's voice he recorded.

Of course, revealing a little girl was kidnapped in broad daylight generated questions.

"Little Red Riding Hood?" Darius struggled to believe what he was hearing.

"I wish it was unusual," Amanda remarked. "There really is no limit to the amount of weird to be encountered in this job."

"But kidnapping a little girl?" Darius protested.

Tempest bumped his hip to push off the kitchen counter and started back toward his office. "Well, it gets weirder yet, I'm afraid."

Darius took a swig of his drink and followed. "How so?"

"The Storyteller called me earlier."

Amanda choked on her wine. "He called you!"

"Yup. We had a lovely conversation, and he read me the gingerbread man rhyme. He's telling a story, and he believes he cannot be caught. He called to tell me I should stop wasting my time."

"What did you say to that?" Amanda wanted to know.

"I promised to make a mess of him when I finally track him down."

"That's more like it," Darius looked ready to hand out some slaps of his own.

Tempest picked up the Dictaphone. "I recorded most of our conversation. There is a part at the end I want you to listen to." His remark was aimed at Amanda, though he included Darius.

He rewound the tape, which he'd listened to more than

a dozen times already, and played the whole thing. It cut in midway through the Storyteller arguing about the legitimacy of his birth line and no one spoke until it got to the end.

"Did you hear the announcer at the end?" Tempest asked, his question once again aimed at Amanda.

"Sounded like a train station."

Tempest agreed, relieved it wasn't just his ears playing tricks on him.

"I've been trying to figure out where it is. It starts with 'The train now approaching on platform one is the 1703 service to F ...' If I can pin down which station that is, I will have a location for this scumbag. A general area, at least," Tempest amended his statement.

They listened again. The announcement was almost impossible to make out and only because he'd played it back so many times had Tempest been able to figure out what was being said. Some words came out clearer and he'd filled in the blanks with educated guesswork.

However, the Storyteller ended the call before he could hear where the train was going or where it might be calling next. The last piece of information would have given him the station in an instant. Now he had to piece it together and had been trawling his contacts to see who knew about trains. So far he had drawn a blank.

"Could the F be Frittenden?" Amanda suggested, her face showing her doubt.

Tempest released a slow sigh. "Or Five Oak Green, or Frogholt, or Fawkham. There are a bunch of F's from which to pick. I could probably narrow that down because they won't all have rail stations serving them, but knowing where it is going tells me roughly nothing about where it is.

That's the thing I have to try to figure out. As things stand, this is the best lead I have."

"Have you shared it with Quinn?" Amanda questioned. She knew from her own time in the police that they had enormous resources and a stack of experts upon whom they could call.

Tempest shook his head, dropping the Dictaphone back on his desk. "No, but I need to. I'm going to record it to the computer and send him a digital file. We've had two run-ins today already. I really don't feel like going for a third."

The trio talked some more about the Grimm case, what could possibly link the three victims the Storyteller could now count, and Tempest showed them his list of potential next characters. Would he go after Snow White or Sleeping Beauty? Would he play the roll of the wicked witch or the evil queen?

There was just no way to know.

Amanda finished her wine, placing the glass in Tempest's dishwasher and announcing her intention to head home for a bath. She still had an apartment in Maidstone town centre. It was her place, though she spent increasingly little time there. Moving in had been discussed, but for now they were content to have their own spaces, and the subject was too big for either to push.

Kissing her at the door, Tempest withdrew back into the warmth of the house and his guest from Australia.

"How's the fatigue?"

Darius shrugged. "I'm bushed, but I'm not about to quit if it's drinking time. How's about some of that quaint English pub you've been telling me about for years?"

Tempest opened his mouth to say that wouldn't be practical – he needed to go drive and break the law yet tonight – but now that he considered it, involving a couple of the chaps from the pub would lessen his chances of getting caught.

He had his phone in his hand moments later, a group text message going out to the fellas a heartbeat after that.

It was pub o'clock.

Pub O'Clock

THURSDAY, 14TH DECEMBER 1957HRS

It came as no great surprise to Tempest to find some of the guys were already there. Basic, Hilary, and Jagjit all lived in the village. Jagjit had moved out for a brief period when he first got married, but the lure of the quiet village life, the cheaper property prices, and his family brought him scurrying back less than six months later.

His wife, the lovely Alice, didn't seem to mind a bit that she suddenly had several dozen of her husband's close relatives living on her doorstep. In Tempest's experience Indian families are just like that; really well-meshed and constantly celebrating life together.

Hilary was the one among them who had been married for years. His kids were at secondary school and in the last year he'd quit his long-term career in telemarketing, at which his friends knew he excelled, for a new role as Basic's business partner/manager.

Basic's real name is James Burham, but he's been introducing himself as Basic since long before Tempest met him.

He's ... well, he's not what one might call bright. He looks like a Neanderthal, spills on himself all the time, has little to offer by way of conversation, and used to park shopping trolleys at a supermarket for a living.

That was until he stumbled across an idea so genius only a truly stupid person could have ever thought it would work – he started selling air guitars on the internet. He sold so many he branched into limited 'signed' editions, and from there made the leap to selling 'wicked air' otherwise known as pictures of him doing jumps on his BMX bike.

Now his list of products ranged from invisibility cloaks to dehydrated water to models of stealth planes where the customer bought a remote control and had to pretend they could see the jet in action.

The pair of them were making a fortune and had recently gotten involved with the Blue Moon team in Boston when a trip there went sideways.

Tempest found all three of them at their usual table just inside the pub door. They were halfway down their first pints and ready for Tempest to buy them another one.

The dogs clawed at the carpet to get to the people they knew, people who were going to make a fuss of them and feed them snacks.

"I'll get these," Darius volunteered after a quick round of introductions.

Moments later the pub door opened again, and Big Ben walked in like John Wayne after too many hours in the saddle.

Jagjit laughed, "Hey, how are the stitches?"

Hilary cocked an eyebrow. "Stitches?"

Big Ben slumped into a spare chair. "Occupational hazard."

"Having sex is not your occupation," Tempest pointed out.

Big Ben shrugged. "I get paid."

The chaps exchanged glances: this was news to them.

"In compliments," Big Ben added with a grin. "Each one I get is thoroughly deserved. Often, it's just pure amazement when I drop my trousers and the lady in question finds herself saying, goodness what a big ..."

"Ego?" Hilary suggested. "What a big ego you have, grandma."

Big Ben took the well-known line and continued with it. "All the better to sha ..."

"Ben!" Darius roared. He was coming back from the bar, his hands filled with brimming pint glasses. "You old dog!"

Big Ben got to his feet, proving he wasn't as badly injured as he might want everyone to think. They shook hands and when Darius had returned from the bar having got one more drink for the latecomer, Tempest had to explain how they all knew each other.

"So, stitches," said Hilary, eyeing Big Ben.

"Yup," Big Ben looked less than happy about it. "A hundred and forty-seven of them."

Hilary's forehead creased in disbelief. "A hundred and ..."

"Could have been much worse," Big Ben sipped his pint. "Only the tip tore. Otherwise ..."

Tempest shook his head. "He's exaggerating, Hilary. Have you never met him before? He probably got one stitch, and they had to make it extra small just so it would fit."

Before anyone else could jump in with a new topic of

conversation – everyone was itching to talk about anything other then Big Ben's genitals – Tempest jumped in.

"Anyone know a train expert?"

He got a round of raised eyebrows.

"The latest maniac I'm trying to track chose to call me this evening and I caught the sound of a train announcer in the background just before we were cut off."

Hilary said, "Play it for Basic. His train knowledge is unparalleled."

Tempest looked doubtful.

"Trust me," Hilary defended his claim. "Basic is a proper trainspotter. He's got notebook upon notebook listing the trains he's seen, the route they were taking, what they were hauling ... I bet he'll be able to help."

Darius asked, "Did you bring it with you?"

Grumpily, Tempest trudged back to his house. He left the dogs with his friends when they made it quite clear they were happy where they were. Of course, not having to stop every few yards for them to sniff something made his round trip quicker by several minutes.

Sitting at the table once more, the chaps all crowded around the tiny Dictaphone to listen when Tempest played the last few seconds of his recording.

Basic crunched on a packet of cheese and onion crisps, his attention unfocused much as it always seemed to be. Nevertheless, when the recording finished and everyone looked his way, he popped another giant round of fried potato in his mouth and said, "That's the 1703 out of West Malling. The final station is Faversham."

Tempest couldn't stop his frown forming. "How can you be so sure?"

Basic shrugged, a motion that saw his enormous shoulders rise and fall like tectonic plates and crumbs spill from his t-shirt.

"There is only one train line in the county that terminates in a place that starts with an F. That means it's a Faversham line. That gives us two options, the trains out of Victoria coming via Maidstone East and those out of Charing Cross via Rochester. The Rochester trains don't stop anywhere at 1703 so it has to be the Maidstone East line and that means it has to be about to arrive at West Malling."

Just like that, the man with an IQ barely high enough to control his breathing and digestion, solved the riddle.

Hilary picked up his pint, a smug grin on his face. "Told you."

"You did," Tempest acknowledged, glad he'd gone home for the Dictaphone.

"Unfortunately, that means I have to cut things short."

Darius had his pint halfway to his mouth. "You want to find this guy right now?"

Tempest indicated his drink. "I was always going out again tonight. There's a chance this Storyteller guy is one of the first victim's patients. He's a psychiatrist," Tempest explained. "But his list of patients is not information I can easily obtain, so I was planning to simply break in and take it."

Tempest gave everyone a moment to voice their opinion, forgetting they all had his back and had been in his corner since before he opened the doors to Blue Moon.

"Now though," he continued. "If there is a chance we can find where this guy is ..."

Darius put his pint down, done with it now that there were more important tasks ahead.

"He's got a little girl. You can count me in."

"Me too," growled Big Ben. "I'm not that badly injured."

Not willing to be left out, the remaining three all voted their inclusion. No one was yet to finish their first pint, so sobriety and the ability to drive were barely in question. Regardless, they were all going and their hunt for the Storyteller's lair was happening right now.

Wrong About Everything

THURSDAY, 14TH DECEMBER 2037HRS

It was agreed that Tempest's proposed excursion to the King Wellness Clinic could wait. They wouldn't need to figure out the Storyteller's identity if they caught him red-handed with two kidnap victims.

Instead, after dropping the dogs at home, they drove to West Malling Train Station where they parked and listened. Accessing a map on his phone, Tempest zeroed in on the local area, eliminating some parts of the town for being too far away for the announcer's message to be heard.

It still left a stack of nearby properties, though exactly how many they were talking about could not be determined from the map.

He was about to suggest they split up when Tempest's phone rang. The suddenness of it cut through the still December air like a claxon, making Hilary squeal in shock.

While the rest of the guys ribbed him for it, Tempest checked the screen, saw the name displayed and thumbed the button to connect the call.

"Ian. If you are calling about the train announcer, we believe we have already figured it out. I am fairly confident it is West Malling. I am there now with some friends. A few dozen officers to help comb the area would be greatly appreciated." Only as he was speaking had Tempest realised he probably could have asked for help the moment they figured out where to look.

"No, Mr Michaels, I am not calling about the recording you sent me. There is no way to confirm its authenticity for a start. The person you were speaking with could be anyone. Have you not considered that it was probably a crank call."

"No, Ian, it was the Storyteller."

"So nice to hear your usual overconfidence in place," Quinn sneered. "Tell me this, Mr Michaels, when you asked him about Dr King and he denied all knowledge, did that not tip you off? Your caller knows about Sophie Banbridge because her abduction has been all over the news this evening. There has been nothing reported about Dr King because there was nothing to gain by doing so at the time."

"Then how did he know to call me, Ian? I note that you chose not to mention my involvement when you gave your press conference." In truth Quinn had confirmed the police had brought in a specialist consultant but omitted to confirm who that was.

"Who knows," Quinn spat dismissively. "He probably took one look at the weird nature of the crime and guessed you were mixed up in it. Enjoy West Malling, Mr Michaels, I shall not be sending you any of my men. They have far better things to do following up real leads."

Biting, Tempest said, "What lead, Ian? Did your team turn up something at the school?" He hoped for some video footage that might have caught the motorcycle. A registration plate, unless the dirt bike was stolen, would lead them straight to the Storyteller's door. All Tempest cared about was the victims. Whether Quinn got there first or he did made no difference so long as someone caught the Storyteller before he could harm the little girl or Dr King.

"He left behind a book," Quinn reported triumphantly. "Just like the one he left with Olga Rudokova. He might have managed to leave no DNA evidence at Dr King's house, but there are fingerprints on the book, Mr Michaels. Enjoy your late evening excursion."

Tempest got the sense that Quinn was about to hang up and had to jump in quickly to stop him.

"Ian why did you call me?" If it had been to gloat about his lead, he would have led with it.

"Ah, yes. I almost forgot. You left the scene outside the school when I told you to wait and thus you missed the other development."

Tempest thought he was going to be forced to beg to know what it was, and was thankful, in many ways, that Quinn thought it too juicy to keep to himself.

"Your insistence that your so-called Storyteller is not after money fell apart. The Lord Mayor of Kent received a ransom demand earlier this evening. For the safe return of Sophie Banbridge, he wants ten million pounds, or the stories will continue. You were wrong about him, Mr Michaels. In fact, you've been wrong about everything since I was forced to let you interfere with this case. Please continue wasting your time though, or don't. The choice is yours, just so long as you don't waste any more of mine."

The line went dead.

Tempest spent the next few seconds strangling his phone

and wishing it could be Chief Inspector Quinn's neck in his hands.

When he took a breath to address the questioning looks from his colleagues, all he needed to say was a single word.

"Quinn."

They were waiting for his lead on what to do next, but he required a moment to clear his thoughts and consider the latest news.

The Storyteller left another book behind, placing it somewhere it would be found but wouldn't be immediately obvious. It was a bit like a serial killer taking trophies from his victims but in reverse.

To Tempest's mind the books worked with his theory that the Storyteller wanted people to know what he was doing. He called himself an artist and claimed he had no interest in money. Was he lying?

Forced to question if Quinn could be right and the caller was nothing more than a well-informed crank, he dismissed the notion. Tempest remained certain he had been speaking to the man on the dirt bike. So why the ransom? It wasn't like he could claim the ten million was needed for publishing, distribution, and marketing.

Or maybe he could. The Storyteller was high functioning, his brain able to conceive complex plans, but it was also a bag of angry cats and just as crazy.

The clues conflicted and it bothered Tempest that he could make no sense of it. If he allowed himself to believe he'd been speaking with the Storyteller, then either the self-proclaimed descendent of Jacob Grimm was lying about his desire for wealth, or Quinn was the one dealing with a crank call.

Except that didn't work either. The police would have corroborated the authenticity of the ransom demand, almost certainly demanding proof of life. Tempest shook his head; the case was chock full of holes, but it wasn't his first time operating in total confusion.

Drawing attention by raising his arms, Tempest chose to do what had always worked in the past: Keep moving forward, believe he will figure it out, and look forward to punching someone deserving in the face.

Door to Door

THURSDAY, 14TH DECEMBER 2059HRS

They split into three pairs, each setting off in a different direction. The area they had to cover wasn't vast, although it was impossible to be precise about just how far away the announcer's message might be heard.

The general opinion was 'not very far' which dictated they explore the nearer properties first.

Big Ben went with Jagjit, the pair setting off toward a collection of large, detached properties across a field. They had direct line of sight to the station and the lack of anything more substantial than a few hedges between one and the other suggested the sound might travel that far.

Basic and Hilary went to the west where a row of houses bore some promise. That left Tempest and Darius. Tempest chose the location he believed held the greatest hope – a small industrial park behind the station. Much of it was abandoned, the businesses moved on, but there were three places that appeared to still be trading.

Two were automotive related, the location perfect for

taking cars apart and using machine tools. The third was an accountant's office.

Tempest and Darius looked around the abandoned buildings first but found no sign of life inside them. Dismissing them quickly, they focused on the businesses still in operation, checking all three for any signs they might house kidnap victims. There were no lights on inside, no sounds coming from within, and no sign of the dirt bike, not that he would have ridden it all the way to West Malling from Greenhithe with a girl draped over the saddle.

Tempest clambered over a fence using a boost from Darius, but the yard on the other side provided nothing worth finding.

After fifteen minutes of searching, they accepted defeat and hoped one of the other pairs might have found something more promising. However, as they were starting their walk back to the train station where the cars had been left, Tempest spotted something that caught his eyes and stilled his feet.

Darius kept walking for two seconds before he realised he was alone and by the time he spun around to see where his partner had gone, Tempest was halfway to a building they had already checked once, albeit only a cursory once over.

It was the door to the side that had Tempest's attention. In their inspection of the buildings, they had looked through the windows and checked the doors, including the one he was now heading for. It was locked up and there was no sign of life, but where the side door had detritus, weeds, and litter built up around it, there was a carved arc where it had all been shunted to one side.

The recent rain combined with the dirt clumped it all together into one muddy mass. He should have seen it when he first looked, but hadn't. Now it demanded his full attention as he knelt to examine the mess on the ground.

How long since the door was last opened?

Using the torch on his phone, he made the area bright enough to see the drag marks indented in the mud. Someone used force to shove the weeds and muck aside.

"It rained today," he remarked, mostly to himself though Darius was standing right next to him.

"Do we break in?" Darius questioned. He wasn't bothered about breaking the law, certainly not when it felt entirely justified, and was poised to put his foot through a door the moment Tempest gave him the go ahead.

Tempest gritted his teeth took a moment to second guess himself. Ultimately though, he couldn't come up with a reason why the door might have been opened in the last year, let alone the previous few hours. Perhaps it was being opened and closed a lot in recent days; there was no way to determine if that was the case, but the building looked abandoned, and it clearly wasn't.

Looking around, Tempest spotted what he wanted.

"Let's use that."

The ten-foot-long piece of hollow metal pipe acted as a perfect lever to get under the steel door's bottom lip. They heaved together, using a rock as a fulcrum to lift the door off its hinges. It popped clear almost without making a sound and could be lifted back into place if they chose to leave the building secure and hide their entry point.

About to step through the threshold into the darkened interior, Tempest's phone rang to almost give both men a heart attack.

"This is tense stuff," Darius admitted, sagging against the doorframe. "You said it can get a little adventurous, but

I didn't expect ..." he wafted his hand around to indicate everything, "... this."

Tempest fished out his phone, made a point of switching it to silent mode while cursing himself for not doing it earlier.

The caller was Big Ben. Waiting outside and speaking at a low volume, Tempest answered.

"This is a bust," Big Ben let him know. "There's nothing here and we stopped being able to hear the station announcer about two hundred yards before we got to the first house."

"We might be onto something here," Tempest reported. "Check with the other guys and come to the industrial park under the rail bridge. We are in the first building on the left, just going in."

He disconnected the call, dropped the phone back into his pocket, and stepped through the door. A pungent scent reached his nostrils, one that was at the same time familiar and unwelcome. He twitched his eyes at Darius, checking to see if he was getting it too.

He was.

Darius dropped his voice to a whisper. "Is that?"

Tempest nodded. "I think so."

"This would be a good time to be armed."

Tempest raised his right fist. Then he raised his left and made a shotgun pump action as though he were loading both.

The moment of dark humour brought a smile to their faces in what they both believed was about to be a very grim situation.

The smell was the very distinctive scent of a dead body. It is the kind of odour that sticks with you, so that once you have encountered it, you know it for life. They were smelling it now, but Tempest was telling himself it couldn't be Sophie.

The scent needed time to develop. He was certain of that, and the little girl had only been taken hours ago. Even if the Storyteller killed her by accident in his escape from Greenhithe ...

Tempest pushed the thought and images from his head, refusing to dwell on them.

Inside the building a muddy footprint showed where someone had stepped in the dirt outside and brought it in. A second less distinct footprint was beyond that, then a third, but by the time it got to a fourth there was almost nothing left to show the person's passage.

Tempest stopped to take a photograph, wanting to be able to show the police what it looked like before they stepped inside.

Dropping into a crouch, he took a small cloth tape measure from a pocket, laying it out next to the footprint to gauge its size.

"A ten," he remarked, rising back to full height to continue onward through the darkened building.

Darius found a light switch, but flicking it up, down and up again changed nothing, the power disconnected long ago.

The sign outside the building had long since given up and fallen off, but with a jolt Tempest realised where he was.

The floor of the building was mostly clear; some boxes piled in one corner and a couple of old desks were all the visible clutter. A steel roller door at the far end spoke of a previous life, perhaps as another mechanics' shop or a tyre fitter's place. However, the walls were decorated with old, tatty, faded posters of muscular men and women posing to show off their physiques.

It was a gym.

"This is where he brought Olga," Tempest whispered. "She described this place. He brought her here, hacked off her hair, and drugged her again before ditching her in Mote Park."

He kept his excitement in check. He could hope for physical evidence here – fingerprints and more, but they still had to find and deal with the dead body they could both smell.

"It's stronger over here," Tempest called, his voice quiet, yet easily loud enough to carry in the silence that held only their breathing and footsteps.

In the back corner, a portacabin that had seen much better days, acted as an office. They only needed to get close to the door to confirm the smell was coming from inside.

The door was shut, so grimly they held their breath and yanked it open.

A rat scurried out, squeaking its fright and they peeked inside, each using their phones to illuminate the interior.

The body of a large man lay on top of a desk in the middle of the office space. It made it look like an autopsy table.

Ducking his head back outside to take another deep breath of cleaner air, Tempest went fully inside. He needed to call in what they had found, but he wanted to check for himself first. He wanted to check he was right about the identity of the body and to confirm there was only the one to be found.

First, he inspected the body, which he did without touching. It had been horribly mutilated and Tempest prayed the damage was all postmortem. The face was a bloated mess, the features all but gone, which in turn made identifying the corpse all but impossible.

All but.

While Darius checked the rest of the cabin, offering a thumbs up when he found nothing else, Tempest found a pen which he used to manoeuvre the dead man's right hand.

Just as he expected, the index finger was missing, lopped off with something crude to leave tattered flesh just like the finger in Verity King's fridge.

They had found **Dr King**.

What About Sophie?

THURSDAY, 14TH DECEMBER 2140HRS

"There's a backpack over there," Darius indicated a direction with his thumb and managed to speak without drawing breath. "Looks like it belongs to a girl."

Tempest checked for himself, using latex gloves to operate the zip and look inside. The Smiggle bag contained textbooks and notebooks, a pencil case, and a lunchbox.

The first notebook he carefully extracted bore the name Sophie Banbridge 1C in swirly feminine handwriting. There were little hearts in place of the dots over the 'i's'.

Finally, Tempest had a tangible link between Dr King's abduction and Sophie's. It made sense for them to both be crimes committed by the Storyteller, but until that point there had remained in his mind a niggling doubt, holes in the case he could not explain. Not that the holes were suddenly plugged, but it was impossible now to deny the connection.

"Oh, my God," spat Jagjit, the fool then taking a deep breath and gagging instantly.

The idiot had come to find his friends inside the building, undoubtedly drawn by the beams of torchlight and lack of disturbing noises that might have convinced him to remain outside.

He was bent over and heaving for air which only made things worse.

Tempest had seen enough anyway and the whole scene needed to be quarantined so the police forensic people could take over. Grabbing Jagjit's arm, he steered his friend back outside and into the cold night air where he pushed him up against a wall and commanded him to breath.

"I can taste it," Jagjit wailed.

Tempest nodded, certain the stench would be on his clothes and in his hair for days no matter how many times he scrubbed them.

Big Ben and the others were just crossing the tarmac of the small industrial park, questioning looks on their faces until Tempest filled them in on the latest development.

"It is going to get boring here really fast once I call the police. I want you all to bug out now. Go back to the pub and have one for me. I'm going to be here for hours. You should go too, Darius," Tempest tried to get his guest to leave with the others. "You need some rest before the jetlag kills you."

Darius argued instantly, "I came here to learn and that is what is happening. Your police might do things a little different from the guys in Queensland, but that's all it will be. I'm sticking around."

"You guys want a car?" Big Ben offered his keys. They had come in his tricked-out utility vehicle and Jagjit's new soccer mum car which the chaps assured him Alice got him to buy in preparation for the kids to start arriving.

Darius took the keys and walked back to the station with the guys. He was going to collect Big Ben's motor and return with it. The guys were heading home, the pub no longer holding the allure it did a few hours ago.

Alone in the dark outside an abandoned industrial unit that contained a dead body, Tempest did what he needed to do and called the police.

He tried Quinn first but wasn't shocked when he got no answer. His second call was to the Maidstone nick dispatch desk and when he hung up just a few minutes later units were already rolling to his location.

Darius got there first, parking Big Ben's car within the confines of the industrial park but off to one side where Tempest said they wouldn't be in the way.

"That your first body since Iraq?" Tempest asked. They were inside the cab with the engine running to restore some warmth to their bodies.

Darius nodded. "You've seen a few on the job, I take it?"

"More than I would like to count."

The cops arrived without their flashing lights to tell the world there was something to see. Just a pair of constables in a squad car sent to confirm the report. They did just that while Tempest and Darius remained outside the abandoned building.

Then came the rest, a procession of vehicles bringing detectives, forensic scientists, and inevitably, Chief Inspector Quinn.

Tempest made sure he was observed by the senior officer before retreating inside the warmth of Big Ben's car.

"We need to stay?" Darius questioned.

"Not strictly. We could have made the call anonymously, assuming I had a burner phone with me so they wouldn't just trace it, but this is a live case with my name on it, so I want to be around to see what happens. At least for a while. And I need to talk with the nice chief inspector to see what other developments there have been."

The next time Tempest looked across, Darius was sleeping. It came as no great surprise, and he couldn't calculate how few hours the big man might have racked up in the last two or three days.

Slipping quietly from the car, he went to see what was occurring.

Quinn saw him coming and dismissed his sergeant so they could talk.

"I do hope you are not looking for a pat on the back, Mr Michaels. Entering the building illegally will have to be explained."

Tempest let a small snort escape his nose.

"How do you know I didn't find the door resting against the side of the building, Ian?" They both glanced at the door which leaned against the exterior brickwork to the right of the frame still attached by the self-closing mechanism which was stretched to its maximum.

"Did you find the door like that?" Quinn sounded genuinely curious.

"Let's just say I did and leave it at that." Tempest smiled sweetly to deepen the aggravation he chose to provide.

Quinn rolled his eyes. "That is hardly how things work, Mr Michaels, and you know it."

"Nevertheless, my statement will record the door was open and I have an additional witness who can corroborate that." *Once I brief him so our stories are straight*, Tempest remarked inside his head. Speaking again before Quinn got a chance, Tempest asked a question, "Is it Dr King?"

Quinn pursed his lips, still unhappy to be made to work with the paranormal P.I.

"It might be," he conceded. "The victim's face is too badly beaten to be certain without further testing. I'm afraid we will have to ask Mrs King to identify him. If she cannot, we will go down the route of dental records, but I feel confident we have found your Storyteller's first victim."

"What about Sophie?"

Quinn hitched an eyebrow.

"We found her backpack in there," Tempest continued. "But there was no sign of her ... no sign she had ever been in there. Have they found fingerprints that could be hers?" Only after he left the office and had time to reflect in the quiet of Big Ben's car did Tempest realise he hadn't seen tiny footprints in the mud that could have belonged to the missing girl. Admittedly, she could have been carried in still unconscious, but kids are heavy and the man he saw was slight and short, not someone who would be comfortable lugging an eleven-year-old-girl around.

"Again, Mr Michaels, the backpack appears to belong to Sophie Banbridge. A photograph has been forwarded to the liaison officer working with her parents, but I think we can assume it is hers and not some clever ruse. That does not, however, mean that she was ever here, and even if she was, she is very much not here now. Unfortunately, Mr Michaels, you might be well-meaning, but you are an amateur. Were you not involved in the case, and had you not blundered into what is clearly an important location to the man we are chasing, we might have been able to set a trap for him and await his return."

The statement was bait, goading Tempest to respond angrily and he recognised it for what it was.

"Were it not for my blundering," he replied, his tone

Modern Fairy Tale

cool, "I doubt you would ever have found this location. For that matter, had you dispatched officers hours ago when I requested them, they would have been on the scene to ensure my 'blundering' could not cause any harm or ruin your precious investigation. Tell me, Ian," Tempest switched subjects, "is the Lord Mayor planning to pay the ransom?"

"That is above my pay grade, Mr Michaels, and most certainly above yours. However, I am sure any decision on the subject will be taken with due consideration."

"Sir?" called the same sergeant Quinn was talking to before Tempest approached. He hovered in the hole where the door used to sit, his expectant expression showing that he needed the chief inspector to see something.

Quinn's feet twitched but he stayed facing Tempest to deliver a final thought. "Your presence here is no longer needed, Mr Michaels, if it ever was." Then, in a manner that was something close to formal he said, "Thank you for your assistance in this case. I shall let the chief constable know that you tried your hardest."

It was another jibe, another brazen attempt to make Tempest snap so he could claim the P.I. was difficult or volatile.

Quinn hesitated for a second, waiting to see how Tempest would respond. When all he got in response to his taunts was an amused grin, he turned to his right and started to walk away.

Tempest called after him, "The case isn't over yet, Ian." The comment made Quinn twitch, if only ever so slightly. Just before he vanished back inside the abandoned gym, Tempest added, "I'll see you tomorrow."

Quinn was trying really hard to get under his skin and he was succeeding. Tempest dearly wanted to slap the stupid out of his 'partner', but doing so would play directly into the chief inspector's hands so he was going to soak it up and keep moving forward.

He was also going to get an answer to a question that started bugging him at the start of the case and was yet to go away.

B & E

THURSDAY, 14TH DECEMBER 2324HRS

"You do this sort of thing often?"

Darius asked the question as both he and Tempest peered through the windscreen of Big Ben's car.

"Not exactly," Tempest replied, "but sometimes needs must and this feels like one of those occasions." He gripped the doorhandle, paused to allow himself one last chance to change his mind, then gave the door a determined shoulder barge, exiting the car with a steely set to his jaw.

Breaking into places is a criminal activity, no matter the justification, so the trick is always to either have a legitimate reason: it's on fire and you fear for the lives of the people inside, you believed you heard someone shout for help, or possibly that you have traced a criminal to the location and can claim to believe they have intent to harm someone they are holding.

None of those held true on this occasion and he wasn't about to start a fire and risk adding property destruction to his list of crimes. Coming up on midnight, there was going to be no one inside the King Wellness Clinic, but that was kind of the point.

Tempest had no good reason to believe the Storyteller was one of Dr King's clients, but something about his job as a psychiatrist and the damaged mental state of the Storyteller made him want to find out. So here he was, ready to sneak into the private clinic to steal the list of clients.

They were back in Kings Hill and watching the premises and the general area around it to be sure there was no one else around. From memory, Tempest knew the same building housed a plastic surgeon, a firm specialising in sonograms for expectant mothers, a physiotherapist, and two job recruitment agencies.

To mask his movements, Tempest made sure to park way down the street where CCTV footage from the businesses wouldn't pick up the car. He then changed into his black clothing and coated his face in camouflage paint; a coloured wax that was easy to apply and remove.

Darius masked his features too, unwilling to wait in Big Ben's car as Tempest suggested.

It could be argued that their actions made their intentions clear and that they were knowingly about to engage in the art of cat burglary, and it was true. It also lessened the chances of being caught, something Tempest held a one hundred percent record for avoiding so far though it had come close a few times.

As ready as they were going to get, Tempest led the way around the back of the building, guessing a narrow passage at the end of the row would lead to a rear yard. They had to climb over three separate walls to get to the right building, and were then forced to guess which set of windows might lead to Dr King's clinic.

Unable to know for certain, even though he had been

inside, Tempest decided they were as well to pick a convenient window and go from there. Balancing on the lid of a plastic wheelie bin gave them enough height to access the first floor.

"The good thing," Tempest selected a long, thin knife from a multitool, "about sash windows, is how easy they are to open from the outside."

Demonstrating practiced ease – he'd practiced on the windows in his original office until he could perform the task with his eyes closed – he inserted the knife between the upper and lower halves, found the catch, and forced it to rotate.

Pulling the knife free, he folded it away, returned it to a zip pocket where it wouldn't fall out, and using gloved hands raised the lower window.

"We don't have windows like this in Australia," Darius murmured.

Donning a pair of plastic overboots to ensure they took no dirt inside with them and left no footprints behind, Tempest slipped over the sill to drop lightly down on the other side.

"That's a shame," he whispered, knowing there was no need to be quiet yet feeling it was the natural thing to do.

The office they found themselves in was not the one they wanted, though the presence of a long couch made them hopeful for a moment. It turned out to be the physiotherapy place. The entrance door opened into a wide landing where they could see a brass plaque boasting Dr King's practice on the other side of the stairs.

"We break in through the door?" Darius questioned, his tone doubtful. Thus far they had left no trace of their illegal entry. Exiting the office they came into was easy because they were inside, but he could see no easy way to access the place they really wanted.

Tempest shook his head and they backtracked, moved the wheelie bin, and repeated the trick with the window now they could be sure they had the right place.

Twenty minutes later they were in Big Ben's car and easing through the streets of Kings Hill on their way home.

In Tempest's pocket, a flashdrive held everything he could find on the computer in Dr King's private office. Like so many people, the idea that he might need to protect his password to the extent that it existed only in his head never occurred and he had it written inside a notepad inside his desk drawer right next to the keyboard.

It was one of the issues with office computer systems, in Tempest's opinion. The built in automations forced users to change their passwords every few months and prevented them from using one they might have employed before. Worse yet, they had to contain numbers, capitals, and symbols to make guessing them impossible for the would-be hacker.

The net result being that the users forgot the stupid passwords and resorted to writing them down, sometimes on a post-it note stuck to the computer screen.

Accessing Dr King's files was as simple as taking books from a library less the danger of late fees for not returning them on time.

"You going to check that out when you get home?" Darius asked around a yawn. He was struggling to stay awake and very definitely going to bed when they got in.

"Yeah. I just need to see the patient names and find pictures of them. If he has photos on file, it will be easy."

Dr King didn't see the need for pictures of his patients

though, Tempest discovered moments after settling into his office chair.

The dogs bounded out of their bed to greet the guys when they came through the door but retreated back under their blankets within seconds of claiming a gravy bone each. Darius took himself to bed and Tempest made a rum and coke, hoping to cool his brain so he might sleep when he finally crawled into bed.

Not having pictures of Dr King's clients was going to make the process slower and Tempest very nearly put it off until the morning when he could approach it with fresh eyes and a clear head. It was just after 0100hrs in the morning, and he was feeling the effects of a long day filled with adventure.

However, he made it a practice to not take drinks to bed simply because he had a habit of falling asleep before finishing them only to be woken shortly thereafter to find two dachshunds balanced on his nightstand with their tongues lapping the tasty liquid.

It was for that reason alone that he stayed where he was, sifting the list of Dr King's patients. For the most part, the names told him gender and he dismissed all the women instantly. The files listed age and that allowed him to further narrow the pool.

Tempest had no experience from which to guess how many clients a psychiatrist might have at any one time, but figured the list of clients would go back years and if the Storyteller *was* one of his patients, he wasn't necessarily a current one.

Dismissing anyone over forty, which he considered was still probably ten years older than he believed the Storyteller could be, Tempest rounded out the list of potentials to ninety-nine. It was a big number given that he now had to look for photographs of each person and cross reference the pictures he found to be sure he had the right face.

It was a task he'd undertaken before, so he knew the proliferation of social media made it easy to find pictures of 'Fred Bloggs' but also that he was likely to find a dozen or more Freds the moment he entered the name.

With a sip, a grimace because the rum was strong, and a sigh, Tempest entered the first name.

His screen, set to display images, filled with photographs in neat rows. Expecting to waste his time and eventually prove the man he saw outside the school in Greenhithe was not, in fact, one of Dr King's patients, Tempest would have spat out his drink if he hadn't already swallowed it.

Staring back at him, third picture in on the second row, Andrew Grimwald smiled for the camera. The photograph was an old one, Andrew looking to be still in his late teens, but there was no denying it was the same person. He even had the same awful 'curtains' hairstyle, his bright orange hair parted right down the centre to hang limply to either side of his face.

Switching from a search engine directly to social media, Tempest found the man's profile. It was littered with quotes from Grimm Brother's Fairy Tales and images of books and toys Andrew collected.

He was a Grimm Brother's nut, his obsession displayed for all to see.

Slumping back into his chair, Tempest eyed the rest of his rum and coke with disappointment. He wasn't going to get to finish it, and he wasn't getting to sleep any time soon either.

The Raid

FRIDAY, 15TH DECEMBER 0517HRS

Setting up a raid takes time. Sure, there are police officers trained for such things, firearms officers who are employed to be ready to react at a moment's notice. They operate as teams, practicing forced entry in a multitude of scenarios so they can anticipate the movements and motions of the other people in the team and be as ready as they can be.

However, when the police receive a tip off from a person who claims to know the identity of a person wanted in connection with a kidnapping of a little girl, some due process is still required.

Higher-ups must first approve the decision to have firearms officers smash their way into the house of a civilian. At night that means rousing said higher-ups from their warm, comfortable bed. The information supplied must be checked, rechecked, and triple checked because past errors are known by the press, and no one wants to be responsible for a raid that targets the wrong person.

Then the area around the address to be raided must be

reconnoitred, the team assembled ... it's a long list of boxes to be ticked before the first cop swings the door breaker and the team rush through the breach.

Tempest needed no such checks, but with a little girl's life on the line, the images of Dr King's dead body refused to leave his mind, he wasn't about to kick the door in himself. He also recognised that it was anything but a one-man job and his friends, while well-meaning, were just a bunch of chaps from the pub. Hardly the making of a team set to raid a house in the middle of the night.

So Tempest accepted it was a task beyond his capability to perform and drove directly to the nick in Maidstone. There he made enough noise to be seen quickly.

Quinn had retired for the night, leaving officers at the abandoned gym in West Malling to continue the operation there, but it wasn't long before he reappeared, his uniform looking just as fresh and crisp as ever.

In the intervening time since they were together at the abandoned gym, Mrs King had identified her husband's body. It was one of the first things Quinn told Tempest, though he seemed to take no pleasure in it.

Tempest accepted the news with a nod, keeping his thoughts to himself. Killing Dr King didn't make any sense unless it was nothing to do with the Storyteller's modern fairy tale. But that couldn't be the case because of the theatrics employed in his disappearance.

For whatever reason, Andrew chose to attack his psychiatrist and kill him. But why then lie about it? If Andrew was behind the frog and the golden goose – both distinctly Grimm characters, why did he deny it? If he killed Dr King as some kind of revenge or because he knew too much about his plans, why leave the frog if it was nothing to do with the story?

It made Tempest's head hurt to think about it and his fatigue was making it worse.

By the time they got to the forming up point a street over from Andrew Grimwald's listed address in Hadlow, the chief constable had joined them. It was his authority stamped on the raid and his vested interest in seeing the case brought to a successful end.

"This is good work," he acknowledged without making it clear if he was addressing Tempest or Quinn. "Well done. I knew the pair of you would work well together."

Tempest had to fight to keep his mouth closed and wondered if Quinn had willingly given him some of the credit or been forced to admit the truth that the paranormal P.I. was behind all the recent successes.

The radio crackled, the armed response unit leader confirming they were about to go in.

"Let's move forward, shall we?" the chief constable suggested. He wanted a closer look at the action.

The command centre was little more than a van and a couple of squad cars in the carpark behind a parade of shops, but they left it and the officers manning the vehicles to get a better view.

They arrived in time to hear the shouts as the firearms officers went through the front door, their loud instructions becoming muffled as they raced inside.

It was all over in seconds, but the hoped-for triumph of the team leader reporting a suspect in custody and a little girl saved never came.

Via the radio, they were able to track the team's progress through the house, so Tempest heard when they found somebody, but the firearms officers sounded more confused than anything else.

Different parts of the team reported clear for the areas

they checked, and it was done, the team leader exiting the house to wave the chief constable across.

Tempest went with him, walking in his wake alongside Quinn though the chief inspector made a big point of being closer to his boss to make it look like he was leading.

Interested only in the end result, Tempest listened keenly to what Sergeant Crow, the team leader of the raiding party, had to say.

"One person in the house, Sir. I believe it's the suspect's mother. That's what she claims at least. There is no sign of Sophie Banbridge though a more thorough search will be needed to determine if she was ever here." Behind him lights were coming on inside the house and curtains were twitching in nearby properties, the people sleeping peacefully in their beds roused by the unexpected sound of men shouting in the street outside.

The chief constable started forward, aiming his feet at the smashed front door; he was going inside but not before the team leader issued a warning.

"It's weird in there, Sir. Scary. The mum is clearly another of Andrew's victims. I already radioed for medical support though you only need to take one look at her to know her worst injuries are on the inside."

Tempest wanted to know what that meant, but when the chief constable went inside, Quinn made a point of stopping in the doorway.

"No civilians." He barred Tempest's entry.

"You've got to be kidding me."

Addressing the Sergeant Crow, Quinn said, "This is Tempest Michaels. He's a paranormal investigator."

"I know who he is," the heavily armed officer replied, his tone carrying no opinion on the subject.

"The press will be all over this case, so unless you want to find yourself being ribbed by the other teams for ghost-busting instead of real police work, make sure he is kept well away from the property."

Sergeant Crow looked Tempest up and down. "I was led to believe he identified the suspect and provided his location, Sir."

"Which failed to yield either the suspect or the little girl he has snatched. You have your orders, Sergeant."

With that, Quinn crossed the threshold, proceeding inside without once looking back at the man he left outside.

Crow watched him go, muttering a descriptive he wouldn't use in front of his kids.

Tempest agreed, "He is all of that and more."

"You knocked out one of his teeth, right?"

A slim smile crossed Tempest's face. "I did. Got me three months jail time. Right now, it feels like I might like some more."

Crow snorted a laugh. "Well, join the queue. You are not the only one who would like to see Chief Inspector Quinn put on his backside."

Tempest started forward, aiming to enter the house despite everything. He bounced off Crow's extended arm.

"Sorry. It's not worth the aggravation I would get."

Tempest acknowledged Sergeant Crow's stance with a nod, stepping back to observe the house before turning around and walking away. He was tired, distinctly overdue some sleep, and in need of breakfast.

Expecting Darius would be awake by the time he got home, Tempest vowed to attend to his own basic needs before putting any further effort into the case.

Sergeant Crow watched him go, waiting outside for his

team members to begin exiting and hoping the ambulance he requested might arrive soon – Mrs Grimwald was in a bad way.

However, his eyes were not the only ones watching Tempest Michaels wander back down the street.

Tom Thumb

FRIDAY, 15TH DECEMBER 0524HRS

Andrew Grimwald seethed with rage. Tempest Michaels was outside his home, and he'd brought the police with him.

How dare he!

Didn't he understand the great work in progress? Had he not explained it sufficiently just a few hours ago?

What angered him most was that he could have been there. It was luck more than anything that meant Andrew was out when the police came. The advice was to move things along, to get the story moving. It made him worry that his sponsor thought he might get caught before the final spectacle was in place.

It was all about the final spectacle. Without that there was nothing.

With a gasp that sent a flutter through Andrew's entire body, he realised his collection was lost to him. The work of a lifetime, all the Grimm memorabilia, including Jacob Grimm's actual hat, signed photographs, and posters displayed in storefronts two hundred years ago when the books were first published. The police had it all now. Maybe they wouldn't confiscate it - it had nothing to do with the case per se, but he wouldn't be able to get to it.

"It's okay, Andrew," he whispered to himself. "This is bigger than all of that put together." He knew it was true, but that did little to quell his desire to wail the injustice into the night.

Maybe when it was done and the world revelled in the majesty of the story he showed them, they would give it all back. They would understand when it was done. That was what his sponsor always told him. Yes, Andrew was going to have to do some things that people might find distasteful, but that was no reason to shy away from them. Each of his characters had an important role to play.

From where he watched in the shadows, Andrew saw Tempest Michaels turn and walk away. It eased his tension a little. Somehow the thought of him touching his things was too much. The police were one thing, but he felt a connection with the paranormal detective. They had spoken. He had given Tempest Michaels fair warning, yet he chose to ignore it all.

Well, Andrew had an idea how to repay his betrayal.

Slinking back to his van, Andrew checked on his latest victim. Tom Thumb was still unconscious, the angry red welt on the back of his head oozing plasma to mat his hair. Andrew felt his pulse, confirming the tiny man would survive before settling behind his steering wheel.

How close he had come to failure. Had he waited to seek his next character, he would be in custody now. As it was, he almost drove straight into them, only spotting the squad cars as he came past them. Had they been closer to the house, it might have been all too late by the time he realised what was going on.

Forcing himself to calm, Andrew turned the key, firing

the van's engine into life and setting off. Heading away from his home and the police, he had a new destination in mind. He would take Tom Thumb to join Little Red Riding Hood. It was always going to end there anyway.

Things were moving faster than he wanted, but he consoled himself by placing a call to the one person he knew he could rely on to say supportive words: his sponsor.

"Andrew?" the familiar voice echoed through the van's speaker system when the call connected. "Is everything okay?"

The voice was guarded. Andrew hadn't heard it sound like that before.

Stuttering and tripping over his words, he managed to say, "The police are at my house." When he got no response, he flicked his eyes down to make sure the call was still connected and said, "Hello?"

The voice asked, "Where are you now?"

"On my way to the cottage. I have Tom Thumb, but I lost the wicked witch! It won't work without the wicked witch!"

Soothing now, the guardedness of the voice gone, it said, "Do not worry, Andrew. A wicked witch can be replaced. This is far from insurmountable. Remember?" he coached, "we talked about setbacks and unexpected obstacles. What you are trying to do has never been attempted before. The world will marvel at your creativity, Andrew, and no great artist achieved their finest work without some pain along the way."

As they always did, his sponsor's words chipped away the rough edges of Andrew's soul, making him feel better, more confident.

"Thank you," he whispered, his voice cracking.

"Now, are you listening?" the voice demanded, the sudden change in tone making Andrew nervous once more.

"Yes! Always."

"Good. The police are drawing closer, Andrew. You must hurry now. Proceed to the final act. Gather your final characters. I already have a replacement for the wicked witch, but you must prepare. Have you identified Hansel and Gretel?"

A grim sneer gripped Andrew's lips, the corners turning up. He knew precisely which siblings he was going to invite to take the greatest honour, a brother and sister whose identity would provide him the sweetest revenge at the same time.

Bacon and Eggs

FRIDAY, 15TH DECEMBER 0746HRS

Darius was indeed out of bed when Tempest got home, his body clock confused enough about the time that he woke after only five hours sleep, and despite being exhausted, when his eyes opened he could not manage to trick slumber into returning.

Tempest found him at the breakfast bar in his kitchen, drinking coffee. A dirty plate that had once held bacon, eggs, and toast if Tempest's nose was anything to go by, sat to one side.

The dogs had been out and their breakfast was long gone. It left very little for Tempest to do and for that he was thankful.

He regaled Darius with the latest developments, skimming over Quinn's behaviour lest it arouse his ire, and made himself a hearty breakfast in deference to the extra calories he burned being up all night.

Darius recharged the kettle, pressing it into service to make more tea. He had no plan for the day other than to trail around after Tempest or one of the other Blue Moon detectives. Since they still had Big Ben's car, Tempest gave him a call.

It was a little surreal for Big Ben not to have women in his penthouse apartment – that was a daily occurrence – yet his 'injury' precluded amorous activities and Big Ben was the sort of man who had very little use for female company unless they were naked or doing some housework.

It was agreed that Darius would return Big Ben's car shortly and he would then drop the Australian back at the office in Rochester where he could find something constructive to do, even if it was just hanging around to shadow Amanda and Jane as they went about daily business.

Checking his understanding of the Grimm case, Darius asked, "The police know who they are after now, but they don't know where he is?"

"That's about the size of it. Andrew Grimwald's photograph will be shown on national TV if it hasn't already, and a manhunt will ensue. He will be encouraged to come forward if he is innocent, but I don't believe that he is. Evidence at his house makes it clear he is nuts for the Grimm's Fairy Tales and while I cannot state that it was Grimwald I saw on the dirt bike with the unconscious girl, he was definitely there. It's him all right. He's our scumbag." It made the German accent confusing, since Andrew was English to the core, but Tempest thought it sounded odd when he first heard it and now he understood why – it was completely fake.

"But you didn't get to go in the house?"

Tempest munched on a piece of toast, the bulk of his breakfast already in his belly.

"I did not. Quinn prevented me from going in because he is petty and small minded. However, I hung around until the armed response unit pulled back to the command unit around the corner and got the low down from them."

"Is this the part about his mother?"

Tempest chewed, swallowed, and washed his mouth out with tea. "She was tied up in the basement next to a cauldron. I think she was playing the role of the wicked witch. According to the firearms officers, she claimed her son had kept her down there for months and that he'd completely lost his grip on reality since he stopped attending his appointments with his psychiatrist, Dr King."

"Who he killed."

Tempest pursed his lips, but said, "That is the natural conclusion to make."

Darius frowned a little. "You sound like you're not convinced."

Was he not convinced? Tempest wasn't sure what he thought.

"I don't know. There is something that doesn't entirely fit. I asked Andrew about Dr King when he called me, and he acted as though he had no idea what I was talking about. Also, he left books at the next two crimes but not one at the first scene where we found the frog and the message about wanting his golden goose. He hasn't mentioned the goose since and when I asked him about money, he scoffed at the idea and claimed to be an artist."

Darius drained his mug and placed it in the sink.

"Could he just be yanking your chain? Muddying the waters by being deliberately inconsistent?"

Tempest had asked himself the same thing more than once and was yet to reach an answer.

"Truthfully, I don't know, but I don't think so." He had to fight to get the last words out as a yawn pushed his lower jaw open against his will.

"You should get some sleep."

Tempest nodded. "I really should."

Darius still had the keys to Big Ben's car, so Tempest made sure he had directions, an address for the satnav, and Big Ben's phone number to ensure he wouldn't suffer any dramas finding his place.

With food in his belly and nothing constructive he could do immediately, Tempest collected the dachshunds and went to bed.

Briefing

FRIDAY 15TH DECEMBER 1412HRS

Roused by the sound of his phone vibrating its way across his nightstand, Tempest rolled over, fumbled for it, dropped it, and had to fight his way out of the duvet to look for it under the bed.

By then the caller had rung off, but they called back before Tempest got the chance to check his call log to see who it might have been.

"Quinn," he grumbled, flopping his head back down onto his pillow and thumbing the button to connect the call.

"Mr Michaels?"

"Yup."

"There has been another development. Another kidnapping, from the look of things. The chief constable is holding a briefing shortly."

Tempest absorbed what the chief inspector told him, then saw what he omitted to say.

"You need me there otherwise your boss will want you to explain why I am not. And you're worried I will tell him what a royal pain in the butt you have been since he assigned you to bring me in as a consultant."

Silence came down the phone. It made Tempest happy.

"Did he question where I was earlier at Andrew Grimwald's house?"

"No, Mr Michaels, but he did ask how we came to know the name and address of our prime suspect all of a sudden. A small fact you chose to gloss over. You are not a reporter, Mr Michaels. Refusing to reveal your source is not a tactic you can employ."

"Good, because I don't have a source. I'm a detective, Ian. I figure things out. The how of it is insignificant. Especially when we have the life of an eleven-year-old girl on the line."

"A girl we are no nearer to recovering."

"That's down to you, Ian. You have the resources. Get your officers out there and find him. Use the TV. Use the internet. Make technology work for you."

"The briefing is in twenty minutes, Mr Michaels. Personally, I don't care if you attend or not. In fact, as I have said before, I think it would be better all round if you stay away."

"But the chief constable won't honour my fee if you can show I was actively problematic as a consultant. That's why you don't want me there, Ian. Or he will, but there won't be any future work."

"Money? You're concerned about money? And there I was listening to you lecture me about how nothing else mattered compared to the life of a little girl."

Tempest gritted his teeth; he'd walked right into Quinn's trap.

A glance at the bedside clock told him time was ticking

by; Quinn happily keeping him talking to reduce his chance of getting to the briefing on time. Well, stuff that.

Tempest threw the phone on the bed, letting Quinn talk to empty air while he ran to the bathroom to freshen up. He had eighteen minutes to get to the nick and that was going to be a push. In fact, it would probably come down to traffic through the town centre and he had no way to control that.

Nineteen minutes later, he shoved open the doors to the briefing room to find the chief constable already talking. All heads swung around to see the figure framed in the brighter light coming from outside. The chief constable paused what he was saying.

"Please come in, Mr Michaels," he invited, his tone neutral which was a heck of a lot better than impatient or annoyed, two emotions Tempest was prepared to receive for his tardiness. "Take a seat anywhere. You haven't missed much."

The briefing provided little by way of new information and appeared to be aimed at bringing a new shift of officers up to speed. That made sense to Tempest as they would need to rotate the previous shift off so they could get some rest.

What Tempest did learn was that he'd been right when he identified possible targets. A popular actor, with the stage name 'Tom Thumb' had been taken in the night, abducted from his house where his wife, also an actor with the stage name 'Thumbelina' was rendered unconscious but left behind.

"We are yet to establish why the suspect chose to take one and leave the other," the chief constable remarked.

Tempest frowned. Did they really not know? Unsure what protocol might be, no one had interrupted the big boss since Tempest took his seat, then deciding he didn't much care, Tempest opened his mouth and provided an answer.

"Because Thumbelina is not one of the Grimm's Fairy Tales."

There were a few sharp intakes of breath from around the room and enough eyes twitching his way to let Tempest know it wasn't normal or acceptable to interrupt the boss when he was speaking.

Regardless, now that he had everyone's attention, he continued to explain, "Thumbelina is a story by Hans Christian Anderson. Tom Thumb was ... well, actually it wasn't written by the Grimm Brothers because they didn't write any of the stories, they just recorded the local folk legends from across Europe. The point is that Andrew Grimwald left Thumbelina behind because she has nothing to do with the story he is trying to tell."

"Thank you, Mr Michaels," the chief constable dipped his head in acknowledgement. "Ladies and gentlemen, if you are not aware, Mr Michaels is helping us as a consultant on this case due to its ... unusual nature. As you've just witnessed, his perspective is proving very insightful."

The chief constable pushed on, outlining the manhunt for Andrew Grimwald, the agencies involved and what they were each doing to ensure his capture and the safe return of the two victims he now held.

When it was done, the assembled officers had some questions of their own which the chief constable called Quinn up to field. In all Tempest found himself immobile for almost forty-five minutes, during which he'd learned the identity of the latest victim – Ivan Barnett AKA Tom Thumb – and that the police had no clue where Andrew Grimwald might be or where he could be holding his victims.

Modern Fairy Tale

The abandoned gym was not registered in Andrew Grimwald's name, nor could they identify any tangible connection between him and it. They had, however, matched fingerprints found there with ones at his house. They also found strands of Olga's long, blonde hair.

Andrew owned no other property and had no living relatives save for a distant uncle of his mother's in Scotland. Wherever he was, the Storyteller had gone to ground and there was no telling how long he might stay that way.

The question troubling Tempest's mind was not so much where they might be, which was a worry, but what Andrew planned to do with them. He was acting out some bizarre story, but it wasn't one that a person could follow by reading the tales.

Quite the opposite. If anything, it was a mash up of many tales, all thrown into one melting pot. But how would it end? Was Red Riding Hood to be eaten by the wolf? Tempest's eyes bugged out, the question sending a horrifying flare of possibility through his heart.

"Have there been any reports of wolves being stolen?" he asked, blurting the question just as the officers were starting to file out of the room.

His question caused some murmurs, eyes looking his way unsure whether to take him seriously or not.

"Hey!" Tempest snapped. "It's a yes or no question. Has anyone in this room heard a report of a wolf, or maybe even a large wolflike dog being taken in the last week or so?"

Still no responses came, which in itself was an answer, but the chief constable forced his way through the press of bodies now milling about inside the door unable to get out because Tempest blocked the exit.

"What are you thinking, Mr Michaels?" the chief

constable was taking him seriously at least. "Is this going to be part of Andrew's plan?"

Tempest sucked on his bottom lip. "That I cannot say, but I'm asking myself what the characters are for. He's calling Sophie Little Red Riding Hood. He's just nabbed Tom Thumb. From what I hear, his mother was supposed to fill the role of the wicked witch. There has been a golden goose and a frog king though the frog king has already been killed. What is his end game?"

It was a rhetorical question, but one Tempest had to air. Andrew Grimwald had a plan, of that much he was certain. He was organised too which was probably the most worrying element of the whole thing. The police raided his house, but they hadn't found little Sophie Banbridge and the hunt for Andrew was already many hours old, his face circulated across the TV and internet. That meant he was able to avoid detection while keeping multiple victims captive.

Was he in disguise? Or did he have a place to go that no one knew about?

Tempest's racing mind was about to voice his question about other properties Andrew might have access to when a harassed looking out of breath constable skidded to a halt outside the briefing room doors.

"There's been another message, Sir!" the young female constable blurted. "The ransom has increased, and the Lord Mayor is waiting for you on your private line, Sir."

She managed to get it all out without drawing breath, then sucked in a huge lungful before she turned blue.

The chief constable strode purposefully from the room, leaving Tempest behind as if completely forgotten.

Quinn was hard on his boss's heels, keeping pace and talking animatedly all the way.

Modern Fairy Tale

Tempest followed behind, once again questioning the conflicting information in his head. Andrew didn't care about money, he was convinced of it. But what did that mean for the case? Someone was demanding a ransom, so if it wasn't Andrew, who was it? They had to be involved. Otherwise, how would they know to make the call?

The chief constable's pace reminded Tempest of Darth Vader, storming through the Death Star with his ridiculously long legs, a tail of stormtroopers jogging to keep up. Instead of stormtroopers, the chief constable left an entourage of police officers in his wake, trailing along like a comet's tail.

Somewhere in the middle, Tempest allowed himself to be buoyed along like so much flotsam.

However, at the chief constable's office at the far end of a corridor on the top floor of the Maidstone nick, Chief Inspector Quinn stopped everyone else from going inside, barring the doorway with his body.

"We will keep you apprised of the Lord Mayor's considerations," he told the swathe of inspectors, sergeants, and constables.

Tempest moved through them, a question he very much felt he needed an answer to poised on his lips.

Quinn held up his hand, palm out. "I don't think so, Mr Michaels." Stepping inside the chief inspector's office as his boss picked up the phone, Quinn made to shut the door.

Tempest put his foot in the way.

"Have they recorded the voice of the person making the ransom demands?"

Quinn's angry grimace almost spat a command to move his foot, but the subtext of Tempest's question sank in.

"You're still pushing the daft idea that your Storyteller isn't doing this for money, aren't you."

"He isn't. I'm the only one who has heard his voice, Ian. How do you know the ransom demands aren't phoney?"

Quinn spat his response without needing to think, "How do you know the fool that called you wasn't the fake? Trust me, Mr Michaels, the ransom demands are genuine and have come with proof of life. We might not share your particular genius for bedtime stories, but we do know a thing or two about police work."

The words came laced with amusement, Quinn's loyal audience behind Tempest tittering obediently.

"Now will you remove your foot, Mr Michaels? Or shall I have you carried from the building?"

Two burly officers appeared either side of Tempest's shoulders, their silent looming enough to confirm Quinn would happily give the command to make it happen.

Tempest withdrew his foot, forcing calm into his mind though it screamed and kicked in rage all the way from the upstairs corridor to the street outside.

Office Work

FRIDAY, 15TH DECEMBER 1500HRS

Gripping the roof of his car, Tempest needed five minutes to calm down. Breathing exercises, mental tricks, and the knowledge that the future would probably prove him right had the desired effect, but it took a while.

Annoyingly, Amanda's words of warning continued to echo in his ears. She didn't want him to take the case in the first place. Anything that placed him in close proximity to Quinn was a bad idea and worse yet, he'd known she was right when she first said it.

In a position of power, Quinn was going out of his way to trigger Tempest. If Tempest quit on the case, Quinn won. If Tempest succumbed to his desires and knocked out another of Quinn's teeth, Quinn won again.

In fact, the only way Tempest could conceive his own victory was to find Andrew, rescue the hostages, and solve the case. Even if it turned out Andrew's motivation was never anything but money, it would be hard for Quinn to gloat when everyone would see who solved the case.

But how was he going to achieve that?

Thus far he'd followed the clues and they allowed him to find not only where the Storyteller had been holding Dr King, but the man's true identity and then his home. Had he been able to enter Andrew Grimwald's home maybe he would have a next clue to follow.

As it was, the trail had gone cold and the only thing he could do was go back to the drawing board to try to figure out the next move or the next victim.

But would there be any more? Surely, Andrew could feel the net drawing in around him. The police raiding his home had to have made him nervous. Would he risk taking anyone else? Or was it simply that he had to. The story had to be told, and Andrew would not rest until it was complete.

Momentarily frozen by the multitude of unknowns, Tempest's thoughts were interrupted by his phone.

Closing his eyes for a moment and taking a breath, Tempest reframed his thoughts – it could be anyone calling, from his girlfriend, Amanda, to the Storyteller himself. Exhaling slowly, he took out his phone, opened his eyes, and checked the screen.

Dad.

"What's up, old man?".

"Just checking you are set for dinner tonight, kid? Your mother is going all out. She's been in the kitchen since breakfast chopping, preparing, and getting dinner ready. Also, there exists a small danger she might propose to Amanda on your behalf if you haven't done it by the time you get here."

Okay, so if Tempest needed any more stress, there it was in the form of his mother's will.

"How small of a danger?" Tempest banged his head against the roof of his car.

Modern Fairy Tale

"Odds are probably about even. I mean, she won't actually propose for you, obviously."

"Oh, obviously," Tempest echoed, thinking it was nothing of the sort.

"But short of stuffing an apple in her mouth, I can't guarantee she won't sit humming the *Wedding March*, or ask Amanda if her ring finger ever gets cold."

Both those things sounded precisely like tactics his mother would employ. He loved her to bits but could recognise her for what she was: a bully. What made it worse was that she would justify her actions and defend them regardless of how much damage she did.

Sighing, Tempest said, "Thanks for the warning. I will be there in a little while to help out. I just need to check on something first."

He was not going to be bullied into proposing to Amanda by anyone, let alone his mother. When he got down on one knee, it was going to be spectacular, a moment he and Amanda would cherish for the rest of their lives. That almost certainly meant he needed to avoid taking her to dinner tonight, which in turn meant he wouldn't see his sister and her kids.

He was the only uncle they had. Well, their father had a brother, but Tempest was the only cool uncle they had, and he wanted to be in their lives more than he was. So he couldn't just duck dinner either.

Pushing thoughts of family drama from his mind, Tempest returned to the very present case and what he could do to find Andrew Grimwald.

Thumbing the call button on his steering wheel to activate his in-car phone system, he spoke to the voice recognition software and connected a call to someone he believed could help.

"Tempest?" The voice of Patience Woods boomed over his speakers.

"Sergeant Woods." Tempest recalled his promotions. How some of them were expected, but that others came out of the blue. Each one came with a pay rise, but it was the recognition that mattered, the advancement above his peers. However, it was only when hearing people address you differently that it really hit home that something significant had changed. So it would be too for his friend.

"Yeah, you can keep saying that. I like how it sounds. What can I do for you?"

"Quinn is up to his usual tricks with this Grimm case. They might catch the guy, but I'm not convinced and I'm not willing to wait. I'm on my way to my office. I have some things I need to look up, but more than anything I need to speak to Andrew Grimwald's mother. I don't think they will let me in without a police escort …"

"No problem," Patience cut over the top. "I wouldn't be here were it not for all the busts you and Amanda helped me to make."

"Yes, you would," Tempest shot back.

"No, I wouldn't, and we both know it. Quinn knows it too and he's going to make my life even harder now that I have three stripes on my uniform. If you need to see Mrs Grimwald, I will make it happen. Just give me an hour, okay?"

That worked perfectly for Tempest, he was halfway back to the office in Rochester and now that his brain was once again attuned to find the answers, he couldn't get there quick enough.

Slotting his car into the hole next to Amanda's, he made another call, this one to his neighbour, Mrs Comerforth. Without the ability to be certain he would get home in time to feed the dogs and let them out/take them for a walk, he wanted to know they would have their needs catered to.

Mrs Comerforth would do that and then some. In fact, the dogs were probably happier at her house than their own. Mrs Comerforth would tuck them up with a blanket, feed them biscuits, and make a constant fuss of them. They wouldn't get taken for a walk, but she had a big enough garden that they would exercise themselves. It wasn't as though they had long legs and needed to go miles.

Entering the main area of the office from the back corridor, Tempest ended the call to his neighbour with a final thank you and a promise to collect them when he got home.

Marjory was at her desk as usual – he got a cursory wave as he swept in and round to check the private offices.

There were three detectives and two offices which meant they had to share. It was rarely an issue as their work meant they were out more than half the time, but every now and then they found themselves having to juggle the space.

Tempest wanted access to what had originally been 'his' office back when it was just him and Amanda. However, Jane was in it, and she wasn't alone. She had Detective Inspector Cassie Munroe with her, the pair bent over the desk to inspect something laid out across it.

"Is that you, Temp?" Amanda called from her office, drawing Tempest to pop his head around the frame.

She was there with Darius, the broad-shouldered Australian watching her contemplatively as she made notes on one of the whiteboards.

"Everything okay?" he asked.

"Amanda's got another case," Darius announced. "One with a real *Pet Cemetary* vibe."

Amanda curled her top lip and shuddered. "Four separate reports of dead pets coming back to life. They've been terrorising people out in Cuxton and one of them is a Rottweiler dog. No one has been hurt yet, but something twisted is occurring."

"Who's the client?"

Amanda popped the lid on her pen. "The parish council. They tried the police and guess what answer they got?"

Tempest didn't have to answer.

Darius said, "Amanda has been explaining how many of your clients come here after the police dismiss their concerns."

Tempest nodded. "That's what happens when a person goes into the nick claiming to have been chased by a zombie dog."

"Or that they have a spectral train running past their house at night," said Amanda.

"That's a real case?" Darius sounded amazed.

Amanda took two paces to her right, moving a sheet of A2 paper to reveal a chart beneath it.

"This is our score sheet. It's just a bit of fun, but we chalk up the mythical or supernatural creatures we come up against. As you can see, I am yet to bag my first vampire case, but Tempest has three under his belt."

Darius squinted at the chart, a series of rows and columns with the three detectives' names at the left-hand edge.

"But you are the only one with a voodoo case," he pointed out.

"Yup," Amand grinned. "Barely survived that one. Almost got to be a human sacrifice." Pushing attention back to Tempest, she asked, "How's it going? Knocked out Quinn yet?"

"Came close," Tempest admitted. Turning serious for a moment, he said, "The Storyteller took another victim and has vanished. The ransom demand also went up."

Darius frowned. "I thought you said he wasn't after money."

Tempest shrugged. "He said he wasn't, and I'm still not convinced he is. Either way, he's gone to ground, and I want to try to figure out where. Patience is going to get me in to see his mother shortly. First, I need to figure out a few things."

Amanda volunteered, "We can help. This case," she aimed a hand at her notes on the per cemetery, "will be someone with some underfed pets. I will need to figure out why they are using them to terrorise a neighbourhood and employ someone in animal services to help catch them - I don't feel like getting bitten by a Rottweiler. It can wait though."

Tempest wasn't about to argue. Dropping his bag, he explained what he wanted to find: history of Andrew and his mother. On social media, there would be pictures and pictures might show them something. He tackled that with Amanda, asking Darius to search for any recent news articles mentioning the word 'wolf'.

Tempest very much hoped not to find the latter.

However, when the call from Patience came just a little more than an hour later, they hadn't found anything.

Patience confirmed which hospital and ward Mrs Grimwald was in and that she would meet Tempest there. In her opinion, she needed to escort him if they hoped to get past the constable outside who most likely had strict instructions not to let anyone in other than medical staff and the police.

Amanda checked the time.

"What are you going to do about dinner at your parents?"

Tempest sucked some air between his teeth. His mother would throw a royal fit if he didn't show up, but this had to take priority. He would make it up to her later, but couldn't help silently acknowledge that he was likely ducking a bullet by not going.

Hitching his bag onto his shoulder, and backing toward the door, Tempest said, "I guess I'm going to be late. Do you want to take Darius instead?"

"Hell no!"

Darius's eyebrows twitched, questioning what might have Amanda so against time in his company.

She laughed at his sideways glance. "Sorry, that's not about you. That's about Tempest's mother."

"She can be difficult?" Darius guessed.

Amanda grabbed her bag, hooked Tempest's arm, and pushed both men from the office.

"Tempest's mother expects us to get married. No, I'll correct that. She expects us to already be married and to be spitting out grandchildren. Come on, we'll all go to see Mrs Grimwald. I think Tempest could use some help on this case."

"Ah," said Darius. "Yes, my mother wants to know why I haven't got a wife and kids too. Her hints can be less than subtle at times."

They waved goodbye to Marjory, who they would not see until she returned on Monday when the office reopened, but left Jane and DI Munroe alone – they were hard at it, both on the phone interrogating someone.

Hustling to get to their cars – they would need both as neither had more than two seats – Tempest, Amanda, and Darius set off to see the wicked witch.

Edith

FRIDAY, 15TH DECEMBER 1623HRS

Medway Maritime Hospital is easy enough to get to from Rochester at the right time of day. This wasn't it. In fact, this was precisely the wrong time of day. The Medway towns might have started out as small villages along the banks of a wide river, but over the centuries, they grew outward, the inexorable onward march of the population demanding new houses be built to accommodate them.

Now those ancient villages formed one giant concrete sprawl, the arteries of which would clog several times a day as parents on school runs and workers trying to get back and forth to their jobs all congested into spaces too tight to allow movement.

"We would be better off walking," Tempest muttered to himself as they crawled into Gillingham.

They were nearly there; he would take the next turning and find clearer roads all the way to the hospital, but the turn was controlled by a set of traffic lights and he'd already watched it cycle on and off three times while gaining less than thirty feet.

Patience called to confirm he was merely stuck in traffic, not still at his office. Traffic posed less of a barrier to her journey – judicious use of her lights and sirens created gaps when she needed them. He would find her in the hospital's reception area when he arrived.

The lights changed again, and the cars surged forward. Tempest had his nose almost glued to the car in front, following it even as the lights changed to amber again. He flicked his eyes to his rear-view mirror in time to catch sight of Amanda flooring her accelerator. She flew through behind him even though the light must have switched to red by then.

At the hospital, they parked, throwing their cars into the first spots they found in the multistorey carpark.

'*We're here.*' Tempest sent a text to Patience.

'*We?*' came back almost instantly, reminding Tempest he hadn't yet told Patience he was bringing company.

Figuring she would see them in the next thirty seconds, Tempest left her to find out with her own eyes and hurried through the hospital reception, his eyes peeled for signs of her uniform.

Patience is short, so she can be lost to sight in a crowd, but she is also loud, and it was her voice that gave them direction when Tempest and Amanda heard their friend cackle.

She was chatting with a tall, black man in scrubs – a doctor by the look of things. In her hands, a large to-go cup of coffee sent steam into the air. Spotting Tempest and then Amanda, she flared her eyes their way and mouthed something lude about the man she was undoubtedly chatting up.

"Her next unwitting victim," hissed Amanda quietly so her friend would not hear. They both knew Patience well enough to know she was happy to date but had never been looking for anything more serious.

Patience, tactile as ever, gripped the doctor's arm, took out a Sharpie pen from her pocket and mumbled around the lid as she wrote her number on the back of the man's hand. When he thanked her and turned away, she smacked his rump, the 'slap' noise drawing the eyes of people dotted throughout the hospital's reception.

The doctor looked embarrassed for a moment, scratching his head as he hurried away. Patience watched him go, staring unashamedly at his backside and making appreciative noises.

"Are you going to drool?" asked Amanda.

Patience tore her eyes away from the target. "I might." Paying attention to Tempest and Amanda for the first time since they arrived, she finally noticed the tall man standing between and just behind them.

She frowned and pointed. "This guy with you?"

"This is Darius," said Tempest. "He's going to open the Blue Moon Australia office shortly."

Darius extended his hand. "Nice to meet you. Patience, is it?"

Dropping her voice to a husky tone, Patience said, "Honey, you can call me whatever you want." She followed her suggestive statement by making a snorting noise like a bull about to charge.

Darius withdrew his hand, his eyes a good deal wider than they had been.

Amanda gripped Patience by the shoulder, turning her around to face the opposite direction and giving her a polite shove to get her moving.

"Will you knock it off?"

Patience twisted her neck to look back over her shoulder.

"Can you blame me? That is one hunky lump of meat. How come you always hang out with the best-looking men?"

"He's married," Amanda lied, knowing full well Darius was single. "Got six kids. Leave him alone."

Patience pulled a grumpy face, but took a left turn, leading them to where they needed to go before Amanda could prompt her.

Mrs Grimwald was in a private ward in a private room with a police officer on guard outside.

"Hey, Chuckie," Patience called out to get his attention before the bored-looking constable noticed she was coming.

"Patience. I mean, Sarge. Sorry." Constable Chuckleton got to his feet just as Patience arrived outside Mrs Grimwald's door. "Um, what are you doing here?"

"Need to see the patient, Chuckie." She pointed at the door.

Chuckie moved to block her, using an arm to stop her getting to the handle.

"Can't let you in there, Sergeant. Chief Inspector Quinn's orders. No one in without his express permission."

Tempest felt the muscles in his jaw tighten.

Patience looped a friendly arm around Constable Chuckleton's neck and used it to steer him away from the door.

Straining their ears to hear, Tempest, Amanda, and Darius all heard something about her putting in a good word with Lori Foster.

"That's one of the girls at the nick," Amanda whispered trying to keep the guys up to speed.

They also saw when Patience removed her arm from around his shoulders and abruptly cupped Chuckie somewhere he might not wish to be, um, cupped.

Chuckie nodded his understanding in spasmodic twitches, his eyes constantly darting to his trousers and the arm of Sergeant Woods.

"Good boy." She finally let go of his goods and returned to her friends, a pleased smile on her face. "He's going to let us in."

Chuckie was leaning against the wall, doubled over a little, and looking a touch winded.

"Aren't you worried he'll talk to HR?" Amanda questioned, her voice too quiet for the words to reach poor Chuckie's ears.

Patience flashed a smile. "Not even slightly. I will have no idea what HR are talking about if he does. Besides, I'm going to set him up with Lori. Her boyfriend cheated on her last week and then dumped her when she got upset. She's looking for some revenge sex."

Her remark would have killed the conversation anyway, but she was already going through the door to Mrs Grimwald's room, and it was time to get serious.

"Remember," Tempest whispered, "This lady is a victim too."

The figure under the bedcovers was a shrivelled, skeletal form. The television was playing quietly, Mrs Grimwald's eyes open and watching and though she rolled her head to one side when her door opened, she rolled it back again, her visitors less interesting than whatever the TV was showing.

"Mrs Grimwald?" Patience spoke softly, her voice like a hug. "Mrs Grimwald, I'm Patience Woods, a sergeant with Kent police. The people with me are from the Blue Moon Investigation Agency. They are consulting for the police on this case and have some questions for you."

Tutting, the skinny woman picked up the remote from

where it lay on the bed next to her hand, and with a flick, the television went dark.

"More questions?" she muttered.

"How are you feeling, Mrs Grimwald?" Patience deflected.

Rather than answer, Mrs Grimwald twisted around to snag the controls for her bed. A whirring noise accompanied the mattress starting to move. She was sitting herself up, which Tempest took to be a good sign.

Edith Grimwald – he'd looked up her name earlier – had a hook nose with a wart on the end. It was a classic kid's cartoon prop for any would-be witch. No wonder her son cast her in that role. In her early sixties, her black hair, shot through with grey, was piled up around her head and had to be many feet long if released. Her skin was pale almost to the point of being see-through and she was missing several teeth which only added to the witchy look.

Once satisfied with her new position, Edith said, "How do I feel? I feel empty. That's how I feel. I have no one left. Nothing to live for. My husband left when Andrew was just a little boy, and he never came back. How does that reflect on me as a woman? I couldn't even satisfy my own husband. Then my child, the little boy it was my duty to raise, grows into the biggest monster you could imagine. As his obsession with the Brothers Grimm grew, so his cruelty toward me deepened. He acted as though everything was my fault. And maybe he was right. Maybe I am the reason he is so twisted inside. Maybe I am to blame for him growing up without a father figure in his life."

No one else said anything, each questioning what strategy they could employ to help the poor woman see beyond the recent terror. Yes, her son was a monster, but was she to blame for that? Perhaps, but to know such a thing would require a lot more information than they possessed.

"You have questions for me," Edith continued, her eyes fixed not on her guests, but on some distant point on the wall above their heads, "but I have no answers. He never shared his plans with me. I didn't know he was going to kidnap a little girl or murder his psychiatrist. The psychiatrist I convinced him to see and who I paid for. That poor man. So ask away, but don't expect great things from me. I told the police detectives the same thing."

Tempest exhaled slowly through his nose, trying to think how to approach the information he hoped Edith might hold in her head.

Rather than tackle it head on, he came from an angle.

"Edith when did your son start calling you the wicked witch?"

If the question surprised her, she didn't show it.

"About a year ago. Right around when he stopped seeing Dr King."

"And what was he seeing Dr King for?"

"He got fired from his job because he couldn't concentrate on it. It was his obsession with the Brothers Grimm. It started when he was younger. I don't exactly remember when, but sometime in his early teens. He came up with this daft idea that he was related to one of the Grimm brothers."

"Jacob," Tempest supplied. His phone buzzed in his pocket, the insistent vibration making him thankful it was on silent.

"That's right," Edith sighed. "He's not of course. I tried to prove it to him, tracing my family back through multiple generations, but the more I showed him, the more upset he became. In the end I just let him believe what he wanted to believe. It wasn't worth fighting over."

"Did he ever hurt you?"

Edith chuckled softly though there was no humour in her sounds. "I should say so, yes. Only recently though. Only in the last year. That was when he really started to scare me. He started talking about his vision. He had this crazy idea that he could reveal himself to the world as the direct descendant of the Grimms. He would stay in his room for days, coming out to eat and nothing else. He got crazier and crazier, started talking about bringing the stories up to date and how his modern retelling would capture the world's imagination." She paused, her eyes locked on some painful part of her past. A tear slipped out.

Tempest kept quiet. He had questions to ask and a sense of urgency to get the answers he needed, but Edith was talking, and he knew she might reveal more if permitted to just get it off her chest. His phone started buzzing again. It was the third time in a row which meant someone wanted to speak with him urgently enough to be persistent. He wanted to check who it was, but with Edith talking he didn't dare step away to answer it.

When she started up again, the tear sat on her right cheek, Edith making no move to wipe it away.

"He woke me in the night. He had a chain around my neck and he was yanking me from my bed. He forced me down into the cellar and I went hoarse shouting for someone to help me. No one ever came. He chained me to the pipes and left me there. He brought me scraps of food to stop me from starving, and he never once called me 'mother' again. I was always the wicked witch. I think he planned to kill me."

Her belief matched Tempest's though he saw nothing to

gain by confirming she was most likely right about her son's madness.

"Edith," he came to her side, "where would he go?" Tempest already knew the family owned no property to which he might have run, but the abandoned gym showed that Andrew would find somewhere to hide out. His phone stopped buzzing but started again immediately.

Edith turned her head, meeting his eyes for the first time. "I wish I could tell you something. I really do. The police asked me all these questions only a few hours ago, and I told them the same thing. I don't know anything about my son. I didn't know what he was capable of, and I have no idea where he might be."

Andrew's possible location was the only thing Tempest cared about. He was going to have to push Mrs Grimwald to deliver a better answer than 'I don't know,' but he needed to deal with the caller in his pocket first.

Without looking, he fished the device out and handed it to Amanda, his eyes imploring that she deal with it.

He turned back to Edith, but Amanda's words stopped him before he could speak.

"Tempest, it's your mother."

That his mother was calling came as no great shock. She was likely trying to confirm what time he would arrive, though that would not explain the sense of urgency to contact him she clearly felt.

However, when Amanda said, "You've got missed calls from your father and your sister too." Tempest's heart started to beat faster.

Both his parents and his sister all trying to call him at the same time. It couldn't be for anything good. With a sick feeling creeping into his gut, Tempest took the phone back, thumbed the button to answer it and stepped outside into the hallway where Constable Chuckleton was back on his chair.

"Tempest!" his mother shrieked in his ear. "Tempest, he's got them! He was here and he's taken them both! Where have you been? Why weren't you answering your phone?"

The level of heartrending panic in his mother's voice sent a shockwave of fear through his body.

"Who, mother? Who are we talking about? Who was there?"

He heard his sister's voice say, "Is it him? Is he there?" She was close by to mum, her voice distant but coming through clearly enough. However, just like with his mother, it was the emotion behind the words, not the words themselves that scared him. Tempest knew his twin sister better than he knew almost anyone else, and he had never heard such gut-wrenching fear in her voice.

When suddenly it was her in his ear and not his mother, he jolted.

"Tempest!" Rachel wailed. "He's taken Fallon and Martha! You have to get them back!" She was shouting, the panic of a mother separated from her children.

Tempest heard himself ask, "Who?" though he already knew the answer.

Rachel was sobbing, unable to speak and it was his father who answered Tempest's question.

"It was this Storyteller fellow of yours, Tempest. At least that's what we think. There was a fire at the house."

"Your house?" Tempest blurted, barely able to believe what he was hearing.

"It started outside. There were newspapers stacked around the back by the bins for recycling and they went up."

Not for one second did Tempest believe that could be an accident. It was December, the temperature hovering around a balmy five degrees Celsius. Newspapers were not known for self-combustion, and certainly not in the cold.

"We evacuated the house, and I went to fight it with Rachel. I ... I don't really know what happened, but somewhere in the confusion the kids went missing."

"Martha and Fallon," Tempest needed to hear his father say it.

"Yes, son. Whoever took them stabbed Chris."

Tempest swore under his breath.

"The ambulance is here now. He's lost a lot of blood. It's a gut wound, son."

That was all the information Tempest needed; he could fill in the rest himself. One of the body's biggest arteries runs through the soft tissue of the abdomen. Slice through it and a person will bleed out quickly.

"There was a book ..." his father began.

"Hansel and Gretel," Tempest breathed the words, stopping his father in his tracks.

"Yeah. Hansel and Gretel," dad confirmed. "How did you know that?"

There was noise in the background, shouting and arguing from his mother and his sister.

"Is the baby okay?" Tempest demanded to know, desperate to get off the phone so he could act.

"Yes. Your mother had hold of the baby when the fire started. She's still holding him now. They've just loaded Chris into the ambulance. It looks like they are going to blue light him all the way to the hospital. Your mum and sister are going with him."

Tempest could hear the mix of conflicting emotions in his father's voice. He was upset, he was scared, and he was very, very angry. Someone attacked his house, damaging it with fire and threatening the people inside. Like being burgled, his home would never feel quite as safe again, but all of that paled in comparison to the kidnapping of his grandchildren.

When Tempest's father spoke again, it was with a low growl of rage.

"Son, I want you to find this Storyteller. I want to you to find him and get my grandkids back. What you do to him after is up to you, but no one will care if he's never seen again. You got that, Tempest? I want my grandkids back."

Tempest felt weak. Adrenaline coursed through his body and his elevated heartrate needed an outlet. They needed something to do.

With a tone like steel being forged, Tempest said, "I'm on it," and ended the call.

When he shunted the door to Mrs Grimwald's room open again, everyone looked his way, Edith included. There was no mistaking the change in Tempest's attitude. He wasn't going to hurt her, goodness knows she'd been through enough, but by God he was going to get a better answer than 'I don't know'.

The Woods

FRIDAY, 15TH DECEMBER 1710HRS

Tempest held onto the cissy handle above his head and wondered if he might wrench it from the roof of the car when Patience lined up to take the next corner. Everyone claimed Patience to be a terrible driver, but he wasn't so sure that was accurate.

With her at the wheel, they had torn out of the hospital carpark on two wheels, powered through the Gillingham traffic, taken every side street and backroad imaginable and were about to enter the Medway tunnel.

Traffic would pick up again on the other side, but the lights and sirens would clear it.

Pushed to start providing answers, Edith Grimwald finally found a thought in her head. Tempest pressed her to tell him where her son felt safe. Where he might go that was away from everyone. Somewhere quiet and secluded.

Unfortunately, Edith's directions were less than accurate. She could find it herself, she claimed, but there was no way they could take the woman from her hospital bed.

They were on route to the woods north of Cobham where Mrs Grimwald promised Tempest her son used to play as a kid. They found an old cabin in the woods on a daytrip for a picnic when he was eight or nine and they'd gone back time and again, Andrew begging his mother to take him to the cottage in the woods.

It was the word 'cottage' that told Tempest this would be the place. A cottage in the woods, just like the wicked witch had in Hansel and Gretel. In the story, the kids kicked her into the oven before she could roast them for her supper, but what Andrew had planned was anyone's guess.

Amanda's car was lost from sight before they reached the tunnel. She'd kept up for some of the journey, weaving through the gaps Patience made with her squad car, but eventually she became snarled in the press of cars and fell behind.

When Patience asked if she should slow down, Tempest insisted they press on. It was fully dark already, and the taking of his nephew and niece to play the role of the famous brother and sister lost in the woods had a note of finality about it.

Andrew killed his head doctor, hacked off the hair of poor Rapunzel, and had since kidnapped four innocents, three of them children.

Patience wanted to radio for backup, to get additional units rolling, but what did they actually know? In a definite sense, the answer was a resounding nothing. Tempest was going on what his gut told him, and while that might be right more often than not, diverting police resources on what could prove to be a wild goose chase would do more bad than good.

Instead, she called Brad Hardacre, a cop she had shared a car with more often than not. He promised to be ready, and to have others standing by, ones who would drop what they were doing if she found something.

Long before they reached the old carpark where Edith said she used to leave her car before setting off into the woods, Patience killed her lights and sirens. They were close enough now that the sound might spook Andrew.

Tempest's concern that they might trigger the Storyteller into acting early or rashly was another reason not to involve a glut of cops. They had to find his place first. Maybe then, if he was there, they could call for backup, but Tempest already knew he was more than likely going to kick the door off its hinges and burst in proverbial guns blazing.

Out of the squad car, Patience and Tempest met each other's eyes over the roof.

"Do we wait for Amanda and Darius?" she asked.

Tempest gave her an apologetic expression. "I can't. But listen, you don't have to come with me." Tempest said the words though he knew they were futile.

Patience offered him a disbelieving face. "This guy is holding three kids that we know of. If he is here, I'm going to arrest him and put my foot up his backside. Probably in that order."

Wishing he'd thought to grab his combat gear from the boot of his car, Tempest looked down at his shiny leather oxford shoes. Hardly the thing for a stroll through the woods in the dark. Recent rain dictated the ground would be boggy, but he wasn't worried about his shoes, or the nice jacket and coat he had on. His only concern was about his ability to fight and how prepared Andrew might be.

"This guy is working alone, right?" Patience asked as they set off. Their route took them under the M2 motorway through a concrete tunnel. It was houses on one side and nothing but woodland on the other.

Tempest opened his mouth to respond, the word 'Yes' forming on his lips when he questioned the concept. Was Andrew working alone? Could he have pulled all this off by himself? What if he wasn't?

He thought back to the footprints he found at the abandoned gym. They were size tens just like his, but Andrew was only five feet six inches tall; would his feet be that big? They couldn't be Dr King's footprints, for even if he was alive when they walked him into the building, he'd been dead too long for the mud left by his passage to still be damp.

"Tempest?" Patience pushed him to answer.

In the dark beneath the canopy of trees, physical gestures could not be seen, so he said, "I'm not sure, but if he isn't, I don't think we are talking about a gang."

"An accomplice though?"

After a few seconds, Tempest said, "Maybe."

Patches of moonlight flickered down through the leaves, but only when small clearings occurred did they find any real change in the amount of light hitting the ground. Their eyes adjusted quickly, which allowed them to navigate between the trees, but they could not see if there were obstacles beneath their feet and both tripped multiple times.

When pushed to give as much detail as possible, Edith described the route she would take from the carpark and provided rough distances. The darkness made it hard to judge distance, so Tempest resorted to counting strides, though it was woefully inaccurate over such broken terrain.

However, the biggest question was not whether they would find the cottage in the woods, but whether Andrew was there. It felt right to Tempest – if a person was to kidnap Hansel and Gretel to re-enact a story from the Grimm's Fairy Tales, there would need to be a cottage in the woods. Likewise with Red Riding Hood and granny's house.

Unfortunately, while Tempest had considered the possibility of the wolf in that story, he'd forgotten the woodcutter.

The Gingerbread House

FRIDAY, 15TH DECEMBER 1727HRS

It felt like an age had passed with the two of them stumbling around in the dark woods when Tempest's phone bleeped with an incoming text message. He read it with one eye to preserve his night vision.

Amanda and Darius had arrived finally at the carpark and were hurrying to catch up. She asked if he'd had any luck. Tempest's reply was short and to the point, but had he waited just two minutes, his report would have been different.

Through the trees, a dim light, which Tempest first believed to be coming from the distant motorway, turned out to be something more promising.

"I can smell wood smoke," hissed Patience.

Tempest could too, and buoyed by the hope they might have found what they so desperately needed to locate, they pushed on.

His feet were soaked, the very first puddle he came to swamping his shoes with great glee and malicious vigour. His trousers were likely going straight in the trash, but he'd barely noticed such was his determination to find his sister's kids.

"How far do you think we have come?" Patience asked, her voice an almost silent whisper.

Tempest didn't know, but guessed, "Half a mile. You're going to let Brad know?"

"Yes." Patience used her radio, the volume turned down to almost nothing, to communicate their rough location. They were going to have to get closer to be able to confirm it was the right place, but equally knew they could be walking into a trap and wanted someone else to know where to come when they brought all the back-up.

Meanwhile, unable to keep his feet still, Tempest pushed onward through the trees. The smell of woodsmoke strengthened, reminding him of winter evenings in his local pub. It was an enticing scent, entirely out of place in their situation.

The dim light took form, becoming a rectangle – a window, no less, and pressing closer, the moonlight catching the wisp of smoke from the chimney became visible. A minute later the trees began to thin and the cottage took form.

Beside Tempest, Patience murmured, "You have got to be kidding me." She echoed Tempest's thoughts, for they were both looking at what could only be described as a gingerbread cottage.

"It's decorated with candy." Patience shook her head with disbelief.

Brightly coloured sweets of all shapes and sizes adorned the outer walls of the tiny, single storey cottage. Tempest guessed they were merely decoration made from wood or ceramic, but at this point his disbelief was so completely suspended nothing much was going to come as a surprise.

Having found the cottage, and there really was no question they had the right location, he sent a text to Amanda, had Patience do her best to relay directions to the cops, and started forward.

His nephew and niece were in the cottage, and he was getting them back. Leaving Patience in his wake, he surged across the open ground, closing the final fifty feet to the cottage at something close to his top running pace. There was no garden wall to negotiate, no outer fence, and the fear he held for boobytraps transpired to be baseless.

Reaching the cottage door, he slowed. With half a mind to crash straight through it, his decision not to came because it looked so solid. Hewn from trees, if it failed to yield, he would injure himself and in so doing become a victim himself. He could not afford to risk it.

Creeping around the side to peer in through the window, he caught sight of a steel cage. Its dull steel bars were thick enough that anyone inside it would never get out. It looked to be less than three feet tall, so again, if there was anyone in it, they wouldn't be able to stand up or move around.

When something moved, his heart jolted. For a moment he thought what he could see was the fur of a creature inside the cage, but when it turned slightly, Tempest saw the face of Sophie Banbridge. It was her hair he had seen, her red hood no longer covering it.

Just beyond the cage a small square table held a chopping board with an axe sticking out of it. The handle angled upward at forty-five degrees.

Risking a better angle, Tempest saw beyond the table and found a pair of legs. They were on the floor, sticking out into the room and looked to belong to an adult female.

Modern Fairy Tale

Tempest didn't know who that was, but doubted she was an accomplice.

Trying to get a better look at the woman's face, he leaned farther into the window and had to snap his head back sharply when Andrew wandered past the window mere inches from Tempest's face.

If his sister's kids were in there, he couldn't see them, but the tiny window afforded only a limited view and the interior was lit only by the glow from the open fire at one end, and some candles dotted here and there. He was in the right place, and it was time to make his presence known. He wasn't armed and Patience only had her baton and a can of incapacitant spray which wasn't ideal for use in close confines where it was as likely to get you as it was the target.

Andrew could have a shotgun easily enough. Or he might have a hunting rifle. These were both legal weapons for which he could obtain a licence. However, persons intent on criminal behaviour rarely care about such nonsense as laws, so gripping the door handle to see if it would open, Tempest accepted he might be about to die.

Patience gripped his arm, making him look at her. "Back up is coming," she hissed. "We should wait."

Tempest shook his head. "I'm going on three," he whispered, counting down three fingers.

The handle turned under his command, the door opened a crack, and Tempest threw his entire bodyweight through the widening gap.

He heard the dull thump of something very solid hitting something not quite so resilient, but by the time his ears registered the sound, his senses were already shutting down and his vision was dimming.

The Fight

FRIDAY, 15TH DECEMBER 1733HRS

Tempest's eyes fluttered open, the light hitting his pupils like drops of acid burning all the way through to his brain.

Children were crying, their terrified wails filling his head like hot knives plunging in and out of his ears. His skull threatened to split down the centre, but as Tempest forced his eyelids to open and accepted the pain, he saw how little time he had to recover.

Andrew was coming for him and he carried a knife. It was his first proper look at the man behind the misery and murder, and what he saw pleased him. Wearing clothes from a bygone era, probably ones made to reflect the early nineteenth century when the Grimm Brothers collected and published their tales, he was short and scrawny.

If asked to guess, Tempest would say his opponent weighed a hundred and twenty pounds – so light he would swat him like a fly.

The kids were yelling, their fear filling the air in the cabin with a sense of cloying anguish. From his position on the floorboards Tempest could not see them, but if they could yell then they were alive and since he was yet to see anyone other than Andrew, all he had to do was disarm one opponent to free them all.

Easy.

Except it wasn't.

Rolling back onto his shoulders, Tempest kicked his legs up and out, propelling himself off the floor in a showy manoeuvre he'd performed a thousand times at the gym. However, the blow to his head left his whole body uncoordinated and he crashed back down in a jumbled lump, his arms and legs flailing.

"Tempest."

The wheezing croak pulled his head around even as Andrew came for him. Andrew was shouting something, making threats and scaring the kids, but Tempest's head full of concussed fog struggled to decipher one sound from another and he was too shocked by the sight of Patience to do anything more than stare at her.

The tail end of a crossbow bolt poked out from her jacket below her left clavicle. Like Tempest, she was struggling to sit up and fighting against pain. Drops of her blood were on the floor where they disturbed the dust.

"Tempest," Patience wheezed again, but her eyes fluttered and closed.

"Think you're the woodcutter, do you?" Andrew shrieked. "Come to save the day?" he stepped over Tempest's uncoordinated legs and started to crouch. He had the knife in both hands, aiming to plunge it down straight into Tempest's chest. The look on his face was one of maniacal glee.

Tempest coughed, the dust from the floor getting into his lungs. He knew how to intercept the knife. He knew he could stop it from reaching his flesh and he knew for absolute certain he was strong enough and skilled enough to pummel the smaller man to a pulp.

But his brain didn't want to connect the dots.

Only at the last moment, when the knife began to swing down, did he manage to flail his arms. They collided with Andrew's, Tempest willing his body to protect itself, but even as he tensed his muscles to force the knife's trajectory to change, he knew he hadn't done enough.

Andrew had put everything into the swing, his intention to drive the tip of the blade into the floorboards on the other side of Tempest's body, but knocked off target, he sliced down into the meat at the edge of Tempest's chest.

Tempest howled in pain and rolled, taking the smaller man with him. Thrusting up with his hips and twisting, he toppled his attacker, but Andrew still held the knife and with a twist, he sent a new torrent of agony into his victim.

Holding Andrew's forearms, the two men were lying on their sides facing each other. Andrew tried to turn the knife again, tried to tear his arms free so he could stab some more, but Tempest was putting all he had into holding his attacker still and now that he was immobilised, Tempest was going to turn things in his favour.

Andrew lashed out. His arms were trapped but his legs were free to move so he kicked and kneed, throwing his whole body into every blow.

Growling his rage, Tempest lifted his uppermost leg, brought his knee to his chest, and kicked outward with all his might. Basic laws of physics commanded that the smaller, lighter object be the one to move, so Tempest stayed still and Andrew vanished backward, sliding across the floor to thump into the wall.

Suddenly there was three feet between them and Tempest could get to his feet. Upright he could fight.

Upright he could move, but rolling to get his feet beneath his body and raising his head sent waves of confusing nausea through him. The room spun like he was drunk and he staggered, staying upright only because his left hand came to rest on the table.

Using his left arm sent a fresh lance of pain through the wound to his chest and made Tempest's head swim. He needed a minute to recover, but Andrew's scream of rage announced his next attack.

Breathing heavily, and convinced he might throw up or pass out, Tempest ducked around the other side of the table. He wanted to fight, but he was in no fit state to do so. He needed a weapon, something he could use to defend himself, but as he tried to pull out a chair to parry Andrew's lunge, his feet caught on something unseen, and he spilled.

Landing heavily back on the floor, he saw what tripped him, the pair of women's legs he'd spotted through the window. They hadn't moved and he saw why: their owner was very dead.

Their owner was Verity King, Tempest realised with a sickening jolt. How she came to be dead was not immediately obvious, but was hardly of paramount importance at that time because Andrew was crowding over him and he still had hold of the knife.

The chair Tempest attempted to pick up had come to rest over his chest and was perhaps the only thing that stopped Andrew from delivering a death blow. He grabbed the chair with one hand, trying to yank it out of his way.

"I'm going to kill you, Woodcutter," he barked, laughter in his eyes.

But holding the knife meant he only had one arm for the chair and against Tempest's upper body strength he was no match.

Tempest's head still swam with concussed confusion, but with his back pressed against the floor all he needed to focus on was his limbs. He wrenched the chair from Andrew's grip and kicked out with his feet, scything through the smaller man's ankles to fell him.

Andrew fell with the knife held out and down, aiming to slice into Tempest even as he toppled. He missed only through pure luck on Tempest's part, and the force driving the knife downward jammed it into the wood.

Tempest scooted backward to get away, moving to the far end of the cottage's single room where the open fire crackled and burned. There, he finally caught sight of his nephew and niece. They were in the same cage as Sophie, crammed in with barely enough room to move. All three kids had their faces pressed between the front bars.

Behind them, a fourth figure, the inert body of a dwarf lay unmoving on the floor of the cage.

The kids' appearance was wretched – puffy eyes and blotchy faces from crying, but he could see no blood or bruising. They yelled for him to set them free, and he would do so the first moment he could. Attempting to do it now would just get him killed though.

Screaming with outrage, Andrew gave up on the knife; it was buried too deep for his feeble muscles to wrestle free. Up and on his feet, he ran across the room, back in the direction of the door where he bent down to collect something.

Tempest seized his chance. Not that he could move fast in a straight line or had full control of his body yet. Nevertheless, and by using the table for support, he abandoned his sister's kids to get the knife. He might not be able to fully coordinate his limbs, but a knife is a knife, and anyone can use one of those as Andrew had so convincingly demonstrated.

Plucking it from the floorboards with a yank, Tempest came back to upright brandishing it triumphantly. A blade would never be his weapon of choice, he much preferred to fight unarmed, but it was time for Andrew Grimwald to die, and he would feel no remorse about ending the crazy man's life.

Wavering on his feet, Tempest spotted another item that might prove useful. Did he have time to grab it before Andrew turned around?

Whether he could or not proved moot. Andrew rose to upright holding a much more convincing weapon than anything else in the cottage and the fog inside Tempest's mind lifted enough that he could see how events had panned out.

He'd burst through the door looking for Andrew, but he'd been spotted outside and Andrew was waiting. On the floor was an old steel skillet, a cast iron thing that had to weigh thirty pounds. Tempest knew it was that which knocked him unconscious, Andrew taking care of him before shooting Patience with a crossbow when she followed Tempest in.

Crossbows are a one-shot deal though, so Andrew dropped it to grab a knife, undoubtedly intending to kill Tempest and Patience both. That Tempest was still alive was nothing short of a miracle though his shirt was getting sticky from all the blood running freely from the knife wound to his left pectoral and his vision still wavered from the blow to his head.

"Drop it!" Andrew commanded, holding the crossbow steady though his breathing was ragged. It was reloaded and there was no chance he could miss at such close range.

For a second, Tempest considered throwing the knife. It wasn't a skill he'd practiced much, but again he was so close, how could he miss? Ultimately, he knew he would never get to release his throw if he tried. All Andrew had to do was squeeze his right index finger.

Fallon and Martha cried for him to keep fighting, Sophie added her voice too, the three kids wanting to be set free from the maniac who held them. They all wailed when Tempest let the knife slide between his fingers. It clattered to the floor and stayed there.

"Now back up," Andrew stalked forward, forcing Tempest back. They were heading into the open space beyond the table where the three children were tied up.

Tempest watched Andrew's hands and eyes, looking for any sign he might pull the trigger. If he could move, if he could make it so that the bolt hit him somewhere that wouldn't instantly kill him, the weapon would be useless again and he might stand a chance. Overpowering the smaller man wouldn't take him long and it was starting to feel like it would be the last thing he ever did.

Tempest wasn't exactly enthralled by the idea, but if it was a case of exchanging his life for the three kids' he would do it.

"Why did you kill Mrs King?" Tempest asked, trying to buy a few more seconds.

Andrew's eyebrows rippled with question and the crossbow twitched.

"You don't get to ask questions, Woodcutter. You were never supposed to be part of this story."

"This isn't a story," Tempest laughed. His head hurt like there were a thousand pixies inside it with drills, but the dizziness and nausea were passing, and he felt okay to be upright. The ability to think straight meant he could rationalise a strategy and his was to provoke the maniac with the crossbow. He wanted to be able to predict when Andrew would fire.

Andrew lived for the story he was trying to show the world – his masterpiece. Nothing else mattered to him and that made him vulnerable.

"This is the greatest story the world has ever seen!" Andrew screamed.

"You're an angry child with no father searching for some meaning in your pathetic life," Tempest shot back, smiling at the killer the whole while. "This story of yours is nothing but a confusing collection of ideas that make no sense. What part did Rapunzel play? Huh? What was the frog king all about?"

"You'll see," Andrew yelled. "Everyone will see. The ending will be magnificent."

"The ending?" Tempest questioned derisively. "You think there is going to be an ending? In a few moments I am going to kill you, that's the only way this shambles of a fairy tale ends." He held his hands to either side of his body, showing how empty they were, but keeping them ready to react.

Andrew sneered, "Oh, yeah?" he brandished the crossbow again aiming it in Tempest's face. "I'm the only one with a weapon, Woodcutter. How do you propose to kill me?"

Tempest made a big show of shrugging. "Oh, I figure since I am the woodcutter, I would use that axe you left on the table for me."

Doubt clouded Andrew's face and he twitched his eyes across to check the chopping board.

It was empty.

From behind his back where he'd tucked the axe head

into his belt and endured the pain of it biting into his flesh for the last minute, Tempest grabbed it and swung.

His right arm came over his shoulder, travelling in a wide arc that picked up speed as it went.

From the corner of his eye Andrew saw what Tempest was doing. He pulled the tigger to release the bolt but did so just as the axe smashed down through the crossbow's wooden frame.

The bolt flew past Tempest's right hip, slamming into the wall a yard behind his body, but the axe was still moving. It smashed a path through the crossbow, taking three of Andrew's fingers with it.

The Storyteller screamed in pain, dropping the weapon to stare at his stumps.

Tempest's wild swing pulled him off balance, but only for a second. Putting his left arm down to correct his motion and reverse it, he planned to swing the axe back up and into the Storyteller's body, ending his reign of terror once and for all.

But Andrew bolted, holding his bleeding hand high as he started to move. His face was pulled into a rictus of pain and horror unable to comprehend his current situation. Not looking where he was going, he failed to see Sophie stick out her leg.

He tripped and stumbled, his arms cartwheeling. Unable to correct himself he fell headfirst into the fireplace.

His screams trebled in volume and his victims had to watch as the now burning form ran from the house with his hair and clothes aflame. He vanished into the darkness outside, his high-pitched howls departing with him.

Aftermath

FRIDAY, 15TH DECEMBER 1815HRS

Tempest didn't know which way to go. Patience was dead for all he knew, the children were all traumatised and begging him to set them free, and the law of cliché's enforced the idea that Andrew would run back through the door to get his revenge if Tempest dared to assume they'd seen the last of him.

His left side was a ball of pain where the knife carved a path through his pectoral muscle. He wouldn't be doing any bench pressing for a while. His head continued to clang like a bell from the blow he got running through the door, but it was all secondary to the sense of relief, bordering on joy, he felt.

It was over.

Making his way to the cage, he lowered himself gingerly to the floor to inspect the lock. Fallon, Martha, and Sophie were all right at the front, their tear-streaked faces a little calmer now their kidnapper was dead or dying.

Martha intertwined her fingers with Tempest's through the bars of the cage.

"Are you all right, Uncle Tempest?" she asked.

"You are bleeding," Fallon pointed out.

Tempest reached through the bars to pat them both on their shoulders with blood-soaked fingers before shifting his gaze to take in Sophie.

"That was a very brave thing you did, sticking your leg out to trip him."

"I hope he is dead," Sophie replied flatly.

"Any idea where the key is?" Tempest lifted the hefty padlock holding the cage shut.

"It's in his pocket," said Sophie. "I saw him put it in there."

Tempest looked at the door. It hung open letting the cold night air creep in and the warmth from the open fire spill out. Closing it would improve things immediately; the kids were shivering inside their tiny cage, but he needed to go outside first.

When he tried to get up, the kids grabbed for his arms.

"Don't leave us," Martha begged, her tone desperate.

"Don't leave us, Uncle Tempest," Fallon echoed.

Sophie said nothing. The older girl was in the back corner of the cage now, curled in on herself where she hugged her knees next to Tom Thumb.

Tempest watched for long enough to confirm the dwarf's chest was rising and falling and tried a reassuring expression.

"I'll be right back kids. I need to find the key if I can." Despite his promises, he had to gently tug his arms free and reassure them all again that he would be right back.

Andrew could not have gotten far; that's what Tempest told himself, but before he went to search for the Storyteller's smouldering remains, he peered around the table at Patience.

Modern Fairy Tale

Convinced he was going to find her eyes open and staring lifelessly at the ceiling, he instead discovered she was distinctly less dead than he thought.

"Patience!" he rushed to her side.

"Sorry," she mumbled, "I think I passed out there for a while. Are you okay? You look terrible?"

"I'm going into shock," Tempest admitted, his voice quiet so the kids wouldn't hear. "You called this in, right? People are coming?"

Patience nodded. "Can you help me to sit up? This thing," she dipped her head toward the tail end of the crossbow bolt sticking out of her chest, "is making things difficult."

Tempest hooked a chair from the table, and together they got her up and into it. There, she took out her radio, waved to the kids and said, "I have friends coming. Don't you worry about anything."

Leaving her to communicate with the back-up, Tempest fought against the growing sensation of disconnectedness his brain felt with the rest of his body. Shock from blood loss and pain was setting in and he needed to lie down if he was to fight it.

First the key though and for once the task was easier than expected.

Andrew had gone about thirty yards before he ran out of ... um, steam. His charred remains were face down in the leaf litter and mud beneath the trees and easy to spot from the smoke still rising off his smouldering clothes.

The key was indeed in Andrew's pocket; the front left one of his breeches since they were too strangely designed to be called trousers.

He checked for a pulse, found none, but angled a quick kick at Andrew's ribs just to be sure. Key in hand, feeling dizzy and disoriented, but jubilant all the same, Tempest staggered back to the cottage.

By the time the first police officers arrived twenty minutes later, Tempest had a hot cup of sweet tea in his body and was feeling better. Amanda and Darius appeared ten minutes earlier, trekking cross country through the same woods to find him, Patience, and the kids.

Mrs King had a blanket over her, so the kids didn't have to see, and Amanda judged that she had been strangled, estimating the time of death as much as twenty-fours ago given that rigour mortis was already leaving her body.

Quite why Andrew might have chosen her and whether she was supposed to be the stand-in wicked witch they had no idea.

Darius inspected Tempest's wounds, playing down how bad the wound to his chest was though he didn't fool Tempest.

"Is it always like this?" he asked. "You know, just so I understand what I am getting into."

Amanda reached out to take Tempest's hand and answered for him.

"No, this was a bad one. Usually, we find the bad guy and he surrenders. Or we find the bad guy and we let Big Ben slap him around for a bit. Then they surrender."

Tempest sniggered, "Or, if it's a bad 'girl' we send Big Ben in and wait for her to repent of her sins and give thanks to Jesus."

It was a moment of light heartedness in a dark environment.

The cottage was more than half a mile from the nearest road which made getting in and out difficult but far from impossible. Paramedics came along with the police, checking the kids over first at the insistence of both Patience and Tempest. Thankfully, there were enough ambulance crews to go around, and the kids were completely unharmed.

Unable to fight the demand that he stay on the stretcher, Tempest allowed himself to be carried back through the woods, under the motorway through the concrete tunnel and out under the streetlights on the other side.

That was as close as the ambulances could get, and there he found Chief Inspector Quinn. He was just arriving, late to the party as he was off duty and at home when the calls came in.

He wanted to see the cottage for himself, of course, but stopped next to Tempest so the press, who were also just arriving, could photograph him with the hero of the hour.

"Well done, Mr Michaels," he grabbed Tempest's right hand and smiled for the camera.

Tempest didn't have the energy to shove him away, but Amanda did it for him, taking Quinn's arm and using it to twist him away. While the paramedics loaded Tempest into the ambulance, she glared.

"Swooping in to grab the glory, Ian? I don't think so."

"It's okay," Tempest called from the back of the ambulance. They were hooking him up and making sure the stretcher wouldn't move in transit. "Ian was leading this case from the start. I'm just a consultant and it's not like I'm in any shape to give a press conference, is it?"

"Tempest, you solved the whole thing," Amanda protested. "You have been leading Quinn from the start, not the other way around."

"Have I?" Tempest questioned, making Amanda worry he might be slipping into delirium. "I'm not so sure." Lifting his head from the stretcher for a moment, he caught his girlfriend's eye and gave a quick wink. Lying it down again before Quinn could spot the exchange, he asked, "Was the ransom paid?"

Quinn fielded the question but faced the camera when he did it. "No. The Lord Mayor of Kent was under extreme pressure to succumb to the kidnappers demands; we are talking about child hostages not adults, but through determined police work, aided," he added quickly because Tempest was right in the shot, "by a civilian consultant, we have been able to end this situation. Unfortunately, the man behind the crimes ..."

Quinn's voice droned on in the background, talking to the press the way he always did, but Tempest tuned it out.

"I'll follow you to the hospital," Amanda promised, delivering a gentle kiss to Tempest's lips.

"We need to get going," the paramedic tending him warned.

"Go with my nephew and niece," Tempest countered. "Get them back to their mother. Then go home and get some rest. I just need a few stitches and some sleep. There's nothing to gain by spending the night next to my bed."

The ambulance doors closed and Amanda watched it pull away. The call to Tempest's sister had gone in more than half an hour ago, so she knew her kids were alive and well. She was at the hospital though with her husband, her parents, and the baby, waiting to hear if he would survive his wounds and both Martha and Fallon were already on route to her location.

Going home held many merits, not least of which were the possibility of alcohol and a hot bath.

But the wink. She needed to know what the wink meant.

Dead and Buried

SUNDAY, 17TH DECEMBER 1103HRS

Throughout the whole case, Tempest had been plagued by doubt. Right at the very start there were inconsistencies. The books that Andrew left at each scene came from a boxed set they found in his house when the police raided it. It was Edith's from when she was young. Little Red Riding Hood, Hansel and Gretel, Tom Thumb, and Rapunzel were all missing from it, yet the Frog King story was still there; he didn't leave it at Dr King's house.

Why not?

He left behind no physical evidence of breaking in to snatch Dr King in the night and his wife awoke to discover the frog in her bed. How soundly did the woman sleep to have not noticed any of that happening?

When Tempest quizzed Andrew about money, he scoffed at the concept and Tempest believed him. Andrew wasn't interested in money. Not even slightly. Yet there was a ransom to be paid if the hostages were to be released and it was clear to Tempest that Andrew never had any intention of setting them free.

He'd blundered forward, following his nose from clue to clue, tracking down the person behind it, but the questions persisted.

However, it was when he found the footprint that the concept of an accomplice first began to take form. Whoever put Dr King's body in the abandoned gym left behind a size ten footprint. Now, a person can put on oversize shoes or force their feet into smaller ones, but Tempest considered that an unlikely scenario.

More likely, he thought, someone who was not Andrew Grimwald placed Dr King's body where they found it. His thoughts went a stage further though because Andrew didn't seem to know anything about the Frog King, the Golden Goose, or Dr King's murder. More suspicious yet, when Tempest asked him why he killed Verity King, he didn't appear to know who she was either.

Patched up and released (at his insistence) by noon on Saturday, Tempest had been in contact with Amanda ever since she found him in the hospital on Friday night.

You see, the case wasn't over.

At a press conference on Friday night, in front of dozens of reporters, the chief constable, aided by information provided by Chief Inspector Quinn, wrapped up the case with a neat bow. It was all over according to the police. Andrew Grimwald, a particularly disturbed individual, had murdered his psychiatrist and then gone on a crazed campaign to re-enact scenes from the Grimm's Fairy Tales.

In his house they found papers tracing his ancestry all the way back to Jacob Grimm. They were forgeries. Andrew's fixation on becoming famous led him to kidnap children and attack adults, but he had very definitely worked alone. Buy who supplied the forgeries? Who would Andrew have talked to about his fantasies? Who might he have told about the cottage in the woods? An answer itched away inside Tempest's head and that drove him to continue investigating even from his hospital bed when the doctors and nurses thought he should be sleeping.

The chief constable gave thanks to Tempest Michaels, naming both him and the Blue Moon Investigation Agency for their part in the successful rescue of the hostages. Tempest had since received many, many requests for interviews, all of which he'd ducked.

For one very simple reason: he was still trying to catch the person behind it all.

He let Quinn hog the glory and the limelight, happy to know he was digging himself a deeper and deeper hole with every wrong claim he made.

Andrew had tiny feet - a size four, Tempest discovered. Certainly no match for the size ten he found at the gym. Andrew hadn't killed Dr King. He hadn't broken into his psychiatrist's house late at night, hadn't cut off his finger, and it wasn't by his hand that the bloody message came to be scrawled on Mrs King's mirror. But it was Dr King's finger they found, so who cut it off?

Tempest revealed his beliefs to Amanda when she joined him at the hospital. Unable to leave his bed, he'd sent her to find his family. Sick with worry that his sister's husband might have been killed, Tempest distracted himself by using his phone to conduct yet more research.

He unearthed several key truths very quickly, but it's always easier to find information when you know what to look for.

When Amanda returned, she came with Tempest's whole family. Chris was going to be okay but was in poor shape and had lost a lot of blood.

"This is your fault," Rachel accused, her voice quiet and tearful.

"That's not fair, love," their father argued. "Tempest couldn't have known any of this would happen. He almost died getting the kids back."

Rachel turned away, unable or unwilling to look at her brother when she said, "Would it have happened if he didn't chase criminals for a living?"

Tempest's mother went after her, shepherding the kids which just left Amanda and Tempest's father by his bed.

"You should go, Dad," Tempest insisted. "I'm fine. They are not."

His father argued, but not for long and not very hard. Tempest was right, Rachel did need him more than Tempest.

With the room quiet again, Tempest showed Amanda what he had found and convinced her to take the baton to finish what he could no longer continue. The danger, he insisted, was that they might slip through his fingers if she didn't watch very closely.

He refused to say who 'they' were though despite threats of violence and withholding of sex.

So Amanda followed his instructions, staking out the person he said she needed to watch. She swapped with Jane, and Jane swapped with Darius, each taking a turn staking out the house of a person Tempest hadn't named though they knew not why.

When Tempest left the hospital, he took a taxi directly to the stakeout location, fighting with Darius to take a turn, though in the end they compromised and both stayed.

Darius confirmed the target was in the house and had not left since they began the stakeout the previous evening.

When she did leave, they followed her in Amanda's

Lotus, tailing all the way to West Malling where they watched her collect some dry cleaning. They tailed her back again and waited all night down the street from her house, Tempest insisting he would allow Amanda to relieve him on Sunday, though by then, he knew he would be questioning the accuracy of his deductions.

When finally the target left her house again, she did so carrying a large suitcase and a smaller one – what one might call carry-on size. It happened just after seven o'clock on Sunday morning, mere minutes after Amanda arrived with Jane to question if her boyfriend had lost his marbles.

Smiling wryly, Tempest suggested they might all like to go for a drive.

There was little question where she was going, Mrs Frobisher and her luggage were packed into a silver BMW marked with 'Gatwick Shuttle' livery on each side. It dropped her at the South Terminal, Tempest and Amanda bailing out a few cars back from her taxi to leave Darius and Jane looking for parking spaces in the short-term carpark.

Her arm looped through his, Amanda walked alongside Tempest, following Dr King's former assistant through the terminal. They watched her drop her bags, checked where she was going, and quickly bought two tickets on an EasyJet hop to Amsterdam – the cheapest the chap at the 'last minute' desk could offer them.

Jane phoned as they were going through security into the departure lounge.

"Just wait by the entrance. Someone else is coming to join us," Tempest advised. Then, after explaining about the need to buy tickets and which would be the cheapest, he put his phone away and smiled at his girlfriend. The ring was in his pocket but now was not the time.

"What are you up to, Mr Michaels?" Amanda studied

Tempest's face, looking for clues. "Who's coming to join us? Why did we just follow that woman here?"

"These are all very good questions, my dear. Would you care for a glass of champagne?"

Amanda jinked an eyebrow, wondering if he was being serious. Seeing that he was, she said, "Sure. Why not?"

Tempest considered that there were a lot of good reasons why a person ought not to imbibe champagne before noon on a Sunday, but having seen Mrs Frobisher enter the Champagne and Oyster bar in the heart of Gatwick's South Terminal, it felt like a perfect cover.

Tempest slipped the waiter a twenty and asked for the table in the corner. It was away from Mrs Frobisher and at an angle. Sitting there they would be able to watch her the whole time.

Sipping her champagne, Amanda placed her glass back on the table and fixed Tempest with a bemused expression.

"I won't say I'm not a fan of your need to act cryptically sometimes, but this is really stretching things. Please tell me why we staked out that woman for thirty-six hours and then followed her to Gatwick."

Tempest flicked his eyes in the direction of Mrs Frobisher's table. "Wait for it. Here comes our mystery guest right now."

Amanda twisted in her chair for a better look, a frown forming almost immediately.

"Wait. Isn't that …"

Tempest nodded. "I do believe it is."

"But …"

"Ah," Tempest interrupted, picking up his drink, "this is where it all gets a little complicated. Have a look at his right hand."

Amanda did so. It was bandaged heavily around the index finger which was quite clearly missing.

"He cut it off himself," Tempest shared what he believed.

Mrs Frobisher rose to greet Dr Mortimer King as he came to her table, the two embracing and kissing as lovers, not friends.

Seeing it for herself, Amanda added up the clues fast. "He faked his own death." A frown gripped her brow the moment the accusation left her lips. "But you said his wife identified his body. Why would she do that if he is having an affair and leaving her for this woman?"

"Because she had no idea." Tempest sipped the champagne and placed his glass back down on the table. "Verity King wanted more from her life and her husband convinced her that he had a way to provide it. You see, he had this one patient who possessed a very unique obsession. Andrew Grimwald believed himself to be descended from the Brothers Grimm and he wanted to be famous like them."

"But Andrew stopped seeing Dr King a year ago."

"Stopped seeing him professionally as a patient. I believe they continued to meet in secret. Dr King primed Andrew Grimwald. I imagine he paid for the makeover the cottage received and helped him find the abandoned gym."

"Where they found Dr King's body," Amanda pointed out, still confused.

Tempest shook his head. "Mrs Frobisher's husband's body. He is roughly the same size and shape as Dr King. I found pictures of him online and the two men look nothing alike, but that explains the wounds to the face of the body we found. Mrs King was under instruction from her husband to claim it was him and once she did so her usefulness expired. I believe Dr King strangled her himself, and delivered her body to Andrew Grimwald at the cottage as a substitute for his mother in the role of the wicked witch."

"What would he have done if the police hadn't raided the house and rescued Andrew's mother?"

Tempest shrugged. "Find another way to dispose of her, I guess. We can ask him, but I'm fairly sure he will lie. He lured his wife into the plan with the promise of millions in ransom money and a patsy to take the fall. When I started to question how Verity could have slept through her husband being replaced by a frog, I concluded she could not have. That left me questioning why she would lie about it. She also lied about her sister coming to stay; her way of getting the cops to leave her alone so she wouldn't have to keep faking her grief."

"Dr King placed Mr Frobisher's body in the abandoned gym for us to find. He couldn't have known we were going to get there so soon, but perhaps he had a plan to tip off the cops himself. Whatever he had planned, he made sure Andrew used the place and left his fingerprints behind. All he needed then was for the police to find his body and make the connection to Andrew."

"But you said there was nothing to connect Andrew to the abandoned gym."

"There wasn't, but I think that is just an example of Dr King's wisdom. He didn't want to make it too obvious. Had he done so even Quinn might have smelled a rat. Instead, he positioned his pieces and waited for checkmate. We beat him to it, hence the two-day delay between closing the case and the pair of them fleeing the country."

Amanda studied the couple with outrage bubbling just beneath the surface. It was all so cold blooded.

Maybe Tempest had some elements of it wrong, but she judged that his version of how the crime played out would

Modern Fairy Tale

be close enough to the truth for the differences not to matter.

They finished their champagne and waited for Dr King and Mrs Frobisher to pay their bill and leave. They walked hand in hand, their hips bumping each other's amorously. They smiled a lot.

Until airport security asked them to come to one side at their gate. They looked a little taken aback, and observing from ten yards back, Tempest lipread Dr King asking if there was a problem.

Airport security officers were going to take them away, responding to a tip they received just a short while earlier. They had instructions to secure the couple and await the arrival of a police officer from Kent.

Dr King would have a fake passport and undoubtedly believed that he was on the first step to a new life in a new country with a new woman. If Tempest was going to introduce himself and say anything, now was the time.

Instead, he turned to the friends who had joined him and Amanda when they left the Champagne and Oyster bar. Jane and Darius were either side of the third person who wore her left arm in a sling.

"Ready?" Tempest asked.

Sergeant Patience Woods grinned a big grin.

"You betcha."

Epilogue

THE WIZARD

Sunday, 17th December 1447hrs

Diane Meacock was blissfully unaware that she was about to die. Walking through a suburb of Luton not far from her house, she had every reason to feel happy and confident. Her company had just closed a big deal that she had been working on for more than a year. The bonus she was set to receive would pay for the new sports car she wanted, not that she really needed it, but what's the point of earning such enormous figures if you cannot buy things you don't need? It would also pay for the family holiday in Aruba she had planned as a surprise.

She walked right by her killer without noticing his presence.

Had she seen the cloaked figure lurking in a side alley she might have given him a second glance simply for his unusual appearance, and she might then have hurried upon her way.

Modern Fairy Tale

As it was, her head was too full of optional extras for her new sports car to notice much of anything.

The shadowy figure stepped out into the street, glaring at Diane's back as she walked away. Anger boiled on his face, his jaw muscles so tense his teeth threatened to crack. Adrenaline made his pulse skyrocket, but he knew well enough to anticipate it; this wasn't his first kill.

"Diane Meacock!" he bellowed her name into the cold, crisp afternoon air.

The woman was thirty feet away, her back to him, but she twitched in surprise as he knew she would, and spun around to face the direction from which the shout came.

Her face wasn't sure what to do. He'd made her jump, but there was no immediate reason for her to feel fear. If anything, her features were set to quizzical, questioning who it might be that had called her name.

Until she saw him, that is.

Clad in black with a cloak that fell to the floor, he knew how imposing he looked. Tall and broad across the shoulders, his face was hidden within the hood of his cloak. It hung down across his eyes so only the lower half of his features could be seen. This was intimidating enough, but Diane's brain barely registered this clothing or size because her eyes were focused on the bolts of lightning crackling off his fingertips.

He watched her jaw drop, her mouth opening in stark horror. That he meant her no good was apparent from his stance, but the combination of his appearance, knowing her name when she had no clue as to his identity, and the unexplainable magic he chose to wield in broad daylight made the message quite unambiguous.

Thoughts of leather stitching colour options forgotten, Diane turned and ran. She was on her way to collect her thirteen-year-old daughter from a friend's house. It was easy walking distance, and her doctor continued to insist she needed more exercise. Now she wished she had driven.

Compelled by fear to flee, Diane didn't see the cloaked figure when he began to move his hands.

There were very few others in the street to witness his actions, but passing traffic caught sight of his swirling arms. The lightning from his hands changed, coalescing into an orb which roiled and rolled between his fingers.

He watched, waiting for Diane to reach the spot he'd selected, and when she did, he unleashed the orb, thrusting his hands out and then apart so the swirling orange light dissipated into the air as if absorbed by it.

The effect it had was not immediately obvious, especially if one chose to watch him and not Diane.

However, from a building site on the opposite side of the street, a stack of iron bars shot from where they rested. Six feet in length, half an inch in diameter, and rusty from the rain, they flew out of the concrete pipe where someone had chosen to set them.

Diane, overweight, wearing impractical shoes, and running slow though her speed was the fastest she'd moved in years, chose to check over her shoulder to see if the man in the cloak was pursuing or not. Consequently, she didn't see the iron bars move, seemingly of their own accord, and only caught sight of them when she swung her head back to around to look where she was going.

By then it was far too late to duck, dive, or dodge the deadly barrage.

More than half the iron bars missed her, passing harmlessly through the air to crash into the wall on the other side of the street. Most bounced off, clattering noisily to the ground though two stuck fast, the tips hitting the ancient mortar instead of the brick.

Diane didn't notice the bars reverberating in the wall to her right because while many of them missed, four did not.

The cloaked figure watched, his jaw still clenched, when his victim's body was flung six feet through the air. Impaled on multiple steel rods, each of which hit her chest or abdomen, he knew she was doomed. There would be no saving her, but she was the catalyst of her own fate. Had she acted differently, there would have been no reason to end her life.

Crumpled awkwardly on the pavement, Diane's limbs flopped or twitched as she breathed her last.

He watched, stalking toward her broken form and savouring the kill though he knew delaying his departure to be foolhardy. Crouching, he checked her absent pulse and nodding to himself withdrew a small white business card from inside his cloak.

He tucked it into the right breast pocket of Diane's coat, making sure to leave it partially visible. It was no good if no one found it.

Walking away, his step unhurried, he pushed all thoughts of Diane Meacock from his mind. There were other targets on his list, more people he needed to kill.

Soon the world would know his name and they would never forget it. They wouldn't catch him, he was too powerful for that, and the name would tell them nothing for it was not registered anywhere.

Smiling to himself, Zephyrus Frostwind turned the corner and vanished from sight.

Next in the Blue Moon Investigations Series

vinci-books.com/no-magic

How do you fight a wizard? You don't. You die.

The city of Rochester is in the grip of fear, a terrifying wizard killing at random just for the fun of it. But is he? Or do the victims have something very specific in common? They each received a business card before they met their ends, and Tempest Michaels soon discovers the dead are not the only ones to have been contacted. He has clients lining up, all of them convinced they could be next.

Turn the page for a free preview…

No Such Thing as Magic: Chapter One

THE VAULT, ROCHESTER

Tuesday, January 2nd 2017hrs

No one noticed the man in the black cloak. He knew they wouldn't. In many ways getting ignored by those around him was a skill, though it took him a long time to see it that way. Throughout his youth, not being seen was a curse. Until he embraced it.

The bottom edge of the cloak touched the floor, and its hood came up and over his head, covering not only his hair but also the top half of his face. The features still exposed were hidden in shadow, so anyone looking would only see the bushy black beard that covered his chin, and his mouth, which he'd set into a firm scowl.

Why would he show the world anything else?

The bar was crowded, just as he knew it would be. It was Rochester High Street on a Friday night, and *The Vault* was one of the most popular places to be. Not that he cared about being part of 'the scene'. No, he was there only to deliver a message.

Modern Fairy Tale

A rather final message, one might say. So far as the message's recipient was concerned, anyway.

Passing through the press of people he got a few glances. He always did. The cloak saw to that. He looked different to everyone else, but that was okay because he was different. At school they called him weird, the older kids and his classmates alike all picking on him. Even the girls.

Except one. Except Elaine.

Striding through the bar, his muscular form and height eased his passage for most people moved out of his way. Nevertheless, the crowd slowed his pace and filled the gap he left in his wake.

A man made a comment, laughing with his mates about the weirdo in the hood, but Zephyrus Frostwind, the name he'd given to this side of his personality, ignored the jibes. Their smiles would be gone soon enough.

His target was here. He knew the man's patterns and habits, but to be sure, had followed him this evening. Attacking him in public and surrounded by witnesses might seem rash or foolhardy, but what he planned required an audience. Unlike the two previous lessons, this one would be seen, and people would learn.

Specifically, they would learn to fear.

Word would spread fast, and soon it would be impossible to walk into a crowded place without being recognised. Tonight, though, tonight the drunken fools had no clue of the danger passing through their midst.

Lifting his head slightly to peer under the lip of his cowl, he searched the crowd, rotating slowly on the spot until he found the person he sought.

Gill Carlson had his back to the room, his eyes focused on the bartender a few feet away. Waiting to be served, he'd been trying to attract the man's attention for more than a minute. The bartender was far too busy serving a trio of pretty, flirty girls in low-cut tops.

Lifting his arms up and out with a flourish that sent his black cloak billowing, he wove patterns in the air at chest height. Purple sparks flashed into existence, trailing where his fingers led and swirling through the air.

Eyes flared and those who spotted the display nudged their friends. Fingers pointed and murmurs replaced the background din of conversation, loud as it was to be heard above the thumping bass from the DJ booth. Unworried, the onlookers assumed they were seeing some kind of show put on by the bar's management.

Despite the music, a hush fell, and the cloaked figure drew a deep breath to fill his lungs.

"Gill Carlson!" he bellowed, the glowing sparkles between his hands coalescing into an orb of light.

Gill twisted his body, surprised to hear his name called out loud. He was one of very few not already looking at the magic being conjured in the centre of the crowded bar. No one was trying to walk past the figure in the black cloak anymore and those nearest had moved away, distancing themselves from the strange display.

Suddenly alone at the bar as the punters to Gill's left and right chose to be somewhere else, he froze. Gill couldn't see the eyes of the man inside the hooded cloak, nor could he guess his identity or understand how he knew his name, but when it finally occurred to him that now might be a good time to run away, he dismissed the notion – one of the bar's bouncers was coming.

Coming from behind, the man with the security badge was tall, muscular, and confident in his ability to deal with anyone not carrying a firearm. Knives could be a problem, but he'd trained to disarm anyone stupid enough to sneak one onto the premises.

Gill watched, opting to lean back against the bar with a confident smile on his face. When this was over, people would want to ask him what it was all about. His mind raced, trying to think of something cool to say.

The trio of flirty girls looked to be unattached; he would target them first.

However, watching the bouncer approach from the rear - what had to be the cloaked man's blindside – Gill's smile faltered.

"That's enough," the bouncer reached out with one meaty hand. "Time for you to be leaving." But when his fingers came close to the cloaked man's shoulder, a spark flew. It jumped through the air, bridging the gap to his outstretched hand with an audible snap. The bouncer collapsed as though someone had flipped his 'off' switch.

The man in the cloak never even turned his head.

"Gill Carlson," Zephyrus repeated his victim's name, this time in a low growl. "It is time for you to pay the price."

Gill's right eyebrow launched itself skyward, a question forming on his lips that he would never get to ask.

The wizard flung his arms in Gill's direction, launching the swirling orb of purple light across the bar.

It flew five yards, striking Gill in the chest, but not with any kinetic force that might have knocked him backward. Instead, it appeared to light him up from within. Purple light shone from inside Gill's open mouth while his whole body tensed.

The bar erupted into chaos. Screams and cries accompanied the patrons, most of whom were stampeding toward the exit. They had to take the long route to get around the man in the cloak, his very presence pinning some into the corner behind him where they were too afraid to move lest they get in his way.

Gill's body contorted, spasming on the spot, his arms outstretched on either side until Zephyrus abruptly ended the spell. The man in the cloak dropped his arms to his sides, watching his victim.

Gill sagged, hung limply in the air for a heartbeat, then collapsed inward upon himself. Falling to the spill-strewn floor like a rag doll, he came to rest where he had stood. Only then did the wizard turn away.

Terrified people were still trying to evacuate the bar, pushing, shoving, and elbowing to get any advantage as they surged as one for the bar's main exit. Wisely, a few had gone out the back, opening the fire doors to escape, but most were still trapped when the man in the cloak began to stalk toward them.

Bouncers from the front door, there to prevent unwanted or unsavoury looking people from entering, had to fight against the crowd to get back inside the bar. The owner employed them to ensure The Vault was the top spot in Rochester High Street. They hadn't had an incident worth mentioning in over a year.

The attack was over and there was nothing they could do to fix that, but they were determined to stop the cloaked man before he could leave. They would hold him until the police came and at least the owner would know they had done all they could. Questions about how he got inside would need to be answered, but that was for later.

Approaching the cloaked man cautiously, the bouncers carried no weapons. Union rules prevented such things, but there were five of them and each knew their stuff.

"It will go easier if you surrender," snarled the nearest, genuinely hoping the fool in the cloak chose to resist so they could pummel him. There were still some patrons trapped in the bar and most of them were filming. They needed to be sure their use of force could be considered acceptable and measured, but that left plenty of room for a few broken bones.

Zephyrus raised his arms once more, pleased for the chance to demonstrate his power.

The bouncers formed a semicircle, pinning him in the middle. Or so they thought.

Flicking his sleeves to better expose his hands, the wizard shouted, "Incindair!" and thrust his arms outward at forty-five degrees to his body. Gouts of flame shot from each palm, lighting the room with such intensity that anyone looking had to turn away.

The fire struck two of the bouncers, igniting their clothes instantly. If further motivation to clear the bar was needed, their screams provided it.

The remaining bouncers dived for cover, terrified they could be next.

His path clear, Zephyrus strode in an unhurried manner to the bar's open doors. One was hanging off. Pausing just inside, he reached inside his cloak, fumbling briefly until he found what he was looking for. Returning to the bar, he found an area devoid of liquid and placed a small white card on the surface. There was nothing on it but a name: Zephyrus Frostwind.

Sirens wailed in the distance, the police responding at speed. They were far too late to save Gill Carlson though. And by the time they arrived, the wizard would be long gone.

No Such Thing as Magic: Chapter Two

TENTACLES (I HOPE)

Tuesday January 2nd 2031hrs

Two hundred yards from *The Vault*, Tempest Michaels heard the sirens and turned his head. Were they coming his way? He didn't think so, but regardless, he was running flat out and now was not the time to be distracted.

Ahead of him, a tentacled monster 'ran' as fast as it could, the tentacles blatantly not part of the creature's perambulation method. They flopped and flailed, shaking with its forward motion.

Tempest yelled, "Stop running!" an instruction he hoped the idiot would obey. It was just three weeks since he took a knife to the chest while solving the Grimm Fairytale case and saving his sister's kids. The stitches were out, and the wound was healed. More or less. However, strenuous exercise hurt, and he really didn't want to push his body before it was ready.

Predictably, the tentacled monster went faster, and from inside the suit, an alien voice made a noise much akin to a flatulent walrus expelling his excess gas underwater. Somewhere inside the odd sound were words, which made Tempest believe he was hearing the voice of the fool inside the costume through a voice changing app.

It said, "You can go *something* yourself." The word Tempest couldn't make out was one he could guess.

Muttering obscenities of his own, Tempest pounded down the street to catch it. He could not see how the alien-looking thing was propelling itself along the street, but he didn't need to see them to know there were feet and legs doing the work. For years he'd lived by a simple rule when it came to tackling monsters: it's always, always a costume with an idiot inside it.

Only once could he ever recall being wrong in this assessment and the surgically enhanced polar bear he encountered in the French Alps still haunted his dreams from time to time.

Closing with the tentacled beast, Tempest couldn't figure out how to trip it — the tentacles stuck out in every direction. If he even tried to trip it, he would be the one sent tumbling. Instead of sticking out a foot, he threw his right shoulder into the middle of the thing's back.

Pushed off balance, it didn't get to stumble or fall for Tempest had chosen the timing and trajectory of his attack with care. As he bounced off and into some handy Georgian railings he grabbed to arrest his forward motion, the idiot in the costume collided with a lamppost.

A rather human "Ooooof!" reverberated out from within the alien being, followed swiftly by a groan of pain and the kind of language one might associate with a bar full of sailors.

Tempest sucked in some air, getting his breath back. Hands behind his head to maximise his lung capacity, he knew he needed only a few moments to recover. Regular fitness training during most of two decades in the British Army ensured he was significantly fitter than the average person.

At six feet tall, he was just above average height, but muscle mass made him stronger. Not that he was a body builder. Far from it. However, like the fitness training, regularly testing himself with heavy weights led to muscular development.

The tentacled monster was on its side ... or was it the creature's front? Or back? Heck, did it have a front or back? There were no eyes that Tempest could see, but what it did have, now that it was no longer upright, was feet. Two of them stuck out from a central tube inside the costume and just in case there was any question left as to the human nature of the feet, they were wearing Nike basketball boots.

Tempest, his heartrate already slowing, was about to get started on the process of extracting the idiot, when a shadow caused his head and eyes to twitch to the right. There he saw two more tentacled aliens.

He didn't think they would prove particularly problematic, but as they closed the distance, coming to the aid of their fallen comrade, the idiot was wriggling free.

Dismissing the one he'd already felled, Tempest turned to face the new threat. These ones looked the same, but they each held two of their tentacles up like arms. Because that is what they are, Tempest surmised. A glint of light hitting something shiny suggested at least one carried a knife.

Lifting a hand to his throat, Tempest growled, "Ben? Where are you! I've got three of these things on me and they appear to be armed. A little assistance would not go amiss."

There was no time to say anything else for the creatures

Modern Fairy Tale

were arriving. They moved swiftly but were not running inside their suits. It was a measured approach, and they also seemed to have better control of their costumes than the first fool, all of which spelled trouble.

When the first creature abruptly split open, the man inside using a knife to cut it from head to ... um, tentacle, it really did become three against one, so Tempest chose the only sensible tactic available: he attacked.

Fight training and a career where he got to practice his moves on live targets who would fight back provided a level of confidence few possess. Knowing how few possessed it furthered Tempest's belief that he was going to do okay even though outnumbered three to one.

The man inside tentacled monster number one was still getting up and since he was closest, Tempest hit him first. He had a rough beard and ginger hair that was a grubby shade rather than the bright orange some people get. Darting forward just as Ginger tried to rise, Tempest ran through him, putting a knee to his jaw in a bid to dislocate or break it.

He heard the man's grunt of pain but couldn't spare the time to check if he was out of the fight. Tentacled monsters two and three were upon him and now they were closer he could see they both had a knife in each hand. The blades were the fold-out kind and about six inches in length – quite capable of killing a person if that was their intent. Their arms protruded through holes in their costumes. It gave them limited mobility, but enough that they were dangerous.

Tempest went left, moving into the middle of the street and making it so the monsters were now one behind the other instead of coming at him two abreast. They would correct that in a heartbeat, so he acted before they could.

"Think you're tough, do ya?" asked monster two, advancing in a self-assured manner. Again the voice came with the underwater fart effect added.

Choosing to believe the question was rhetorical, Tempest watched and waited.

"I will carve you up with my testicles," the monster threatened, moving in for the kill.

Certain his ears had not deceived him, despite the alienesque voice alteration, Tempest felt his eyebrows rise in question.

"I'm sorry, your what now?"

He didn't get clarification and felt somewhat relieved when the monster slashed a knife-wielding tentacle in his direction. Stepping back, he surged forward as it lunged, and as the next arm swung in, he used an elbow to block it. That left the monster with both arms spread wide and its 'face' open for attack.

At such close quarters, Tempest had multiple options. He could step in to kick out a leg – kicking through a knee joint ends a fight fast, but the mass of confusing tentacles hid the targets – the man's legs were in there somewhere. He could deliver a hard punch to the solar plexus, another good move to wind an opponent, yet the costume dictated that his blow either wouldn't land at all or would miss its target.

Stuck for what to do next and with monster three coming around the side of monster two, he employed a move he could not remember ever using before: he head-butted it.

It was as his forehead connected that Tempest learned the costume, the head part of it at least, was not made from the same rubber as the tentacles. In fact, as his brain reverberated inside his skull, he wondered if perhaps it had been hewn from granite.

"Ha!" monster two burbled in its weird sounding underwater bubble voice. "Now you get all the testicles! We make mincemeat of you!"

Tempest staggered back, his vision blurring. His feet felt wobbly and disconnected. His arms were up to ward off the attack, but from the corner of his eye he could see Ginger getting back to his feet and knew he was in serious trouble.

He would be able to outrun them. Probably. He was a good runner, conditioned for long periods of exercise, but sprinting had never been a strength. If he turned tail and ran, there was a strong chance one might catch him if they were bright enough to ditch the costume. That was a risk, but it wasn't in Tempest's nature to run away, not from three idiots who had been terrifying people while burgling their houses for the last month.

His opponents spread out, Ginger coming into the middle so the idiots still in their costumes ended up to his left and right. They were all armed with knives and all Tempest had was his wits. His Kelvar vest would stop a blade, but it didn't cover his whole body so if they got him to the floor his survival chances were slim.

Ginger brandished his blade and sneered, "Maybe coming alone wasn't so bright, eh?" Now that he was free of his costume, Tempest got to hear Ginger's voice without the filter. It was eastern European for sure though he couldn't pin an exact country. "Probably should have brought a friend."

"But he did bring a friend!" yelled Big Ben, arriving at a run.

Like the three idiots, Tempest twitched his head around to see the newcomer arriving.

Big Ben got his nickname because he stands six feet seven inches tall and is almost as wide across his muscular shoulders. Unlike Tempest, Benjamin Winters *is* something of a bodybuilder and his physique is nothing short of startling.

Arriving at a run, he leapt into the air. Opening his legs like a pair of scissors, he hit the nearest monster with his groin, riding him to the ground and using his momentum to land with his right fist flying forward into Ginger's shocked face.

That left one final tentacled monster who, upon seeing what happened to his friends, chose to drop the knives.

"I surrender!" it burbled in the hard to decipher alien voice.

Big Ben punched it in the face, proving the hard shell covered the top half of the costume's headpiece only. "Did you say something?" he asked, standing over the now prone form.

"I surrender," the monster repeated.

Big Ben stepped forward, his giant right foot finding the softer, rubbery lower part of the costume. There, he guessed roughly where his opponent's testicles (not tentacles) would be and applied some downward pressure.

"Sorry, couldn't quite catch that. Can you try again without the stupid voice?"

Grab your copy...
vinci-books.com/no-magic

About the Author

When Steve Higgs wrote his debut novel, *Paranormal Nonsense*, he was a captain in the British Army. He would like to pretend that he had one of those careers that must be blacked out and generally denied by the government, and that he has to change his name and move constantly because he is still on the watch list in several countries. In truth, though, he started out as a mechanic - not like Jason Statham in the film by that name, sneaking around as a hitman, but more like one of those sleazy guys who charges a fortune and keeps your car for a week even though the only thing you went in for was a squeaky door hinge.

At school, he was largely disinterested in all subjects except creative writing, for which he won his first prize at the age of ten. However, calling it the first prize he won suggests that there were other prizes, which is not the case. Awards may yet come, but in the meantime, he enjoys writing mystery and thriller novels and claims to have more than a hundred books forming a restless queue in his mind because they are desperate to be written.

Now retired from the military, he lives in southeast England with a duo of lazy sausage dogs. Surrounded by rolling hills, brooding castles, and vineyards, he doubts he'll ever leave, the beer is just too good.

www.ingramcontent.com/pod-product-compliance
Ingram Content Group UK Ltd.
Pitfield, Milton Keynes, MK11 3LW, UK
UKHW041855120925
462873UK00003B/99